BELOW THE HORIZON

John Wingate

SAPERE
BOOKS

BELOW THE
HORIZON

Published by Sapere Books.

20 Windermere Drive, Leeds, England, LS17 7UZ,
United Kingdom

saperebooks.com

ISBN: 978-1-80055-637-9

To our fishers of the deep

Three fishers went sailing away to the west,
Away to the west as the sun went down;
Each thought on the woman who loved him the best,
And the children stood watching them out of the town.

— 'The Three Fishers', by Charles Kingsley

AUTHOR'S NOTE

If the world powers continue to utterly plunder the harvests of the oceans, world calamity is inevitable unless the nations begin to share the planet's bounty.

The deep-sea fishermen hold in their hands the balance between hunger and plenty for all nations of the world; it is the world's politicians who must be the arbiters as to whether the oceans will be able to yield their harvest. On decisions of such moment, the existence of the planet will depend.

The author is deeply indebted to the British Trawler Federation for the encouragement and co-operation he has received.

He has encountered the comradeship of the sea, wherever his research has led him. He is deeply grateful to the friends he has made, both afloat and ashore, for their unstinted contributions.

John Wingate, DSC
February, 1974
Revised October, 1979

1: THE MORNING TIDE

She could not sleep. Her man had lapsed finally into fitful unconsciousness by her side, his arms now slack around her as she lay on her back, her eyes wide open while she stared at the red glow on the ceiling above her — Peter liked to look at her, and they enjoyed the intimacy of their bedside light.

He was always restive on their last night together before a trip. She recognized the signs as he suggested putting Nicola and Peter Junior early to bed. She knew by now all the signals: she felt thankful, as well as resentful, both emotions mixed inextricably. Yes, she could be thankful that her man was different to most of the husbands of her fellow trawler widows. The first night: incapable — too tired; the second night: incoherent — too drunk; and on the third — well, they were off to sea.

Jeannie stared up at the red glow, too numb inside even to cry. In the corner stood his blue canvas kit-bag, *P. Sinclair* painted in white across it. She had packed it so lovingly, with such care, but on this last day he was already apart from her, thinking of his ship, the cause of the ugly pain swelling between herself and her man.

Peter jerked restlessly beside her, his arm binding her tightly. He nestled to her breast as the nightmare woke him and she felt the thick hair of his head beneath her chin. She stroked his forehead, her heart aching with the agony of parting. She knew that the alarm would be ringing soon at two-thirty and she gripped him so that he could never go. 'No,' she whispered, 'I won't let you go…' She woke him then, deliberately, to take him once more to her. In silence, he enveloped her, virile as ever, responding to her every artifice. She need never worry about her Peter's responses … ah, never — and from the far corners of their world, she heard the distant ringing of that bloody alarm. She felt him go limp as he withdrew from her, already not hers — no longer her man, but devoted to that damned ship, one of the top earners in the port.

'Peter…' She raised her mouth to him and felt him brush her lips as she drew his face down to her.

He stood before her, her man, beautiful to her in his manhood. He bent down quickly, pecked her on the forehead and hurriedly slipped into his sea-going gear: trousers, dark blue polo-necked sweater, short jacket and shoes. She slipped into her housecoat. He led her by the hand down to the kids' bedroom, where she put her arm around his waist as he leaned over their Nicola's cot. He touched the child's brow, then tiptoed across to Peter Junior's bed. He kissed him, left the room and hurried silently down the stairs.

She shuffled after him in her slippers; it was best to remain silent, better not to open the old wounds now: there were other jobs better than going to sea for earning the mortgage that supplied the roof over their heads; an easier life for all of them — at least they could all be together if he took up something else. They'd argued it all out before, but now, as on each previous occasion when he sailed on a trip, she began to realize that she was stronger than him. As she crushed him to her breasts, she felt his fingers running through the hair at the back of her head; she knew the anguish in his heart, the pain that always wrenched him asunder. He pushed her gently from him as the doorbell rang. She switched on the light and watched him slip into the taxi waiting outside. She raised her hand and flexed her fingers. The last she saw of him was a white face peering through the back window. His face cracked as he tried to smile. Oh, God: he looked so young.

Peter Sinclair stood motionless, staring at the ship's side rearing above the quayside. She loomed above him, all 330 tons of her, her ugly squareness a reproach to any shipbuilder, the rust beginning to show through her blue sides. *English Campion* was stencilled on the red and white lifebuoy in the rack at the after end of the starboard wing — and he, bloody fool, was her mate. He was twenty-four years old and had now served nine months in this bastard.

A car door clunked behind him and he turned to see the skipper picking his way across the railway track. Peter would recognize that rolling gait and that huge figure anywhere. He took his hands from his jacket pockets and extended a fisherman's morn-of-sailing welcome.

Skipper Walker grunted somewhere from the depths of his gargantuan body, then, using the rope of the gangway as a trapeze, propelled himself, Tarzan-like, over the ship's rail. There was a *crash!* from the deck and a muffled obscenity. Sinclair scrambled after him and helped him to his feet. Another grunt and the skipper removed himself into the bridge structure.

Peter glanced aft at the working-deck. A group of men huddled there, still in their shore-going suits. They talked little, fresh from their beds as some of them were; others, the younger men, had not allowed sleep to rob them of their final hours. The bosun was already on the foredeck to cast off the head rope. His square silhouette was a reassurance as he leaned over the high rail to see if the tug was creeping up yet from the port quarter.

A quick check below to account for the crew: each man-Jack was on board, which in these days of crew shortage was a miracle. If *Campion* had not been a good ship with decent owners, the skipper would have had to take the sweepings of Fleetwood. As it was, Skipper Walker, being the character he was, could select his crew, so a mutual respect had been built up over the years. Peter nipped into his berth below the bridge, flung his anorak onto the bunk and ran up the bridge ladder.

In the subdued lighting which had already been switched on by the sparks, Ewan Massey, he could see the skipper leaning over the bridge rail to watch carefully the tug taking the stern line.

'All ready, Skipper,' Peter said. 'All the crew on board.'

'Oh, aye — we'll go then, Pete.' The skipper turned and for a moment his tired eyes lit on his mate. 'Stand by to let go the ropes.'

So, after three days in dock, the ship was theirs again as soon as the shore lines were let go. The little diesel tug pulled off her stern from the dock, before moving up to take the headrope. She then went astern and, by using the shortened line as a spring, plucked *English Campion* from the wall.

It was 0315 by the time the stern trawler entered the lock. Already Peter could feel the wind blowing from off the sea and he buttoned up the collar of his jacket. It was pitch dark tonight: the buoys ahead, winking red and white, seemed unfriendly as they beckoned the little ship to sea.

She cleared the lock, the leading light on the beacon slipped astern and the dark silhouette of the North Eastern hotel passed down their port side. When the skipper adjusted the propeller pitch to Full Ahead, Peter felt a sense of finality.

Three days in port — it went too bloody fast — and now they were off again, as regularly as a stockbroker catching the seven-twenty-five.

Dawn was breaking when the bosun came up to relieve Peter for a spell. Joe Dilkes was a big man, solid and reliable, who knew his job backwards. His voice was harsh, like a corncrake's.

'The bloody fitters still haven't done those hatch clips, Peter.'

Peter felt the irritation. He knew that the chief had reported the defect. He'd heard him talking to Ernest Chapman, the engineering superintendent, who had promised that they would be repaired before sailing. The figure of the chief now appeared at the head of the bridge ladder: he leaned on the rail, disgust on his face as he listened to the conversation.

'It's that commie, Snakey Deane: now he's a shop steward, he causes nothing but trouble.'

'It'd not be so bad,' Joe added, 'if our lives weren't at stake.' His hand smacked down on the ledge around the bridge console. 'Some of the lads refused to go to sea, if those clips weren't done. I feel I've let them down, now.'

'The Old Man says he'll go back if they feel like that about it, Joe,' Peter said.

'Yes, I will.' The skipper's voice rasped from the head of the ladder. 'Go and ask the lads, Pete.'

The huge frame heaved itself up to the wheelhouse and, leaning against the roll of the ship, neatly propelled itself into the skipper's chair which was fixed amidships and facing the console.

Hooky Walker was in command and for ninety per cent of the hours during the next twenty-two days, he would be the arbitrator of all their lives. As a seaman, he knew the danger of a badly fitting upper-deck hatch. 'It's their lives at stake; they should decide,' he said.

Peter nodded to the bosun and both of them slipped below to the berths. The cook was desultorily toying with the hopeless idea of offering up some sort of breakfast, a lost cause on the first morning after sailing. A general foist through the berths and the reaction was somewhat brusque: six o'clock in the morning, and the morning after, was no time to be asking such a damn-fool question.

'They'll sail, Skip,' Peter reported when he returned to the bridge.

'Oh, aye.'

Peter couldn't help but smile as he regarded his skipper. A mountain of a man, six feet five in his socks, Skipper Walker lolled back in his chair, his thoughts horizons away as he pondered the fishing strategy for the trip. Peter recognized all the signs, as he regarded that rugged profile which could have belonged to a Viking captain steering his longship across the North Sea to plunder our eastern coastline. His craggy nose beaked, almost touching the pugnacious chin. His slab ears were concealed behind tufty ginger sideburns, emphasizing the heavy jowl — and the wide-set, ice-blue eyes, which stared through the windows to the horizons beyond, were framed by the shock of rusty-red hair which topped the square face.

Hooky was still in his shore-going rig, but he was loosening his tie, the first indication that he was beginning to accept the reality of being at sea again. In a few moments he would be off below to his cabin where he would slip into his seagoing gear, the oldest clothes he could find: an old woollen striped shirt without a collar, and a pair of grey bags with two fly buttons missing. With his craggy face, it was not surprising that throughout the Fleetwood trawler fleet he was known as Hooky Walker.

'Those shore gangs still haven't marked the warps correctly,' Peter said. 'Best do it ourselves.'

The bosun swore and the chief jerked his head contemptuously. 'At least we'll know it's done properly,' Hooky growled from the chair. 'I'll stop before we reach the fishing grounds and you can measure up then, Pete.' A smile played at the corner of his mouth. 'At least we'll be ready for the gunboats.'

Skipper Walker, one of the up-and-coming skippers in the Gunn Fishing Company's fleet, was not a happy man as he slumped lower into his bridge seat. While steaming to the fishing grounds, he made it a rule to do much of his thinking. Apart from sharing watches with the mate and bosun, there was little else for him to do than to weigh up the factors involved in the impending trip. Resentment was eating away inside him, and he knew the reason for his discontent.

He was a lucky man, he knew, because 'Walker's luck' was a byword in the pool ashore, where men queued to join his ship. His luck began with the men he chose to serve with him — and Ewan Massey, his radio officer, was one of them.

'Ewan, what's the latest on the Cod War front?' he shouted over his shoulder to the radio officer on the starboard after corner of his wheelhouse. A man of thirty emerged, well built, pale from his continuous imprisonment in the artificial light of the radio office. He had an intelligent, disciplined face with thoughtful, grey eyes. He was the intelligence maestro, responsible for feeding his skipper with the facts that he plucked out of the air: the twice-daily schedules of fish caught by other trawlers; the summary of conversations between skippers about where the cod were appearing; and encoding, in their own personal codes, the information passed by the secret syndicates formed by groups of individual ships. Ewan, The Brain, was what the crew called him. The skipper's man, he kept himself to himself and did not mix with the others: his was a twenty-four-hour job, and he always looked tired.

'We're waiting for an announcement from the BTF — something's afoot, I reckon.'

Hooky nodded. 'Aye, them talks again. Reckon we're no better off than a year ago.' The large head subsided into the massive chest. Hooky Walker was thinking.

Though this conflict was known as the Third Cod War, it was, in fact, the fourth of the disputes, the first, in the fifties, being short and vicious. This Third Cod War had now been going on for too long — and what progress had there been? Damn all — and Hooky twitched involuntarily, impatience making him wince with disgust. The world should have learned its lesson from the Second Cod War, back in '73. It was so different then and a tea-party in comparison with this, the Third Cod War: this time, the Russians were very much against the British.

The Communist Icelandic Prime Minister had recently been re-elected on the promise that, once and for all time, he would clear the seas around Iceland of British trawlermen. Without consultation of any kind, his Foreign Minister was proclaiming that Iceland intended once again to take all the fish in Icelandic waters — and, as far as Iceland was concerned and without reference to anyone else, the Icelanders were extending their twelve-mile limit to one of fifty miles.

Hooky squirmed when he thought about it, even now, with this third dispute nearly two years old. For these past two winters, British trawlermen had been fighting this damn Cod

War — all alone and no one at home caring much. If one was to ask anyone in the Southern Counties what this Cod War, the third and most bitter, was all about, they couldn't give you an answer.

'Hell's teeth, Ewan; what's up with this nation of ours? We're too bloody soft.'

Sparks leant across and handed his skipper a message he had just typed. The announcement had come in on the key from the Owners' Federation. Hooky read it twice and handed it back to his operator.

'So the Prime Minister is trying to organize talks with them, is he?'

His operator was silent, waiting for him to continue. Hooky heaved himself from the chair, moved a pace to his right and crouched over the radar visor to pick up Galloway.

'I hate these bloody Icelanders, Ewan. They'll never give up their demand for a fifty-mile limit. They've been massacring their own fishing grounds for years, so what have they got to lose?'

'Nowt, Skip,' Ewan replied. 'We'll give in, I suppose — as we always do.'

Hooky's fist smashed down on the console top. 'Where's our Churchill? By God, we need someone to put some guts back into us — someone who can say "no".'

'Without giving a reason — just *no*,' Ewan said. 'Remember that magnificent Navy chap, Barry Someone-or-other? Skipper of the frigate and Fleet Commander in the First Cod War.'

'Bloody good bloke,' the skipper continued. 'The gunboat was harassing *Topaz* when the frigate came tearing up. Barry shouted through his hailer, "Cover your gun within five seconds or I'll blow you out of the water!"' Hooky's eyes gleamed, but Ewan's face was serious.

'He would have, too,' the operator went on, 'but the Icelanders never moved so fast in their lives.'

'Barry was removed smartish, given a medal and kicked upstairs into the Admiralty,' Hooky snorted, his face flushed with indignation. 'Can't do that sort of thing today. Mustn't hurt anyone's feelings, even though they're chucking all sorts of muck at us.'

'What hurts me is that every time a gunboat chops someone's gear, surely that's an act of piracy or war, if committed in International Waters?'

'Not today, Ewan —' Hooky snorted. 'Not poor old Britain. We're too bloody wet. Take the Russians: the Icelanders would never have dared take them on — they know the sort of answer they'd get in return.'

He looked up to see Ewan moving swiftly to the after window. The operator was shouting, as he pointed across to the port quarter: 'Man overboard, port side — there's a lad in the water, Skip.'

Hooky slid from his chair. With his right hand, he flicked the autopilot over to port; with his left, he pulled the pitch control to zero. He reached the verandah door, as the mate beat him to the port lifebuoy. Peter wrenched it from the rack and slung it far out, spinning outwards and splashing ten yards clear of the ship's side.

'Watch him...'

Hooky had absorbed the emergency instantly. He'd seen the white-faced brassy, Wee Willy, pointing over the side. His mouth was open, but his words were inaudible against the clatter of the gear and the wind. A cable to port and threshing in the wake, he'd seen the flailing arms of a seaman.

'Stand by the lifeboat, Peter,' the skipper yelled. 'I'll try to get alongside.'

Leo Huys, the Belgian deckie, was rolling out of his bunk when he heard the cry of '*Man overboard*', and a banging and clattering on the metal deck. Without donning his boots, he slipped along the passage, up the ladder and through the screen door to the break by the trawl winch. A cluster of men were bunched at the rail, where the bosun was pointing aft across the port quarter. As Leo rushed up the port verandah ladder to get a better view from the bridge, he felt the ship tremble when the skipper went full ahead under full port rudder.

Leo saw the lifebuoy chute was empty and he glanced aft for signs of the man in the water. He saw him immediately, where a pair of arms flailed wildly in the swishing green waters of the tide-race off the Point of Ayre. There he glimpsed, bobbing in the swell, the blond head of Curly Thompson, the lad that was replacing old Bill who was taking off a trip for holidays.

Leo felt his stomach heave — Curly was a friend, and he could barely swim. Leo had attended his wedding only three months ago and they had laughed together when the little boy had arrived two months later. Curly was a good lad, but why was he in the water fighting for his life — and, hell, why was no one going in after him to help?

The terrified face was towards them now, less than fifty yards from the ship's side. Curly seemed incapable even of attempting to swim for the lifebuoy which was now less than twenty yards from his grasp — he was drowning through panic: if someone would only stand by him, he might be restored to his senses — but *why* was no one trying to save him?

As Leo clambered over the rail of the verandah, the reason was plain to see — the confusion of the race and the breaking of the turbulent seas stopped men in their tracks. 'It's too bloody easy to be a dead bloody 'ero —' yes, he heard the words, as he climbed up the ladder. Then it was that Leo Huys — the twenty-five-year-old son of the Belgian who had come to England from Dunkirk — reacted illogically and without reasoning, to save a fellow being's life. He plunged from the verandah deck into the ice-cold sea, thirty feet below.

He felt the shock as he hit the water, felt the dark element sucking him down until he swooped upwards to break surface ten yards from Curly. He struck out with all his strength and remembered to turn away from the breaking seas as he gulped for mouthfuls of air. As he reached the struggling seaman, he saw the blue and white side of *Campion* looming above him, her quarter rearing high in the swell, white foam threshing at her stern.

'For God's sake, Curly —' Leo yelled above the threshing of his frantic efforts. 'Hold on, Curly. I'm coming.' He saw the terror in the lad's face and then, as Leo came up behind him, Curly seemed deliberately to plunge his head under water. The body slowly sank from sight.

Leo acted through instinct. He knew only that Curly was a goner, if he couldn't be reached now. The Belgian gulped a lungful of air and plunged down after the sinking man. It was suddenly dark. In the green gloom, he caught sight of a pale light where the youth was kicking his death throes. Leo reached out and clutched at the dark, struggling mass.

Leo never knew how deep he was, when that grotesque struggle took place beneath the waves. He must have been at about twelve feet, because his ears were bursting; when he grappled with the flailing arms, he knew then that Curly was mad. The man was intent on drowning himself and, in spite of Leo's efforts, would be taking his rescuer with him. The Belgian felt his world spinning about him: with a last, desperate kick, he freed himself from the mortal clutches of the madman.

The last Leo glimpsed of the one-time bridegroom was a willowy shadow, tumbling and rolling over sideways away from him, down, down — then a mere shade, darker than the surrounding water, to disappear utterly.

Leo burst to the surface. He lay for an eternity on his back while he regained his breath and his composure. He had never felt so weak: the length of his body ached, his limbs trembled and his teeth chattered uncontrollably. He knew then that he could so easily die. 'Don't panic — I mustn't panic —' he kept repeating the formula over and over to himself — 'Sophie, my dearest English wife; I can't leave you now —' and in that flash he saw her gazing down at him as she often did, a smile at the corner of her lips; and somehow, from far away, he heard their little Louis's cry — so clear it was.

He shook his head as he gulped the first intake of water; then he felt the bite of a rope rasping across his face. He lashed out instinctively and felt the rounded surfaces of a lifebuoy slipping through his fingers. He clenched his hand, and, thanks be to Jesus, the bight of the buoy's handhold slid tightly into his grasp.

He lay on his back as the line tautened. The water surged past his ears; a wall of red anti-fouling flashed across his sight, blotting out the sky. A row of faces peered and shouted from the white rail: the ship's side swung away again and he felt the rough metal and barnacles tearing the skin from the calves of his legs.

The side swung down on him and there, hanging from the Jacob's ladder, was Wild Bill. A huge hand grabbed the collar of Leo's shirt, a bowline was slipped over his shoulders and he was yanked inboard.

2: A TRIP OUT

Sophie Huys closed the glass-fronted door with both hands. She had watched Ted Bayley walk briskly away, hands stuffed deeply into the pockets of his grey raincoat. *Suppose he's used to errands*, she thought. *It's his job.*

The door clicked shut. *Mustn't wake Louis. He needs his sleep, now that he's teething.* She sat down on the bottom stair, leant forward and cradled her face in her hands, her elbows on her knees. Then the tears came; she let them course uncontrollably.

So her Leo was a hero. The whole of Susan Bennett Street would know by dinnertime, so she must hurry up and tidy the house before the first knock on the door. *Leo is safe: dear God, Leo is safe.* She closed her eyes tightly and tried to see her Lord — He was so close, she could almost feel Him. *Dear Lord, thank you, oh thank you, my man is safe. Our home is secure again: and we can continue the mortgage and Louis still has his father.* Guiltily, she wiped her wet cheeks, dabbed at her eyes and slowly climbed the stairs to little Louis's cot-room. She'd pop him in the pram and walk round to dead Curly's Fiona. She'd need solace now. Fiona would take comfort from her: they had both shared confidences and admitted to each other their fear of the sea — those great oceans that claimed their men.

'It's a bloody trip out.' Hungry Mitch was sitting in the mess room, head down and six inches from the cigarette he was rolling between his fingers. 'Bloody trip out.' He was a superstitious man.

There was silence round the tables where the watch below were sipping their tea before going on watch.

Mitch's chin was beginning to show the first day's stubble. 'We should've gone back,' he said. 'This trip has begun with blood — you know what they say.' He was talking to no one in particular, morose and sorry for himself, as sobriety slowly cleared his befuddled brain from a monumental 'bevvy' now twelve hours old.

'Belt up, Mitch,' Joe the Whip said. 'The skip couldn't have done ought else.'

Wee Willy, the sixteen-year-old brassy, his elbows splayed across the mess table, looked up, his pale face serious as he rested his chin on the lip of the fiddle. 'He was mad when he done it,' he said. 'He showed off to me and told me to watch him walking along the rail. Thought he was joking, I did.'

'Weren't happy at home,' Ben the cook said quietly, his spaniel eyes looking across at Joe. 'Told me so, and I warned him not to be so daft.'

Silence descended again. The ship bucked as she plunged, outward-bound for Iceland, into the northerly swell.

'There'll be an inquest,' Knocker said, the spare, quiet man from Market Street. 'There always is.' He looked across the table at the Belgian. 'You'll be chief witness.'

Leo tapped the ash from his cigarette. Ten minutes ago, he'd descended from his bridge watch. Ted Bayley, the gaffer in Fleetwood, had been on a link call with the skipper. Decent bloke, Ted Bayley: he'd asked on the R/T to speak to the deckie who had tried to save Curly. So Leo had talked to Bayley and asked him to tell Sophie he was okay. 'I'll do that,' the gaffer had said. 'But the trip goes on,' he had added when the skip had gently taken the telephone from Leo's fingers.

'What'll you say, Leo?' Joe asked.

They were all staring at him now, these six men of the watch, with the level, clear gaze of seamen used to gazing towards the horizon.

Leo lowered his eyes and flicked again at the ash on his cigarette. 'It was an accident,' he said quietly, as he looked up at them all. 'Wasn't it, lads? An accident.'

The silence in the mess room was broken only by the background pounding of the diesel.

'Aye, lads: 'twas an accident.' The deep voice of the bosun reflected all their feelings.

'Aye, an accident,' Joe repeated. 'It must 'ave bin.'

Leo rose from the settee and quickly left the mess.

'C'mon, you lazy, good-for-nothing bastards,' Joe growled. 'Off your arses. There's work for you on deck.'

'I'll have to check the marks, Skip,' Peter said. 'The shore gang have got 'em wrong again.'

'Aye, Pete,' Hooky Walker replied. He walked over to the winchman's control cabinet and stared at the working deck, where tomorrow all would be bustle as they fixed the nets for the next ten days' fishing. Without Curly Thompson, the deckies were one short in the port watch. This would make a difference over the hauling and shooting, but at least they'd enjoy the benefit of a larger share-out if the trip was a good one. Though Hooky was content that they had decided to continue sailing, he was unhappy that they had already condemned the trip as 'a trip out'. He'd need to show 'em — he'd make a good trip and not spare himself. If the gunboats let him — that bloody *Hekla*. He had a personal hatred of that blue-grey Icelandic gunboat which had shadowed him all one night last trip. 'I'm going for my dinner, Pete,' he said. 'Take her straight up: Mull of Galloway is fine on the starboard bow.'

Peter watched the skipper vanishing down the stairway. At last he could snatch a few minutes' quietness. It seemed an age since the Isle of Man had slipped away under their port quarter and the radio masts of Burrow Head had passed down their starboard side.

He tried to wipe from his mind the race off the Point of Ayre where Curly had been lost. Port Patrick was now on their starboard quarter, the county of Galloway beautiful in its soft mauves, greys and greens, even on this October afternoon. To port and clearly visible was that mysterious and unhappy land of Ulster. It was hard to believe that amongst the softness of those blue hills, men and women once hated each other so bitterly that, under the hypocritical banner of religion, they had blown themselves and their children to smithereens. With a sigh, he adjusted George, the autopilot, and steered for a point in the North Channel, midway between Rathlin Island and that western bastion to the Firth of Clyde, Argyllshire's forbidding Mull of Kintyre.

As he settled in the bridge chair, he took a final look astern to the country he loved, to that haze in the distance which enfolded all that he cherished and owned. Jeannie would be feeding Nicola now: he closed his eyes for a moment to recapture the joy he always felt when he watched their own handiwork suckling at her mother's breast. If ever there was a miracle of creation, that was it.

He heard the ponderous breathing of the skipper reclimbing the bridge ladder. It had been a hateful forenoon, but now Peter was left hungry: he'd see what he could do below to restore the lads' morale.

Hooky Walker always steamed 'outside', as he called it, when outward-bound for Iceland. Only during the winter, when on passage for the White Sea or Iceland, did he pass through the Minches, inside Islay and Mull in order to dodge bad weather.

He had easily picked up Dubh Artach on his radar — and he always smiled when he thought of the 'Du-Arctic Ghost', as the lads called him, the skipper who never fished elsewhere but on the banks surrounding that lighthouse. Skerryvore next, where he had fished as a boy, then Barra Head to starboard and finally goodbye to the UK for three weeks, except to leave St Kilda to starboard and that last desolate rock of the British Isles, Rockall, to port.

It would soon be dark, now that winter was closing in. He wondered how many more hard winters he'd be able to stand up here. The bad years seemed to run in cycles: last year had been exceptionally mild, which was just as well, with these bloody Icelanders harassing the trawlers every moment of the day.

He'd had a bellyful of this Cod War. It was all very well Whitehall being so tolerant with these bastards, but it was not only his and Molly's livelihood that was at stake. There were ten thousand trawlermen involved in this fishing industry and nearly four times as many wives and families. Hell's teeth, they had a hard enough task fighting the elements in order to hunt for fish, without being molested on the high seas. What the hell were the Government and the Navy doing about the sacred freedom of the seas? There was much on Hooky Walker's mind, as dusk fell that evening.

He realized that he was only thirty-seven, still young as skippers went, but he reckoned that at fifty, all skippers were over the hill. If he ever reached the pinnacle and became a top skipper, he'd quit before the rot set in. His beloved Molly, a year older than himself, had stood by him all of those difficult years of marriage — she'd worried every minute of the time he'd been away at sea. She had tried not to influence him, knowing that it was useless to try and lure him back to land. It was even worse now for her, since Mark, their only son, had joined *Foxglove*.

Hooky had been twenty-two years a trawlerman. His dad had been a damned good skipper, and his granfer afore that. With his own career eased by the tradition of his family, he owed it to them, and to his own professional pride, to try and become one of Fleetwood's top skippers.

There was no sentiment in the trawling industry. Owners, skippers and crews were in the hunt entirely for the money — with the proviso that no fisherman, under the inevitably harsh conditions, would have gone to sea for the money alone: he would also have to love the sea, of that Hooky was certain.

He stared at the grey swell beginning to build up ahead of his ship. He had been given the honour by Gunn's to commission *English Campion*, the most modern in their fleet. Implicit in the commission was that Hugh Gunn and his brother, Geoffrey, the two managing directors, both considered him as having the potential to become one of their top skippers: but this was where the stress entered into his life: 'the higher you climb, the harder you fall,' was the saying in the port.

Lucky Hooky, they sometimes called him, partly because of his luck and partly (he'd better assume no false modesty) because he did think more than most. With his intelligence, plus his flair for finding the fish, he had won the reputation of landing high earning catches. He had fought his way up over the years — he had been sacked twice as a young skipper, when he had returned after two consecutively bad trips. No profits, no job — and everyone appreciated the fact. Owners could not run ships unless they earned profits.

One of the pleasures of being a 'three-quarter' skipper was that, with a good ship, he could pick and choose the men who served with him. A good ship earned good money, and that meant high poundage for the crew — in addition to their weekly basic wage, they were paid 6p for every £100 worth of fish. If a good trip earned £25,000, a deckie could take home £150 poundage after three weeks' work. All the crew shared in the enterprise and in the value of the catch when it was sold in the Fleetwood fish market on the morning of docking — not a bad principle, and one which might well apply to the nation, if it wanted again to be prosperous.

Yes, he, Hooky Walker, had been lucky so far, but these harassing tactics of the Icelanders were beginning to cause a deal of bitterness. They might succeed in chopping *Campion*'s gear, but they'd never board her. He hated those bloody gunboats, and *Hekla* in particular. Jolted by this thought, he realized that he'd better snatch some sleep while still steaming, so that he could be fresh for the fray in sixty hours' time.

'Knocker,' he said, inclining his head towards the tall and reliable man from Hampshire, who always shared his watch, 'ask the mate to come up, please. I'm going below.'

English Campion reached the fishing grounds off the east corner of Iceland on the afternoon of the third day's steaming. Twenty miles outside the fifty-mile limit off Reydarfjord, Hooky Walker exercised a trial shooting of the trawl, not only to balance the fathom marks on both trawl warps, but to ensure that all was efficient in case they ran into trouble with the gunboats. He had to be able to haul quickly, then, if he didn't want his gear chopped — it was expensive, so he didn't want *that* to happen often.

From the winch room, he watched the mate and bosun: good men both, each very different in temperament. Pete was a good mate, reliable, and a man who knew his job. He'd fished well, when he, Hooky, had been on holiday. Returned £20,000, he had — and no trouble at all. Joe, the bosun, was good 'un, too. A rattling good seaman who knew his job backwards; strong as a horse, respected by the crew for his knowledge: *Campion* was lucky to have them both. Hooky sighed. He had a sixth sense that this *was* going to be a trip 'out' — he shared the feeling with his crew, but he was damned if he was going to allow them to see his doubts. He was thinking quietly to himself, on the way to Workingman's bank, when the sparks appeared silently from his office.

'They're in trouble up at Hari-Kari, Skip; *Corrina*'s had her gear chopped.'

Hooky's nose almost met his jutting chin as his jaw set. 'Anything else, Ewan?'

'No. Skip, It's *Hekla* apparently. He's told the bunch up there that if he finds any more of 'em fishing within the fifty-mile limit, he'll chop all their gear.'

The volcano erupted. A massive hand smashed down on the bridge console. 'He will, will he? By God, let the bastard try it on me. He'd better not be in my area tomorrow.'

3: MAN OF WAR

Maria Karlsen lay motionless for a few more moments, her body half-turned on the bed, her arm outstretched towards the windows which looked across the playing-card city of Reykjavik. It was barely seven o'clock, but already there was bustle in the clean streets; across the gaily painted roofs, she could see the white-flecked waves curling across the green-greyness of the bay — and that was where she froze her thoughts.

She wished she could steal a tiny fraction of the new day. For a moment or two, she wished that she could savour the joy of fulfilment which Sven and she had shared, before he had suddenly slipped out to shave. He was always thus, a wonderful lover, when he was going back to *Hekla*, the ship of which he was so proud.

Ever since they'd been married some eighteen years ago, he'd always been a good seaman when he'd been in the fishing trawlers; but he had soon realized then that his career would be wasted after he had made the big decision to try for an English degree at Cambridge. Maria sighed, still feeling the warmth of his presence as she looked at the indentation on the pillow where his head had so recently lain.

She'd best get up, because he'd want his breakfast promptly. He always liked to be on board in time for 'Hands Fall In' — and it was a good hour's flight to Nordfjord where the ship lay now. A frown creased her serene forehead, as the harsh reality of present-day politics bit into her mind. Before this wretched Third Cod War with the British, the *Hekla* had always been alongside at Reykjavik: she'd seen much more of him then.

She began to feel flustered. The neighbours would soon be bothering her, now that Sven had become something of a celebrity in the town. He was always in the news and being sent for by the Director and the Ministers. She didn't relish the publicity, because it interfered with her home life and the education of their two sons, now fifteen and seventeen. She slipped out of bed and stood for a moment before the mirror on their dressing-table.

She must watch her weight — her breasts were showing signs of heaviness, but Sven... She smiled to herself, locking away the memory, so that she could, when she had time, savour the moment. Her hair was black and silky and tied at the nape of her neck — he liked it like that and created hell when she tried to alter the style.

'Hey, Maria — do I get my own breakfast or are you up?' The gruff voice floated up from the hallway below. 'I'll miss the ship if I don't look out — the heat's being turned on again today.'

She gave a little cry and hurried into her housecoat, running down the stairs in her flip-flops.

The dark blue Volvo brake slid gently to a rest in the lay-by overlooking Nordfjord. The man who quickly wound down the window was incisive in his movements; the neatly bearded face that peered out at the village nestling in the fold of the point was typically Icelandic, yet there was a fineness about it that suggested a broader experience than that enjoyed by the average islanders. The naval officer, for such he was by the uniform he was wearing, had a finely cut face: his appearance suggested a man of intelligence, quick reaction and decision, but there was also an air of authority and ruthlessness about his bearing.

Captain Sven Karlsen had dropped into the habit of pulling the hired car, in which he drove from the landing strip, into this lay-by for five minutes; from here he could watch his ship and ponder about the coming day, and so avoid being steamrollered by the rush of events that always beset him.

He looked down with appreciation on his sleek gunboat lying so prettily at the jetty. In her blue-grey paint, she merged into the fjord, but he could see that Olaf Hagander, his First Lieutenant, was already on the helicopter deck and talking to the Buffer about the day's routine. He smiled to himself because they were probably trying to anticipate his orders for the day's operations. He knew he was regarded as a taut disciplinarian — he could afford to be, with so many volunteers queueing for his ship — and they feared his anger. Olaf was a good Number One, but too much of a gentleman: an Icelander couldn't hate enough those Britishers out there.

He jerked his head seawards, to the grey seas surging past Nordfjordaharn point where the white lighthouse jutted upwards. His gaze was sweeping the pencil line of the horizon, when suddenly he stopped and screwed up his eyes. The crow's feet wrinkled as the green marble of his irises reflected a small black smudge, visible for an instant and then disappearing in a white smother of foam in the long swell that originated from the Barents Sea.

His jaw tightened; he felt his fingers bunching in the palms of his hands. Well, he'd had definite orders from the Ministry today — this was his chance, and he wasn't going to miss it. He twisted the ignition key, the engine purred and he stamped on the accelerator. Gravel spurted from the rear wheels as he sped down the hill to the village quay where lay his beloved *Hekla*.

'Ready for sea, Skipstjóri. All hands on board.' The first lieutenant saluted and moved to the starboard wing of the enclosed bridge. Karlsen acknowledged the courtesy and nodded at his Number One.

'Single up,' Hagander ordered through the mic cradled in the palm of his hand.

Captain Karlsen watched with approval the efficiency of his ship's company. Trained as they all had been from the days of their childhood to live their lives in the fishing boats, they were instinctive seamen. The ocean that lashed this desolate island was in their blood. Eighteen months in command now, Karlsen felt a quiet satisfaction as his seaman's eye absorbed every detail of his taut ship. *Hekla*, named after Iceland's biggest volcano, was the finest in their fishery protection service. The others, *Laki* of 187 feet and with eighteen knots; and *Stóri*, 206 feet and with seventeen knots, were both armoured with one 57 mm gun, as was *Hekla*. But it was *Hekla*, 204 feet and with her nineteen knots, that those British trawlermen out there most feared. He smiled again to himself, but on this occasion there was a coldness to the glint in his eye. He leaned over the bridge to regard, with a frustration that was a physical pain, the 57 mm on the raised gun deck.

The gunlayer was putting the finishing touches to the weapon of which he was intensely proud. He'd greased the training gear and was replacing the heavy plastic gun cover. The long, blue-steel barrel gleamed from the light film of oil with which it had been carefully cleaned.

Below the gundeck, the fo'c'sle stretched forward to the neat, pointed bow with its white bull-ring. The deck was efficiently clear of any unnecessary gear and was flush so that a big sea could wash straight across it. The bows were finely flared to fling clear the mass of water she took when ploughing headlong into the long swell of these inhospitable waters.

An unusual feature of the design was the unstayed obelisk of a boxed foremast which reared vertically from the centreline of the fo'c'sle. Its purpose was to take the main W/T aerials which ran from the top of the radar tower; a mainmast was therefore unnecessary aft, so that a clear area was available for the helicopter deck. The two 'choppers' ashore had proved invaluable recently, not only for reconnaissance of the fishing grounds, but because even British seamen needed emergency medical treatment sometimes.

'Let go aft,' Karlsen ordered. 'Back up the back-spring.' He strode to the starboard wing and watched the water boil as her stern moved away from the jetty.

A small group of fishermen and their wives stood waving luck to their guardian ship. A youth with long flaxen hair cupped his hands and shouted across the widening gap of water: 'How many are you going to chop today, Skipstjóri?'

Karlsen smiled, waved and concentrated on the job in hand. 'Let go,' he ordered. 'Half-ahead together. Starboard ten. Steer for the buoy, coxswain.'

He watched the steely-black water of the fjord curling along *Hekla*'s waterline. He entered his warm bridge, for it was better in here with the winter coming on (it was already 17 October); the mountains and fjords were white and blue with the first falls of snow.

'Both search radars operational, sir,' Bjorn Knudsen, his navigating officer, reported, 'but the long range 701 is still not working properly.'

'Why not?'

There was an involuntary pause before Knudsen answered. 'The Americans hadn't got a spare condenser, sir. They're flying one over from the States.'

Karlsen said nothing, biting his tongue. The delay wasn't Knudsen's fault. The whole bloody situation was what was wrong.

'Take her, pilot. Telegraph Bank.'

'Aye, aye, sir — Telegraph Bank.'

'Fifteen knots.'

'Fifteen knots, sir.'

Karlsen heard the turbos cut in, then turned to watch the sudden vibration from the black cowls of the two squat funnels set side by side and athwartships of each other. He was impatient to be after that brazen trawler — she must be just inside the twelve-mile limit. He clambered onto his bridge chair, flung his gold-braided cap to the signalman standing by him, and stared moodily through the clear-view screen now twirling at high speed in the wheelhouse windows.

Those British trawlermen were so bloody obstinate: thirteen months now, it was, since his Prime Minister, Pétur Jacobssen had taken that courageous step. It had been about time that he spoke up for the majority. It was pleasant to be an independent Communist state, whatever the anomalies might be. He chuckled quietly to himself as he pondered the absurdity: a Communist independent nation, similar to Yugoslavia, but inside the NATO Alliance which was designed to combat the spread of Russian Communist imperialism. How ridiculous could the situation be, particularly with the Yanks utterly committed with their airbase at Keflavik and with their radar chain complex?

As a senior captain — his thirty-eighth birthday was next month — he was supposed to keep out of politics. His job was to obey orders: if he failed, there were plenty of others itching to jump into his shoes. 'Cut as many trawlers' trawls as you can,' he'd been instructed that morning. 'World sympathy is on the side of the little man, and a few incidents will be a great help to our cause.'

Ever since those frigates of the Royal Navy had appeared on the horizon, things had not been as easy as during those first few months. The sight of those White Ensigns streaming from the British masts always made him pause to reflect what he was taking on, before he cocked a snook at them.

Hekla began to heave as she dipped into the swell running across the entrance to the fjord. As soon as he had cleared the point, he altered to starboard to pass inside Reykjabodhi rocks — he would cut the corner and save time to be after those bloody British trawlers.

Iceland was in the right, he was sure of that. The British fishermen had been plundering the banks off the island for the past three hundred years; but of what relevance was that, when he and his ancestors had been living off the fish for eleven hundred years? He had to admit that, in recent years, Icelandic fishermen had been greedy and were overfishing, without regard for the consequences of cleaning out their own grounds. When the British accepted the twelve-mile limit, no one had realized how short-sighted the Icelandic policy of overfishing had been. His people were now paying the penalty and there would soon be an end to fishing, as they knew it, within the twelve-mile limit. His Prime Minister was right, but it was difficult to justify a unilateral and arbitrary ultimatum of fifty miles — particularly as the British were past-masters at diplomacy and double talk.

He smiled ruefully — that Hague decision against Iceland, way back in the seventies, hadn't helped, particularly as she had torn up the 1961 agreement with Britain. But, as the Minister yesterday had told him privately, in 1973, there was little danger in how hard Iceland twisted the lion's tail. If she barked loud enough, Britain always gave way. Compromise was what the British called weakness. He laughed out loud and Knudsen looked up from the chart table at his captain.

'I'm not really round the bend, Bjorn,' Karlsen said. 'Just thinking about those British trawlers — over a year now, you know.'

'Take a bit of shifting, don't they, sir? Just as well they weren't the Russians.'

The captain snorted. 'They would have sunk us outright — and, anyway, we wouldn't have dared to harass them in the first place. It's lucky they're on our side this time.'

The seas were breaking over the fo'c'sle now, sheets of water spewing over the wheelhouse windows.

'How far's that trawler?' Karslen demanded.

'Ten miles, sir.'

'And that large one to starboard?'

'Just over twelve, sir.'

'Steady on the first. Report when the First Lieutenant is ready with the cutting gear.'

'Aye, aye, sir.'

'And Pilot…'

'Sir?'

'Tell the gunnery officer to stand by the gun.'

4: PAWNS IN THE GAME

It was the seventeenth of October, *Campion*'s second morning on the fishing grounds to the east of that chunk of misery known as Iceland. Knocker Wright was on the forenoon watch with the skipper, and he was leaning over the fishing chart to identify their position — fifteen miles east of Nordfjord and sharing Telegraph bank with their sister ship, *English Primrose.* It was lumpy here and, as always, Knocker disliked the bucking motion of this new ship. These stern trawlers were ideal for the job but, in short seas, they bumped like hell when slamming into a head sea. He sat down on the wheelhouse settee, lit a cigarette and mentally relaxed to soak in the pleasure of being allowed to think in private for a spell. He'd never felt completely accepted in Fleetwood, ever since he'd come up from Portsmouth after he'd finished his National Service in the Navy. He hated Fleetwood, but it was his fault and nobody else's, he supposed.

One of the consolations of being a trawlerman was, he knew better than anybody, the advantage of working amongst men who asked no questions. At sea, a man relished the solitary moments with his thoughts. If a lad wanted to be silent, he was left alone and no one thought him moody. Thus it was this morning, but four days out of dock usually snapped him out of his moroseness.

If it was not for his Sheila, now growing into a beautiful teenager — she would be twelve next year — he would have left Linda years ago, as soon as he had discovered that she was made that way. He should have suspected, when he'd originally agreed to take on little Michael; though the kid wasn't his, at least he'd thought she'd keep her promise and give up the other blokes.

He'd known for two years that she'd been carrying on with Alf Tuscott; they'd all three met in The Plume one evening, but it had not been long before the swine had been round at her door when *Campion* was at sea. He flicked out the ash of his roll-up and stared distantly out of the wheelhouse side window to the grey seas breaking to the north.

Alf was a slick bastard, two-timing and always contemptuous in Knocker's presence. 'You poor fool,' the sod was almost shouting from the rooftops. 'Don't you know I'm having it off with your missus — and she's enjoying it too?' It was too easy for him, a commercial traveller and always free at the weekends — no wonder Linda, who could never resist a male's attentions, took off for dirty weekends with him. But taking their Sheila with them — it was *that* which made him seethe inside.

Linda knew his weakness too — he wanted her like hell and he hadn't the guts to chuck her out. She still came to meet the ship and was always there when *Campion* bumped alongside the dock after a trip. He felt nauseated as he dragged deeply on the cigarette; that way, she was backing both runners, and she still believed he didn't know about her goings-on. She must often have acted a good part in the marital bed. He ground his cigarette end into pulp in the metal tray. He rose from the settee and glanced at the clock. The skipper would be hauling any minute: he was into the fish and he wouldn't let them slip through his fingers.

The mate always came up to the bridge early in the forenoon. The skippers were fond of this hour (they had recovered from the shock of coming to after a few hours' sleep) because they enjoyed passing the time of day on the R/T and swapping information, particularly if one of them was newly arrived from Fleetwood. Peter Sinclair stood at the for'd windows and peered at the side trawler fishing a couple of miles inshore of them. She was bucking in the swell and was shooting her trawl. He could see the for'd door lowered: by the lines of her, she must be the *General Gordon*.

In Peter's opinion, the side trawler was the epitome of a good sea-going ship: her sleek lines merged with the element in which she belonged. The flared bow, the low freeboard amidships, and the high poop-deck aft distinguished her from all other ships: she was a fine work-horse, with superb functional lines for the seas in which she carried out one of the toughest jobs afloat. Peter shivered when he recalled his 'deckie' days in one of the old oil burners, though in these diesel side trawlers working conditions were no better.

In side trawlers, the nets were hauled in over the rail, the trawl being towed from the two gallows on the starboard side. When hauling or shooting the trawler lay-to, almost stopped, beam on to the wind and seas. In this position, she would drift to leeward and so allow the trawlers to stream to windward of her. The trouble came if there was a cross-tide and when there was no wind.

Though the side trawlers had been for so long the backbone of the British deep-sea trawler fleet, there were two disadvantages which now made them obsolete in comparison with their successors, the stern trawlers and the big freezer ships.

The side trawler was a conventional ship and, because the working deck was sited forward, her foremast and derricks had to be stepped well forward on the foredeck. This rigging was high above the water-line; the bridge structure was also of necessity high above the deck so as to provide a clear view over the fo'c'sle head for the wheelhouse personnel. These two requirements were a potential hazard to the ship's stability during wintry bad weather, because black ice and icing immediately attacked these, the worst two areas. This additional weight, high up, rapidly decreased the ship's stability; in wintry conditions, this was the worst hazard with which the skippers of the side trawlers had to contend.

For the crew of the side trawlers, the main hardship was having to work on the open deck. Crouched for hours over a heap of fish; keeping one's feet on the heaving deck as numbed fingers tried to gut the frozen fish; the continuous splash of hose water over the pile of fish to prevent them from freezing; and, all the while, washed down by flying spray and solid sheets of seawater: these were memories that Peter preferred to forget. But the side trawlers were recording big catches and were still top earners.

Peter shook his head and felt a deep content. The modern stern trawler was a dramatic contrast: the gutting was carried out under cover in a heated gutting room. There was no real top-weight hazard in icing conditions and the accommodation was superb: each man lived in a modern berth and he was even protected from his own stupidity. On the last trip, Wild Bill had fallen asleep in his berth with a cigarette still burning in his hand. He had been rudely awakened by a deluge of water swamping him and everyone else in the berth. The fire-drenching sprayer in the deckhead had operated automatically at the first detection of smoke.

In the passageway outside, Soupy Ben had been carrying a tray loaded with sausage rolls. When the fire protection system was automatically triggered off, the spring-loaded fire doors had automatically slammed shut, with considerable force.

Soupy Ben caught the full impact as he was passing: after he had picked up himself and his sausage rolls, the pastry (the bosun said) had been scorched by the violence of Ben's language. The stern trawlers were superb ships and Peter would never willingly return to the old 'sidewinders'.

He stifled a yawn as the skipper returned to the wheelhouse — he'd been up since Hooky had turned in at two o'clock. When the mates, they said, went on watch in the fishing fleet, order was restored from chaos — but they caught no fish. He could see Iceland away to starboard, white now in its late October habit, cold and forbidding. Thank God this wheelhouse was always pleasant, even in mid-winter, warmed by the heat from the engine room which percolated upwards.

The Old Man seemed in his element today: he'd hauled a good bag of fish last night and he liked a trip to be off to a good start. He was holding the R/T telephone upside down in his huge fist as he lounged back like a walrus in his bridge chair. His belly shook as he chuckled with glee at Roddy Mules, the skipper of *Gordon*, who was spinning a yarn about his three days ashore in Fleetwood.

'Took me missus to the films at the Tivoli,' he was saying. 'It was so bleeding cold that me bloody feet was bloody fruzz. When I came out, I said to Doreen, "If it had been a film on the bloody Arctic, I'd have come out with black frost."'

'Ruddy 'ell,' replied Hooky over the R/T.

'Yeh, yeh, yeh,' Rod rambled on over the telephone. 'How've you got on? Playing Hooky, as ever, eh, boy? Any fish, 'ooky? Nowt 'ere.'

'Not so bad, Rod; not so bad — about a hundred and fifty baskets a day. Mostly cod.'

Peter always listened with delight to the intrigue that went on during these forenoon chats between skippers. Each knew that everyone within twelve miles would be listening in to discover whether they could glean any scrap of information as to the whereabouts of the cod. Some, it was sad to say, were definitely evil. They delayed reporting their hauls, but they were always truthful: it would not have paid them to be otherwise.

Hooky was lolling in the chair, his steady blue eyes gazing at the fog banks rolling up from the southward, while Rod continued to ramble on by himself. Hooky slumped motionless, his vast belly heaving slowly up and down as he breathed, his mind active as it sifted all the information his acute brain had digested. When Hooky was thinking, and that was most of the trip, he spoke little.

Skipper Rod was waxing strong about the state of the Icelandic dispute. 'It's about bloody time the bloody Navy was called in,' he was saying bitterly. 'Chopping a man's gear in international waters is plain ruddy piracy, isn't that so, Hooky?'

'Aye, that it is,' Hooky Walker replied, always alert when it came to beating the Icelanders at their own game. 'There's been a fair bit of chopping going on off Langanes. *Laki* got *Richmond Lass*'s gear yesterday. No one's seen…'

Hooky was working himself into his daily rage over the subject of gunboats, when Ewan slid into the wheelhouse. Like so many times before, he held the flimsy sheet of paper before his skipper's nose, while the recumbent figure continued to chatter over the phone. Peter watched the bushy eyebrows shoot upwards.

'Oh, aye,' Hooky said. 'Looks like things are happening, Rod. See yer —' and he slammed down the instrument into its nook. 'Bloody gunboat. Navy says she's just leaving Nordfjord.' He half-rolled, half-propelled himself from the chair and leaned against the motion of the ship to stare aft, across the port quarter towards the snow-capped mountains to the westward. 'Binoculars…' He was holding out his hand towards Peter. 'I think that's her…'

Peter grabbed the pair of binoculars from between the two radars and gave them to the skipper. The mate was peering into the visor of the long-range radar when Hooky shouted, 'There's the bastard.'

Peter picked up the echo at a range of five miles. The gunboat was on the correct bearing for a ship which was steering towards them from Nordfjordaharn point. He continued to track the echo for a full two minutes.

'Five miles,' Peter reported. 'Echo closing rapidly.'

Hooky was stumbling his way back to the bridge chair. As he reached for the telephone to warn Rod in *Gordon*, he glanced at Peter. 'Haul,' he said, 'bloody quick. I'm going to close Rod — and it'll be a race against time.'

Peter sent Knocker to call out the watch, while he himself began the task of heaving in the trawl. His pulse quickened as he turned the control wheel to 'heave' and snapped off the winch brake. He heard the crackle and clink of the wire rattling over the drums and rolling on to the winches. He moved the control wheel to 'full speed', then paused for a second to sight the cross-trees and upperworks of the blue-grey gunboat: she was growing larger at every second, as she climbed up from below the horizon. Then he slipped down the ladder to don his oilskins and fisherman's thigh boots.

'Last fifty, Skip!'

Peter heard Knocker's yell, even from the working deck where he now waited in the break by the winch. The lads were gathered about him and, when the short mark of three strands came in, he moved aft by to haul the nets, as the sea crashed on board from the port beam. Skip was longing to open up to full speed but could not do so until the cod-end was safely on deck.

'This,' Peter yelled across at Tommy Ballance, the relief deckie, 'will be our fastest haul yet.'

'It'll seem the slowest,' Hungry Mitch said, the words barely audible from his toothless mouth. He pointed to the blue-grey warship surging up on their port quarter, sheets of spray shooting upwards as she plunged at full speed through the heavy seas.

Campion's doors climbed out of the sea, but the operation of hanging each one from its stern gantry seemed abysmally slow, Mitch, in the emergency, being all fingers and thumbs as he unclipped the independent wire. Peter waved his green glove impatiently and the bridles began to heave in, but once again it seemed a lifetime before the bridle chain came up to the bollards. It was music to hear it loosed on to the steel ramp to begin its last journey up to the warp-tension rollers; the banging of the dan-lenos as they thumped home was the signal for the frantic shackling on of the inhaul.

Peter looked aft to the green belly of the net, now swaying drunkenly in the streaky astern; to the orange buoys swooping downwards in the swell which, as always, seemed to be overtaking them to mount the ramp in anger. There was the cod-end, with a few fish protruding through the mesh: above it swooped and glided the molly birds and, no further than a mile now, the spray-drenched bows of *Hekla* were leaping through the seas.

Hooky Walker had increased the pitch of his propeller and the revs to full speed at 750, as soon as he'd seen the gunboat emerging on the radar. He'd called up *Gordon* on the R/T and told him he was closing as rapidly as he knew how. But the interminable waiting for his own trawl to be hauled had been hard on his patience, never easily controlled at the best of times. He had watched through the window of the winch control room as Knocker had hove in, but the mate seemed damned slow, just when *Campion* needed a quick haul. Now the cod-end was slithering up the ramp but, for the first time in his life, Hooky was not interested in the bag of fish. He picked up the mic: 'Close the doors.'

The red rear doors, which sealed off the ramp, swung to and were bolted shut. He looked up and judged that the bucking gunboat was less than half a mile on his starboard quarter. *Campion* was a mile from *Gordon* now.

He moved to the autopilot and flicked the knurled knob five degrees to starboard. If he could judge the distance right, he would settle dead astern of *Gordon*, who was struggling with her haul. But if *Campion* took station too close to her, there was the hazard that *Gordon*'s cod-end would surface immediately under *Campion* and perhaps foul her propeller or rudder. He decided to concentrate on the job in hand and place his ship in the right position. *Hekla* (he was certain that the gunboat was her) could then not swoop across to cut *Gordon*'s warps without danger of ramming *Campion*. He'd leave the worrying as to who would win the race to someone else.

'Get the mate up here,' he shouted. Ewan, always at the skipper's right-hand in a crisis, slipped from the wheelhouse and yelled aft to the yellow-coated deckie.

When Peter Sinclair reached the bridge, Hooky was slumped back in his chair as usual, silent and motionless, his seaman's eye concentrating entirely on judgement of bearing and distance.

'Watch that bastard, *Hekla*, Pete,' Hooky said. 'And don't give her the chance to board. See the lads are ready with axes and hoses.'

'Right, Skip.' Pete nipped to the verandah to yell down to the watch on deck who had manned the rail to watch the fun. '...and turn out all hands,' he shouted above the wind and the rattling of the bobbins. 'This is an emergency.'

Hooky was on the blower to Mules in *General Gordon*: 'What's your speed, Rod?'

'I'm still stopped, Hooky — don't ram me up me arse.'

'Try not to, Rod — it would be a painful procedure.'

The skipper's laughter was a trifle forced over the air, but the conversation was interrupted by a guttural but incisive voice speaking perfect English on 2182, the international broadcast frequency: 'Get out of my way, *English Campion*. I shall hold you responsible if you interfere.'

Hooky looked out of his starboard bridge window. *Hekla* was less than a cable off his port quarter and almost ensnared in the stern wave of his wash.

Hooky paid no attention but calmly went to the pitch control and moved the lever to stop. 'Take over the wheel, Pete,' he said, steady as a rock. 'Put her "in hand".'

Peter jumped to the wheel, shut the by-pass and grasped the wooden spokes.

'Keep her bang in the middle of *Gordon*'s stern,' Hooky ordered. 'I'll work the speed.'

Peter concentrated on the rusty black stern of the side trawler, which now lay rolling beam-on to the seas as she hauled in her trawl. *Campion* was less than two cables from her but still overtaking fast. He could hear the *crash!* of the gunboat surging up on the starboard beam, less than half a cable distant. From the corner of his eye, he could see her seamen huddled together, waiting to slip their cutting gear.

'Get out of the way!' *Hekla* shouted, as she tore up to within a cable of *Gordon*'s quarter. For her to cut across the warps now, between *Gordon*'s stem and *Campion*'s sharp bow, would be hazardous in the extreme, as the gap continued to narrow.

Hooky picked up the telephone. He felt cold anger mounting inside him as the gunboat slid past his starboard bow.

'I'll ram you if you cross my bow,' was all he said. He moved to the pitch control and went half astern. Peter felt *Campion* shuddering as she rapidly lost way; she settled herself down gently within half a cable of *Gordon*'s stern.

Hekla could not now slide across *Campion*'s stern without slicing *Gordon*'s quarter, or risking being savaged by *Campion*'s flared bow. Peter watched the gunboat heeling suddenly to port as she sheered off to starboard, her wake frothing as she swept by. She steamed close to the old side trawler and passed swiftly up her side.

'How's that for size, Rod?' Hooky said over the R/T.

A figure came out of the trawler's wheelhouse, waved and pointed to port. The gunboat had gone 'hard-over', beautifully handled, and was crossing *Gordon*'s bows. She came tearing down towards them on the opposite course now, her captain on the wing of his bridge. As he swept past *Campion*, he was shaking his fist at his adversary.

'You English bastard,' he shouted over 2182. 'Get outside the fifty-mile limit or next time I will board and arrest you.'

Peter could see the Icelandic captain clearly. He was bearded, tall, and clad in a blue wind-cheater. Of one thing there was no doubt: he might be a right stinker himself, but he could certainly handle that gunboat.

Hooky moved to the port side of the wheelhouse and stepped on to the verandah. From his hand trailed the crinkled cable of the R/T phone: 'You'll only capture this ship,' he snapped, clearly and calmly, 'if you either sink me or I'm dead.'

He slammed the door shut behind him; rolled across to his bridge chair, and slumped into it, like a savage sea-lion returning to its floe after being irritated by a polar bear.

The encounter had a heartening effect on the morale of the crew of *English Campion*: they knew, as far as their skipper was concerned, exactly where they stood. Hooky meant what he said, and he had never yet retreated on his word. Ewan Massey was the first to realize this, when he witnessed the Old Man's resolution on the day of the *Gordon* encounter.

The trip, as forecast, materialized into 'a trip out'. After the excitement with the gunboat, the fishing was abysmal. Other trawlers had their gear chopped, but only once, when Hooky steamed up to Langanes after a day's steaming, did *Campion* sight *Hekla* again — and then at over a mile's range. Hooky had watched his adversary through binoculars, and Ewan had seen the anger welling inside his skipper. Ewan had already chiakked him for his obsessional hatred of Hekla, but this time Hooky turned on him, stabbing a horny finger into Ewan's chest. 'But I do hate him — I really do hate the bastard.'

No, they had made no catch at Langanes for, by the time *Campion* reached Vopna bank, the eighteen trawlers already there had fished it dry and driven away the cod. The gamble had been fruitless; Hooky and his men had felt the disappointment keenly. By the time the seventeenth day had arrived, they had just 'made a trip' — but no more. Now they were homeward bound, course 150 degrees and, if the weather held, they should be in the Minch by Tuesday night.

Ewan knew that Hooky was taking it badly. It was a lonely perch, near the top. *Campion* was well up in the earning stakes and might possibly realize Hooky's life-long ambition to make her one of the top-earning ships. His only rival was his good friend, Husky Tranto, in *English Cowslip*, a sister ship of *Campion*'s and the latest of Gunn's stern trawlers. The two skippers were three-quarters of the way up the ladder and both were fighting for the privilege of being commissioned as skipper of Gunn's next new ship.

Ewan had waited two hours for the link call. He had grown so used to putting the lads through to their wives and sweethearts that he often missed his own. He was sitting in his chair in the radio office when the friendly voice from Portishead broke the silence. Ewan had no need to tune the receiver, for Gunn had done him proud in the office: the main receiver was crystalled for all frequencies, so he had only to select the one he wanted. The voice from Portishead was familiar, for much traffic had flowed between Ewan and Portishead during the last eighteen months.

'Good afternoon, *Campion*, putting your call through now.'

Ewan picked up the black receiver. His heart always quickened, even after all this time, as he waited for his Katie to come on the line. The line clicked and she was through to him, as clearly as if she was in the next room.

Ewan Massey did not only have to maintain and operate all the wireless equipment, from automatic distress transmitters for the life-rafts to the main transmitters to Gunn's office, but he was also the electronics man. As such, he had to maintain the mass of electrical and electronic gear with which this modern trawler was equipped in order to hunt fish. Two deep echo sounders; a sophisticated auto-steering pilot; a track recorder;

two modern radars; a Decca and a Loran Navigator.

In addition there were the modern monitoring systems, one of the most useful being the tension meters which measured the pull on each warp, so that the skipper would know when the trawl was fast on the seabed: warning bells rang if the tension became dangerously high.

In the old steam trawlers, if the trawl came fast on the bottom, the winch would pull back against its own steam pressure when the ship rolled away from the warps. In the design of the electric motors in the first diesel-electric side trawlers, power was cut when a magnetic brake, like a clutch on a car, snapped on to lock the motor in position. The brake was held off by a solenoid which was energized when the controller was switched to the 'ON' position. When the trawl came fast, and the current was cut off through an excessive load, then this brake snapped on, making it impossible to pull the winch back against itself.

This was what had happened to Gunn's first diesel side trawler, which was fishing with her hatch covers off in very bad weather. She took a list when the trawl came fast, because the wires were taut and were pulling on the side of the ship from the top of her gallows. A sea came on board and filled up the holds through the open hatches. She rolled over and sank immediately, taking the skipper, the wireless operator and several hands with her.

Since the inquiry into the tragedy, manually operated emergency release levers were fitted in the wheelhouses, so that the wires could be immediately tripped against the pull. This accident could not be repeated in stern trawlers, because the wires ran over the stern of the ship and not from the side. The tension meters and their monitoring system were of great value to Hooky.

Ewan knew that the crew regarded him as a cold fish and a loner. He had developed amongst his other operator friends a simple code which they used between themselves, so there was a distinct feeling of segregation between him and the rest of the crew. A man could not be on the ball *and* matey, Ewan had decided early in his career, so he tended to remain efficient and somewhat aloof. He cultivated this image because, otherwise, he could never have coped with the twenty-four-hour treadmill nature of his duties.

He lay on his bunk and closed his eyes. After a link call with Katie, he tried to find a moment to seek the seclusion of his berth, a cabin he had to himself at the top of the accommodation ladder. He always allowed himself this one luxury each trip, the pleasure of lying on his bunk to treasure for a few minutes the music of her voice still lingering in his consciousness. He closed his eyes.

She must have been holding Michael on her knee, because he hadn't quite reached the crawling stage. There were, probably, the remains of apple puree smeared over his face, and Katie would be desperately trying to prevent his weaving hands from plastering the phone with the stuff. 'Hullo, darling,' she'd said quietly, with the softness of the west wind in her voice. 'Day and time?'

'Wednesday afternoon,' he'd said, 'if we catch the tide.'

'I'll be waiting,' she said. 'We're all well here.'

'See you Wednesday.'

'See you, darling.'

And the phone went dead.

'Two minutes, *Campion*,' Portishead said. 'Good afternoon.'

Ewan smiled to himself. So few words, so expensive in money, so rich in love. His Katie was a wonderful wife: his perfect complement, so utterly different to him. Vivacious, scatter-brained, warm and loving — what more could he ask? She was even preparing for the house-move next week. He opened his eyes and a shadow crossed his face as the worry of the mortgage clouded his thoughts.

He'd taken on too much, he realized, but she had fallen in love with the little house, a gem of a place with three bedrooms, just outside Fleetwood. He'd given in, provided she didn't nag him for being at sea. This life was in his blood (his cousin had been a skipper) and, on each trip, he had to earn the money. He was lucky to be in *Campion*; if Hooky continued to climb up the ladder, all would be well. His radio operator would do his utmost to keep him there — there was too much at stake.

He rolled out quickly from his bunk: it was time to give the forenoon forecast to the Old Man. He nipped up the bridge ladder and, sliding past the bridge console, entered his office.

This weather machine, Ewan thought, *is the greatest safety factor of this decade — bloody miracle, even though the Nips have produced it.* He pressed a button and up sparked a printed twenty-four-hour weather map. Another button, and, as a forty-eight- and a seventy-two-hour forecast chart of the northern Atlantic emerged, Ewan glanced quickly at them and whistled: the perfect finale for 'a trip out'.

The skipper studied the weather charts for at least a minute.

'What about that ice chart, Ewan? Surely there're icebergs all the way from here to the Butt of Lewis?'

The stubby forefinger stabbed at the concentric circles, so close that they were a black blotch at the entrance to the gap between the south-east corner of Iceland and the north of Scotland.

'We're in for a gale of wind,' Hooky said. 'Hell, but it's come up fast — it's that bloody high off Greenland again.' He looked Ewan in the eye. 'We're caught out this time, Ewan,' he said. 'Better tell the mate. It'll be hurricane stuff.'

Dusk was stealing across the western horizon when the first impact of the depression hit them. The seas had built up rapidly and when the gusts hit *Campion*, Hooky and his men were ready for it. The skipper watched his mate, balanced at the rail which ran across the bridge windows, and tried to weigh him up.

After Peter had left the Merchant Navy, he joined the trawler fleet; he first served as a deckie under Hooky Walker, who had just taken over his first ship as skipper. Sinclair had shown promise and when he had passed his mate's ticket, Hooky had asked him to join as *Campion*'s mate. They had sailed together ever since — for three years now. He'd grown much in stature, so much so that, last year, Pete had taken over as skipper when Hooky had taken two months' holiday. He'd made good trips, too, and the crew had faith in him, which was what mattered.

The ship was plunging now, her flared bow walloping into the head seas. At each slam, she shuddered from stem to stern and Sinclair was flexing his knees at each impact, to reduce the shock on his legs.

'Better reduce the pitch even more, Pete,' Hooky shouted above the din.

Sinclair, Hooky thought, could not have been more than six feet, but his shoulders were powerful. He was the right age — twenty-five — and a good mate, because he didn't bawl out the men, as some did. When he did raise his voice, they jumped — and that was what mattered. His face was open and there was an amused expression about the brown eyes. The large ears, spatulated nose and generous mouth made him look an 'honest

Joe', and there was a trustworthiness in his make-up — *and that's what I need at this moment*, Hooky thought.

Storm force winds always unnerved him. He hated bad weather and loathed the discomfort of a ship being hurled about in heavy seas. He ducked instinctively as a black wall of water reared vertically ahead of him. A white veil drifted across the bridge windows to blot out all vision. Slowly the water drained away to reveal a foaming mass of breaking seas. Force nine to ten now, he judged, and there was worse to come.

The misery of waiting for a gale to pass through was one of the crosses a seaman had to bear. In these tough ships, Hooky had decided that, if he was ever caught out, he would shorten the agony by steaming straight through the eye of the hurricane. She was virtually hove-to and barely maintaining steerage way as she dipped into the trough before mounting the dark mountainsides which heaved upwards to meet them. She was taking it green now, shuddering and shaking herself as she flung the water clear before plunging onwards again to meet the next wave. He glanced at his watch: dark already, yet only six o'clock. The lowering black clouds, sweeping over the trunk of the mast, danced crazily across the storm-smoked sky. Then it was that the alarm bell shrilled behind him: a red lamp was glowing on the monitoring panel.

Hooky felt fear, as he stabbed at the release test button: the hazard seemed to be in the ship's main bilge suction. Water must be flooding in: the level was becoming significant or the alarm would not have operated. He turned to his mate and yelled above the shrieking of the wind: 'Water's rising in the bilge, Pete. Tell the chief and see what's up.'

At that moment, the ship began to climb. Hooky could feel her movement, like the elevation of a skyscraper, climbing the mountain of water that curled, boiling at the breaking crest, roaring towards them. She swooped upward, poised for a second as the maelstrom foamed about her: then, balanced on a knife edge, her bows dipped suddenly to swoop down into the cavernous, black void beneath her.

The impact flung Hooky from his chair. The crash of crockery and the roar of the sea drowned all other sounds as the little ship struggled for her life. When finally she emerged, shaking herself like a half-drowned terrier, there was a strange, sudden calm.

The main engine had stopped dead — a hunk of metal. Kaput. The bridge was plunged into darkness and alarm bells shrilled. The gyro had gone off the board and the autopilot was useless. Hooky was stunned, unable to assimilate the magnitude of the disaster. Then he dashed to the wheel, slammed over the by-pass and spun the wheel amidships. He swore — long, loud and obscenely: without the engine, there could be no way on her, no steerage. He realized then that they were lost: his spine tingled and for one of the rare moments in his life, he knew the meaning of terror.

5: A BREEZE OF WIND

There was no need to call the hands. The shattering blow on the ship's hull, as the freak wave overwhelmed her, sent her sheering off to starboard; the ensuing darkness when the diesel suddenly stopped; and the flickering of the auxiliary lighting as the emergency generator cut in, woke even Knocker Wright, the somnolent Hampshire man from Pompey. Sensing disaster, he fell out of his bunk, thrust on his thigh boots which lay on the tiled passage outside, grabbed his oilskins and rushed on deck. The lads were huddled by the winch, sheltering from the cascades of water that flung across the working deck. The tall figure of the mate was there, and he was securing a bowline around himself and Joe, the hefty bosun. Then, backed up on the line by Mitch and Wild Bill, the two yellow figures, illuminated by the half-light from the white water breaking over the rail, staggered across the deck to inspect the hatch fittings. The bosun threw up his arm and they hauled him back to the shelter.

'The hatch is busted open,' he gasped, dashing the streaming water from his face. 'Those bloody clips have shot up and the hatch has sprung open. Water's pouring in.'

There was fear in the bosun's voice. The hands tending the mate's line knew then that they were fighting for their lives. Peter was hauled back to safety. He had been battered and the wind had been knocked from his lungs.

'Four of you below with the bosun,' he gasped. 'Fix a strong-back on the hatch, fore and aft. Use a tackle and bowse it down in the fish room.' He turned to Knocker. 'Come on,' he yelled. 'We've got to get those hatches back on —' The lads could see only too well what little time they had. Lashing each other to lifelines which they belayed to the rail hooks, they slithered and staggered to the dislodged steel hatch covers.

Peter heard shouts from his party below in the fish room. Using long bars, hammers and ropes, they worked with a frenzy born of terror to lever the hatch covers back into position.

The ship, now out of control, was wallowing crazily, beam on to the seas. Gear smashed across the deck as it snapped free from its side lashings. At any moment, men could be crushed to pulp by a coil of wire, by the spare doors or a heap of bobbins. They worked in silence, terror adding impetus to their frenzied struggles.

In the engine room, Barnie, the Chief Engineer, had been reading the temperatures when *Campion* took the sea. He ended up by the grille surrounding the generator, where he picked himself up from the deck plates. The engine room was wreathed in a dense vapour, the whole compartment being covered in a film of oil.

He felt nauseated as he had rushed at the source of the oil burst, a fractured main fuel line running immediately alongside the main exhaust. Not only was there the catastrophe at this moment of the shutting off of fuel to the main diesel, but the atmosphere was a highly volatile explosive mixture: one spark could demolish the whole compartment.

He had rushed to the exhaust fan motor and reset it. The emergency generator staggered at the extra load, but mercifully stayed on the board while he hauled himself towards the fractured pipe. He shook his head to clear the dizziness. He had to pull himself together if anyone in this ship was to survive.

He struggled to his feet and fought his way back to his stores locker. The only hope was a quick repair — he could make a good job of it later. He was lucky in finding first time the right size polythene pressure hose — a couple of jubilee clips and he would be home and dry. He heaved himself back to the burst pipe and slid the polythene onto the for'ard end of the fuel pipe; he hacksawed four inches off the after end. He slid on one clip, opened it up and fitted the pipe. Then he tried the other clip, but he could not reach the after end of the break from his side of the manifold. He had to crawl underneath the mounting in order to reach it, but he knew his body was too thick for it. God! He did not often blaspheme, for he was a religious man; but now he almost wept with exasperation. Then he knew the answer — Wee Willy, the Brassy: he was small and he could crawl underneath.

Barnie slithered to the ladder and clawed his way up it. He dashed down the passage and yelled at the top of his voice. 'Brassy! Willy! For God's sake, someone find me Willy.'

Knocker was standing by the screen door, white-faced and backing up a purchase which the mate had rigged.

'If you want to live, Knocker, send Willy down to the engine room — NOW!'

Barnie remembered Knocker's open mouth bellowing against the hurricane wind. No sound came. The chief engineer waited a lifetime until, suddenly, through the door, the yellow oilskins of a diminutive body fell to the deck. Barnie helped him to his feet and propelled him down the ladder to the dimly lit engine room.

'Quick, Willy, underneath there — for God's sake, hurry.'

Terror was etched into the young lad's face. He was white and shaking with cold, but he tore at his oilskins and flung them to the deck. Without a word, he slithered beneath the mounting and reappeared on the other side, a query on his peaked face.

'Hold that and do as I tell you.'

The chief worked fast. On went the second jubilee and, the hose held by Wee Willy, Barnie was able to tighten both clips. The ship suddenly was hanging on her beam ends: Barnie held his breath, praying as he had never prayed before. Then, gently at first, she suddenly sprang upwards to catapult him towards the control console. He started the fuel pump and waited for the precious liquid to fill the reservoir; he lunged at the green button on the starter panel.

Barnie kept his finger on the button — it was now or never. He heard the hiss of air then, oh God, the *thunk!* as the engine fired. The engine roared to life, her life-blood once more coursing through her veins. He leapt back to the repair, saw that it was good, and scrambled to the bridge voicepipe. He blew on the whistle and a voice answered, calmly with no trace of anxiety.

'Oh, aye, Chief. Okay, now?'

'Yes, Skip.'

The skipper turned her at full speed, back into the surging seas. He reduced then to dead slow, and with power again on the steering, it was possible to hold her head up, safely hove-to and stemming the fury of the storm. If the mate could secure that hatch, they could yet survive. She was sluggish in the seas now, so heavy with floodwater. The pumps were soon sucking on the bilges, but unless that damned hatch was tightly shut, she could still founder with the water gaining fast on the pumps. At that moment, a yellow oilskinned figure hauled itself slowly up the bridge ladder.

Hooky wondered whether the mate was going to pass out. Blood was flowing from a cut on his forehead and his fate was drained of colour.

'Hatch is shut, Skip.'

'Making water?'

'No, she's tight.'

Hooky hauled himself back to his chair, his eyes fixed ahead. 'Lads all right?'

'Yes — but a few near shaves.'

'All below?'

'Yes, Skip.'

Hooky sat there a moment. He was fighting this monster, this tempest, every nerve strained to meet each new challenge. He would move to the telegraph with surprising agility to adjust the pitch; then he'd slide quickly to the steering, which was again on the autopilot.

'I'd like to get hold of the bastard who made such a bad job of those hatch clips,' he said, turning to Peter. 'Can't understand a man in the shore gang letting down his mates like this.'

Knocker, the winchman, had been listening from the chart-house settee. 'If we get out of this, Skipper,' he said, 'I'll find the bastard myself and wring his bloody neck.'

6: LAUGHTER AND TEARS

Muriel Dilkes was proud of her bosun husband. She knew they respected him in his new ship, *Campion*, but he could be sullen and bad-tempered if he was crossed. He had been at sea since his National Service days — and in trawlers from the moment he left the Navy.

She pulled the pillow tighter to her and pressed her eyes shut — she loved her man, and he must be home soon. They must have missed the afternoon tide, and that meant a knock on the door at any time between a quarter to three and half past in the morning.

They had been married for nigh on twenty years, and had been tolerably happy. She had borne him their two, Johnny and Debbie, but now that they were growing out of their teens she was more on her own when Joe was off to sea.

She sighed and turned on her back, unable to sleep. She thought she heard a car down the road, but it must be that Jaik's boy, back from the town again, she supposed: bad 'un — well in with Slippery Sal, Joe had said. Poor Sal, she'd been a good-looking girl at school, but she had drifted downhill to claim the distinction of being the town's most successful tart.

Men: strange creatures, she thought. They were content, usually pliable as long as you gave them their sex. If a sailor's wife couldn't satisfy her husband when he came home from sea, she might as well say goodbye to him. Three weeks, under those conditions and without seeing a woman, was asking a lot of a normal man. She had always understood that and given all she could — but some women just weren't so hungry for it, that was all.

Joe was good to her — he never came home drunk, but he liked a drink with the lads. Though she missed not seeing so much of the kids now, she had not reached the stage of finding that the companionship of her husband filled the gap — and particularly when he was at sea so much.

He'd been a bosun for seven years now and with Hooky for three. Joe Dilkes had tried a spell ashore at the factory once, but he had stood it only for nine months before being off to sea again. Funny how he had the sea in his blood, particularly after being in the Navy. He'd enjoyed those years: she always suspected he'd been quite a lad before he'd married her.

She recognized the sound of the taxi now, revving up round the corner and rattling to a halt outside, with its squeaky brakes. She snapped on the light, slipped out of bed, and threw on her housecoat. She paused for a moment by the mirror: going grey, she had to admit, and putting on weight a bit. 'But I'm still your bird,' she whispered to herself. She smiled as she dabbed a spot of scent between her breasts.

Skipper Walker had known he would miss yesterday's afternoon tide at Fleetwood so, with time to kill, he had made his return passage through the Sounds. He always loved this route home, out of the weather, out of the swell after thirteen days on Iceland's tide-ripped fishing grounds.

That first sighting of Suliskey, the pinnacle of rock thrusting upwards out of the Atlantic, remote and dangerous, always stirred him after the long steam across the ocean. He had already lost half a day standing by *Seabreeze*, a side trawler which had taken a sea south-east of the Vestmann islands.

Even more welcoming was the first sighting of his homeland which, even in mid-October, greeted him with warmth. The cluster of Scottish crofts, set in the midst of brown fields that ran down to the silver strands at the water's edge, always seemed to be beckoning him. There was the Butt of Lewis, good to see in spite of the dangerous seas running across the outcrop of rocks below the cliffs. Even the clouds seemed different to those over bloody Iceland — here, off these lovely Scottish islands, the clouds were warm and fleecy, soft and rounded. But up there off Iceland — long, horizontal tables of icy grey cirrus and stratocumulus — cold, forbidding, with always the threat of icing, icebergs and gales — ugh!

He'd enjoyed coming down through the Minch again — it was over a year now since he'd sailed that way. He'd never forget the passage down the Sounds: he'd run them since his teens, he and his dad, like a ferry boat, once or twice a fortnight.

He'd stopped in at Gairloch, where the joys and sadnesses of youth had been spent. He'd anchored there and the village folk had come out to welcome home the lad who was now a celebrity, an up-and-coming Fleetwood skipper. The brothers Bruce, ageing now after a lifetime's fishing, came out for him in their immaculately kept fifty-foot boat. *Sea Flower* was carved in rolling, italic letters, into the wide wash-strake at the bow. Her white upperworks, against the emerald green of the hull, looked a picture, Hooky thought — and the faces of those two brothers reflected serenity itself. Calm-eyed, clear-skinned and with wind-driven complexions, their life had been one of work and patient skill. Out in all weathers, these men were true fishermen, men of God, who found a contentment and happiness in their lives through the quality of acceptance. Hooky wondered then whether he would ever reach that stage in his spiritual life — as an ambitious skipper, he was obsessed with reaching for the top, always trying to make a better trip, and fighting to preserve his money from the voracious taxman.

Ye cannot serve God and mammon — he'd known then, when he'd seen the serenity in the Bruces' faces down in the warm fo'c'sle of *Sea Flower*, what the Lord had meant.

The village had turned out and given him a basket of freshly cooked crabs from the small factory which exported these delicacies all over the world. The manager had been unable to comprehend why he could not inveigle more labour to help — he was limited in his production, only by the lack of this human commodity and not by the scarcity of crabs.

Hooky had brought off beer for the crew and, after weighing, he'd piloted his *Campion* down through the Sound: the narrows of the Kyles of Lochalsh, with only half a cable to spare on each side; the Sound of Sleat, then Mull, with Duart Castle, gaunt and black in the moonlight, the Lady's Rock guarded by its flashing buoy. To this stake on the rock top, it was said, they had tied the faithless Chieftain's wife. The tide had done the rest.

Down past Seil and onwards; *Campion* slid past the Corryvreckan, the awesome whirlpool at spring tides. Hooky had been up all night, until the dawn had broken over the Cuillin; he then had handed her over to the mate to bring her down to Galloway and the North Channel. He docked at 0200 on the next morning's tide, Thursday, and he had stayed to see the lumpers open up.

Hooky had a distinctive walk. With all his bulk and weight, he walked lightly on his feet, taking small steps, the habit of years of balancing across a heaving deck. His chin jutted, his hair blew about his face and his lower jaw protruded like a bulldog's. His restless blue eyes were everywhere, missing nothing; when he found himself at the entrance to the fish dock, where his beloved *Campion* still lay alongside, he paused:

these were the last few moments of each trip, the vital minutes which decided whether the hardships of the last twenty days had been worthwhile. Even after all these years, this was still the crunch moment for Hooky: so many factors affected the market price of each variety of fish.

He gazed at the ship, of which he was no longer in command while she lay alongside in the dock. Four hours earlier, she had been the pride of his crew's life. Up to the last minute they had been cleaning her: shower rooms, galley, berths, passages, bridge, working-deck — even her verdigrised ship's bell had been polished by the brassy. His name derived from the brass buttons on the uniforms of the apprentices who first went to sea in 1915, during the years of the Great War. Until recently, the brassy entry had been the sole means by which a young man could start his trawler life. Hooky hoped that the new cadet training scheme introduced by the owners would be given a chance to work. Good recruits were always needed in the industry, and this new scheme was attractive because it raised the status of the officer structure. The big freezer ships were providing the ideal opportunity for launching the scheme.

When she had docked that morning, she was internally as clean as a new pin. Even the working deck had been hosed down, limed and washed again. Her rusty sides and her Red Duster, now shredded by the wind so that only the Jack remained, were the only evidence of the hard work and heavy weather she had endured. That seemed hours ago now, after he had swept on the first flood into Fleetwood's narrow channel.

He enjoyed entering harbour under perfect control. Using his two steering motors, he relished handling the ship with the verve of a destroyer captain. He knew he had the touch of a born seaman: he enjoyed displaying his professionalism to the dockers and harbour officials who, seeing a 330-hundred-ton ship bearing down on them through the locks, with eighteen inches to spare on either side, tended to retreat smartly. When laying his stem on the dock, he had nearly boobed this morning. In his impatience, he had entered too fast: the pitched propeller had managed to take off her way only at the last second. The impact would not have cracked a watch-glass. Out went the springs, over went the brow, and a minute later his crew had clambered ashore: neat and smartly turned out, they were a credit to the ship. They'd be in their homes within twenty minutes.

He always watched them go. He could not help comparing these men with the crews he'd signed on only twelve years ago who, even now, had to be accepted by some of the older side trawlers. If he had his way, he'd make sure that all trawlers were as modernly and decently equipped as *Campion*, and if there was no dole for the layabouts there'd be no manning problems. Happily, the crews of the good ships shared a mutual trust with their owners; each respected and expected the best of each other. At the moment, the penal tax a skipper was forced to pay on the earnings of his trip helped to keep those layabouts alive. He bitterly resented such a system; and he regarded with patient resignation the 'lumpers' who were unloading the fish he had caught with such effort — he had enjoyed only three hours' sleep every twenty-four hours during fourteen days of the trip.

He had to dock his ship within twenty days because of the perishable cargo he carried. The oldest fish would be sixteen days old, and this was the maximum time for fish to be kept in ice; the shelved fish — those that were laid on ice but with no ice on top of them — looked fresh and in prime condition if *Campion* docked at the right time. Four days late, because of the weather or because there was no vacant berth alongside, and the fish could deteriorate in appearance by as much as a hundred per cent. The blue of the eyes would turn grey and the shiny, greasy skin of the cod would begin to turn white — then the price of the market would tumble dramatically.

Hooky stepped briskly across to the white-coated buyers and salesmen now beginning to congregate around the first batch of boxed cod. This was always an agonizing moment for him, because it was always the price of King Cod that called the tune. He waited, the coldness from the mucky ice, barely thawing on the concrete, seeping through his shoes and into his very being.

The auctioneer, a man employed by the port's group of owners, had started the bidding. As each batch of boxes went down, the merchant who was buying it claimed the boxes by throwing on top of them his named tallies. Hooky felt pleased that the cod were holding the highest price so far but, surprisingly, the codlings were fetching even more.

The mixed bag came next: the bergylts, those somewhat obscene spikey red fishes, much prized in Germany, should sell well because today was a Jewish religious festival. The blue ling was also selling highly; and, to his amazement, those coleys with which he'd been so disappointed, haul after haul, had reached an all-time record. He walked slowly from the shed, relieved by the reversal of fortune. He was beginning to feel he might be slipping: he had felt so tired — and he had certainly made some wrong decisions. He had been convinced, at the time, that he should have remained south, on Hari-Kari, but he had risked the long steam and charged north to Langanes only to find the cod gone. If the coleys hadn't fetched such a price, he'd never have made the trip — and even now it could still be touch and go. He'd know the result after breakfast, when he reported for his routine discussion with Ted Bayley. Ted was a good guy and, having worked with Gunn's since he was a boy, he knew his job backwards: he was always sympathetic when he listened to the skipper's reports.

Hooky yawned. He was tired, even though he'd snatched those few hours of sleep in Molly's arms. That was the beauty of a truly good marriage — at this fishing game, a man needed a woman who understood. God, he was tired — and always was on this first morning: he'd had little sleep during the past forty-eight hours.

A finger tapped him on the shoulder. It was Gunn's 'runner'. 'Wanted on the phone, Skip,' the man said, before darting away, intent on catching a likely deckie for the next trip.

'That you, Ted? Hooky here.'

The skipper listened to Ted's dismal report: the shore gang refused to undertake all *Campion*'s defects.

Hooky drew himself up to his full height and took a deep breath. 'It's no good, Ted, I've made up me mind,' he said, putting down the telephone.

Hooky threaded his way through the fleet of refrigerated container lorries, that massive transport enterprise brought into being by British Rail's closure of the line.

He shoved his hands deep into his open great coat and lumbered back to his new Merc: silver grey, it was — a beautiful car and, secretly, he was proud of it. The throng moved out of his way as he drove out through the dock. He peeked through his rear mirror and smiled as he saw them pointing him out. He put his foot down and drove fast. He'd enjoy a quick breakfast and be at head office before Hugh and Geoffrey arrived at nine o'clock. He'd be all ready for them.

He let himself in through the front door and went into the kitchen, where Molly was cooking his first breakfast — the ritual that never lost its savour after three weeks of Soupy

Ben's food. He tiptoed up to her silently, turned her round and kissed her fully on the lips. As she dropped the oven cloth, the telephone shrilled.

'What are your views, Ted?' Hugh Gunn was asking.

Edward Bayley, Manager of Gunn's Fleetwood office, turned from the window through which he had been watching the departure of the salesmen, the buyers and the refrigerated lorries from the fish dock. Another trip for *Campion* was over; he and the Gunn brothers were discussing the vital man who made the whole operation possible — the trawler skipper. It was Hooky's turn to be scrutinized beneath the microscope, and Ted sighed as he turned to face his owners. He hated criticizing the skippers: from an office desk it was too easy to forget what the conditions were like during the winter off Iceland.

'Hooky's had bad luck, Mr Hugh,' Ted Bayley said, addressing the elder of the two Gunn brothers. From the corner of his eye, he glimpsed the impatience that flitted across Geoffrey Gunn's stern face: it was always more difficult to placate the younger brother, a very different character from the elder: tough, with a memory like an elephant, and uncompromising when dealing with the union — the ideal complement to Hugh who, a dreamer, loved his ships, the development of trawler design and the steady building of a modern Gunn fleet. Hugh, it seemed to Ted Bayley, might be the more intelligent of the two; his disarming vagueness concealed a needle-sharp mind.

'I rather agree with you, Ted,' Hugh said from the corner of his grandfather's oaken desk, which he straddled. 'A good skipper can't win every time.'

Geoffrey turned to them both, and his grey eyes were steely as he glanced at each man. Ted always felt uncomfortable beneath their searching gazes. 'Father wouldn't have been so tolerant,' he said.

'I think you're wrong,' Hugh said, his voice gentle but edged with exasperation. 'He would have realized the strain our skippers have been working under.'

'This Third Cod War's been going on for over a year now,' Ted chipped in, always trying to compromise. 'And Hooky's been one of the leaders to hold out against the gunboats. His trips are bound to suffer, with all this harassment.'

'You can't have it both ways,' Geoffrey snapped. 'We're either in the game to make a trip or we're out of business.' His jaw was set as he stuffed his hands into the diagonal trouser pockets of his pepper-and-salt gentleman's tweed suit. 'We can't make exceptions.'

'Here he comes now,' Ted said as he watched Hooky's burly figure sauntering across the road.

'Let's not pre-judge him,' Hugh said. 'Let's hear what Hooky has to say: he's trying all he knows to reach the top.'

As Skipper Hooky Walker closed the oaken door behind him, he felt the atmosphere of generations of Gunns and their skippers closing in around him. For decades now, skippers in from the sea would make the journey to the office on the morning of their arrival: first the fish market, then home for breakfast; and finally back to the office to discuss the trip with the 'gaffer', Ted Bayley or one of the Gunn brothers. Mistakes, successes, repairs, suggestions for the future: all would be analysed in detail — frankly, but with no rancour. The system demanded that everyone, from the owners down to the brassy, should contribute all he could to the enterprise. This morning would be one of those Hooky detested: he'd be forced to have a row, and that meant that his seventy-two hours ashore would be ruined. He dreaded altercations, for they twisted him up inside: he always had to screw up his courage before making the assault. So he wasted no time when he turned to face the Gunn brothers and their manager.

'Nearly lost the ship, Mr Hugh,' he growled. 'Never yet been so near to being overwhelmed.'

The three men kept silent, as they waited for the storm to blow over.

'Your maintenance gang bodged the job on the fish room hatch — didn't even finish the clips, so we filled up when we took a sea.' Hooky told them in a few choice words what had happened. 'If we can't depend upon the repair work being done properly, Mr Hugh and Mr Geoffrey,' he said, facing them squarely, 'we're going to lose even more time — the harassment by the Icelandic gunboats is bad enough.'

He was amused to see that, now that everyone's pocket was being affected, a seriousness had enveloped them all. No one was smiling now: Geoffrey began filling his Dunhill pipe, while Hugh stared out of the window, hands thrust deep into his jacket pockets. It was Ted Bayley, with his dour and canny face, who broke the silence.

'How'd the harassment go, then?'

'Bad. The gunboats were chopping gear whenever they could — and that wastes time.'

'And money,' Geoffrey snapped.

'It's the time off fishing that affects us all so badly,' Hooky went on. 'This last trip was a case in point: standing-by *Seabreeze* lost me a day's fishing.'

'Any worse than the others?' asked Hugh. 'The harassment?'

'Yes; damned sight worse.' Hooky felt the frustration mounting inside him. How difficult it was to put into words, this feeling of helplessness when out there off Iceland. It was one long stress, an endless round of decision-making: whether to compromise fishing time in order to foil the gunboats.

As in the '73 Cod War, the Icelandic Communist Government had already made it known to the world and to their friends, the Russians, that they would arrest anyone whom they found fishing inside their declared fifty-mile limit. The fact that neither the British nor anyone else accepted this limit made no difference to them.

'We all know,' Hooky said, as he glanced at his employers, 'that the Icelanders desperately want to arrest one of us: they can then show us up as an example to the world. What else could I have done under the circumstances,' he asked, 'though I had to waste time and stop fishing?'

'What happened, Hooky?' Hugh asked quietly.

'The weather got up,' Hooky went on, 'and one-hundred-and-eighty miles south-east of the Vestmann Islands, at about tea-time *Seabreeze* took a bad sea. She flooded her engine room and swiped her bridge and boat deck, carrying away everything. She sent out a Mayday and the first person to answer was *Laki*, the Icelandic coastguard. In spite of this damned dispute, she set out immediately from Ingolfshofdi, a hundred miles from *Seabreeze*'s position. "I'll be with you at midnight," she signalled and set off into this appalling weather. She was running down a beam sea, but she sailed without hesitation.'

Hooky shook his head and rubbed the side of his face with his huge hand. 'You've got to give it to 'em,' he said, 'they're damned fine seamen and will always help any ship in trouble. They still put the lore of the sea first.' He could see that the others were listening now, their imaginations alive to that wild night, the shrieking wind, the roar of the seas and that stricken trawler, out of control and almost overwhelmed.

'A tricky situation was developing, can't you see?' Hooky said impatiently. 'Though *Laki* could never have boarded, she could have passed a line across by a line-throwing gun. She would have taken *Seabreeze* in tow and, as soon as the wind had moderated, would have towed her back to Reykjavik — not to the UK. Then they would have arrested her because, a week previously, *Laki* had chopped both her warps.

'By sheer good luck, I'd decided to come home with her, because I'd made my trip; I was thirty miles to the north-east of her, so I hauled and turned round to try to find her. She had no D/F by now and no wireless transmission. It's a darn big ocean, as you all know, but I was lucky and found *Seabreeze* first shot. When I hailed her, she had just sorted herself out: they'd pumped out the engine room, started the engine and, still with no lighting, managed to proceed again under their own steam.

'Things weren't as bad as they had first seemed, but when you see your bridge smashed in, the engine room full of water, and flooding everywhere with men shouting, things always look worse, don't they?'

The two brothers were nodding their heads. Hooky had prevented disaster, even though he'd lost a day-and-a-half's fishing. 'We steamed slowly downwind until the gale blew itself out. *Laki* wished us well and turned back, but the point is, she *did* try to help *Seabreeze*, as they always do, even though they would have arrested her.' He regarded the others who, silent now, were each engrossed in their own thoughts.

'This war,' Hooky concluded, 'it like all wars. I'm not worried about the politicians: to them, it's just a game of chess. They don't give a damn. It's the men that are carrying it out who are the chessmen in the game. We are the pawns, *Hekla* and I, and it's our battle. He's taking away our living and driving us off the grounds we've fished for centuries.'

Hooky had made his point. Geoffrey exchanged a glance with his brother, and Hugh turned towards his manager.

'We've been thinking you need a rest, Hooky,' Ted said. 'Best take a couple of trips off.'

Hooky stopped in mid-flood, unable to believe his ears. They weren't giving him the bum's rush, were they? His lowered head was like an angry bull's. From beneath his bushy, sandy eyebrows, he peered at each man in turn. 'You don't mean that, do you?' he asked, unbelieving. 'I'm not tired.'

The silence was embarrassing.

'You might as well know,' Hooky went on, the anger welling inside him as the dam began to burst, 'the lads won't put to sea until a proper job has been made of the hatch clips.' He looked at them and they met his challenge, facing him squarely.

'Ted's right,' Hugh said. 'Why don't you take a couple of trips off after Christmas? Then you'll be ready to get into the spring fishing.'

The skipper quietly left the office. Fred opened the swing doors for him, down below. He stepped out onto the pavement and walked across the road to where he'd left his new Mercedes. Unseeing, he drove slowly down Dock Road, past the markets and along the seafront. Out there the tide had slipped away, leaving the vast expanse of mud and sand that stretched across Morecambe Bay to the Cumberland hills beyond. 'Fleetwood,' he murmured quietly to himself, 'town of laughter and tears.'

Since the port had been built a hundred years ago, Fleetwood had earned that name. For him, it would certainly mean unhappiness in sixty-five hours' time, if the next trip was not a good one.

7: THE WHITE SEA

Susan Braithwaite stood at the assembly line that fretted eternally past her: the slabs of fish fingers, golden brown from the breadcrumb spreader, were now piling into their required units, ready to be sealed off into the final packaging. Over the months, miles of fish fingers had slatted past her, so that she had begun even to dream about them when her Yorkie was away.

'C'mon luv — stop yer dreamin'.' It was Big Ann, the supervisor, who was everywhere, popping up where she was least expected, checking and helping the girls as the lines sped by.

Susie (for so Yorkie called her) smiled in contentment. It seemed not long ago since he'd left her at two o'clock that morning. 'My Yorkie,' she whispered, hugging the memory of him to herself. She had persuaded him to give up Hull and to bring up their family in Fleetwood instead — which was why the lads had given him the name they had.

He had resisted, but then, after two years of courting, he'd agreed to move as soon as they were married. Now that little Carol was two-and-a-half, Susie could come out to work when Yorkie was at sea. She could thus ease the pain of his absence and earn some money for their home at the same time.

Luckily, she'd picked a good 'un in Yorkie — he'd fallen for her golden hair, she knew, but not many men now would tolerate their wives being away from home when their ship docked. He did not like returning to an empty house, but they had agreed to put up with the disadvantages in order to earn the money: the HP payments on the new Fiat weren't too damaging, and the car had given them a new dimension when he was ashore. They could just about manage it, on top of the house mortgage, so long as he remained with Skipper Walker in *English Campion*. The crew knew that Hooky Walker would one day become a top skipper; they were drawing good money. If the tax was not so savage, they'd cope much better.

Susan sighed: she wondered sometimes whether they were missing out on life. Yorkie seemed so obsessed with giving her *things*, that he saved very little. She didn't want to end up like Sandra Wilkins next door, who was so houseproud that she had even refused a child, even though her Ted yearned for one. Sandra was going to enjoy herself while she could, she confessed, and was going to make their home beautiful while she could: there remained only the deep-freeze to acquire, and then she and Ted would think about a family…

At least she, Susan, wasn't like that: Yorkie had wanted little Carol from the first night of their honeymoon. They had been engaged for nearly two years; they had seriously discussed these things, so there'd been no stress between them, as there was between so many of her friends who were the wives of fishermen. Yorkie had only one worry: that he could keep his place in *Campion*. So long as he ran his fish room properly, the mate, Peter Sinclair, would remain happy: if he pleased that hard men, Yorkie would be all right with the skipper.

Poor old Skipper Walker — Yorkie had said that he'd not swap places with Hooky for all the fish in Fleetwood. His job was one long worry, particularly now that the trawlers were restricted to those boxes off the east coast of Iceland. Yorkie was sure that Hooky was worried about this last trip — he had mentioned the White Sea one night to Knocker Wright. There'd be cod there, he'd hinted: he was fed up with being hemmed in and with not being his own master off Iceland.

The coffee-break whistle sounded, its shrill call shattering her dream. She patted back her hair beneath the blue nylon cap they all had to wear. *Campion* would be well into the Minch now and taking Yorkie to Russian waters: she always felt apprehensive when she thought of those icy seas.

The mate always recognized the signs: Hooky was thinking — and shortly there'd be a decision. His lips were pursed and, though he sat in the bridge chair, he was allowing Peter to take the ship right up to the North Channel. Ulster seemed so close today, those misty blue hills fifteen miles away — and up that lough that led into the distance was Belfast.

'Bloody madmen, aren't they?' was all that Hooky murmured today as the lough slid astern. 'How can they murder each other on a day like this and in such a beautiful land as that?'

Peter Sinclair nodded. It was a relief to escape to sea, away from the strife of landsmen. The ship was thudding beneath their feet today, *Campion*'s first day out. The crew were all turned in, taking it easy on the first day's steaming northwards: tomorrow they'd be once again in their sea-going rig and cleaning up the ship after the shore-gang had fouled her up.

'I heard today that Iceland is going to tell the Yanks to pack up their NATO base and tracking station,' Peter said. 'That'll make things worse around the coast.'

'Russian orders,' Hooky said. 'What else can you expect with a Commie Prime Minister?'

'The Americans have told the Icelanders that they'll leave the island as they found it, so that should make Jacobssen think twice.'

'Yeh, yeh,' the skipper drawled, 'the Yanks have given the island a hell of a lot, including a road running right round the island — but generosity does not necessarily make friends.'

'They're fine people, the Yanks,' Peter said. 'The most generous on earth, but people aren't grateful.'

Peter was watching the skipper: he knew that the parting of the ways would be upon them within the next hour. The high jump of Ailsa Craig was almost on their starboard beam, at the feet of which still lay the submarine, *Vandal*. The craggy Mull of Kintyre was broad on their bow and…

'We'll try the White Sea, this trip,' Hooky said, settling down at last as comfortably as he could in the bridge chair. 'Turn to starboard and take her up the Sound of Jura.'

'Right, Skip.' Peter flipped the knob of the autopilot, which was set to alter course by using five degrees of rudder; the blue and white trawler swung slowly to her new course until, ahead, on the Oa of Islay, the TV masts of Carraig Fhada pierced the clouds.

'We've had a rotten catch for the last two trips off Iceland,' Hooky was saying. 'It's time we made a good trip, or I'll get the sack.'

Peter detected a trace of anxiety behind the laughter that rumbled from the skipper's belly. They all had much at stake, from the brassy to the skipper — damn it, even Jeannie was beginning to worry about their commitments, since he had been bringing home less money after the last two trips. 'We're too spoiled,' Peter had laughed. 'It's tough near the top, you know — we'll have to do without, lass.'

Hooky was still sharing his thoughts with the mate. 'We did well in November last year, before you joined me — we caught a good trip off Novaya Zemlya. I'm better on my own, Pete. My father was just the same.'

They fell silent as the beauty of a tranquil November evening gradually enveloped them. The islands were red from the dead bracken, and the serenity of the Scottish scenery induced

Peter's mind to wander to those far-off days when British fishermen first began trawling.

Peter Sinclair gazed across to the barren hillsides of Jura, rust-brown and gold in the evening shade. As he handed *Campion* back to the skipper for the passage of the Sounds of Jura and of Luing, he knew that this beautiful part of the world must never be altered: but with the national search for oil, could its safety be guaranteed? Life in the east coast of Scotland had never been the same since the oilmen had invaded the coast.

Peter always enjoyed watching the skipper making the passage of the Minches. It was dark now and there was no moon. As Hooky took the throbbing *Campion* up the Firth of Lorne and into the Sound of Mull, Peter had to envy the sure touch of his skipper's seamanship and his pilotage. They left Duart Castle to port, before swinging to the northward as Loch Linnhe, at the entrance to the Caledonian Canal, came abeam. Ardnamurchan Point next and then northward, through the Sound of Sleat and the Kyle of Lochalsh, that exciting passage barely two cables wide. Northward, always northward now, through the Minch until the desolate Butt of Lewis reared up out of the night, close on their port bow.

Midnight came and went. Then the long swell hit the little ship as she began her 680-mile passage; on a course of 041 degrees, she should make a landfall off Skomva at the southern tip of the Lofoten Islands. During the late afternoon, two and a half days later, Skomva stole up from the horizon and was left to the westward, the Devil's Cauldron, twenty miles further on, being given a wide berth: this fearsome whirlpool had swallowed up many a small ship.

As the bleak Lofotens slid past them, Hooky Walker's mind travelled back to his father's recollections of the wartime commando raids on these islands. The attack up Vestfjord had achieved complete surprise: the fish oil factories, of benefit to the Germans, were destroyed; and over 300 Norwegian volunteers had returned with the force when it withdrew.

The jagged peaks of the Lofotens looked down menacingly upon the little trawler when she stopped to pick up the Norwegian pilots for the inshore passage of the fjords. Hooky felt relieved now that he was in the lee of these high mountains. He detested the outer passage up the Norwegian coast, for the weather seemed always to be appalling; the prevailing winds were against the current in the Gulf Stream and the seas were always abominable.

By making the passage through Vestfjord and turning to port for Lodingen, where he was now picking up the pilot, he could take his *Campion* past Harstad and right up to North Cape through sheltered waters. He always savoured the grandeur of this beautiful scenery and enjoyed the company of the pilots. These Norwegian pilots were grand people, working six hours on and six off, while they navigated the ship through the hundred miles of fjords. Passing beneath the bridges and through the narrows of Finnesness required the highest skill. Finnesness was always bitterly cold at this time of year: the ship would often be iced up by the end of the passage.

With the mountains receding astern, dawn broke pale and clear as Hooky took *Campion* past the barren scenery above Tromso. All was white with snow now, an isolated farmhouse scarring the dreary scrub-covered landscape. A few cattle eked out an existence, but they seemed to be the only living creatures on this bleak November day.

They passed Altenfjord, notorious once as the German fleet anchorage where *Tirpitz* lay until she was finally sunk. They travelled up Soroysund and on to Hammerfest, where Hooky again took over his ship until the pilots, enjoying a busman's holiday, could be dropped.

The Norwegian trawler fleet operated out of Hammerfest, its 120-foot modern stern trawlers being able to withstand the hard winters. Up here at the North Cape, only first-class seamen could survive, a fact that was brought home clearly to Hooky when he took *Campion* out of the final shelter of the Honningsvag passage and into the long swell of the Barents Sea. Grey, bleak and cold were the seas that broke over the ship's bows: he felt better when he altered course to the eastward for Russia — and so was able to take the seas beam-on. It was here, in mid-summer, that the cruise ships brought busloads of tourists to stand on the cliff of North Cape to view the Land of the Midnight Sun, where the sun never sets: the pale orb sinks to some ten degrees above the horizon and then climbs again into the ascendant.

Hooky decided to ignore the North Cape Bank, because he needed time to chase the 'flats' (plaice) away to the eastward in the White Sea. He felt relieved now that he was making his easting — but when he reached 33 degrees longitude East, he knew that he would feel again the apprehension he always suffered when leaving astern the friendly Norwegian waters.

He crossed the meridian as the cold, moonless night stole upon him: one more day's steaming and he would be able to shoot his first trawl. He smiled to himself for, at 33 degrees East, he always practised the same ritual. He turned to the watchkeeper beside him. 'Knocker,' he said, 'my cigars.'

Knocker Wright's unshaven face broke into a grin. 'Right, Skip,' he said, glad that the first milestone of a White Sea trip had at last arrived. Once the aroma of cigar smoke pervaded the bridge, all knew that the skip was himself again. Knocker returned up the ladder and handed over the box. 'You put 'em in a different drawer, Skip,' he said. 'Need a light?'

The glow from the match illuminated the two men's faces; one, craggy, entering middle-age and old before its time; the other, lined, tired, and with eyes that reflected sadness and resignation.

Hooky took a long pull at the cigar. He sighed with pleasure as he watched the smoke curling towards the deckhead. Knocker was staring towards the stern.

'See that, Skip?' he asked suddenly. 'A flickering light — I'm sure of it.'

Hooky turned aft and peered towards the western horizon, where a streak of daylight lingered. An orange light danced there, like marsh gas, without form in this deserted ocean. He moved over to the radar screen — but there was no echo. He returned to the after end of the bridge: the light was still there.

Strange, Hooky thought. *There's no one fishing there — or am I being followed again?*

On his last trip to the White Sea, he was sure that he was being shadowed: he never lost the uncomfortable feeling that he was not alone.

'Probably a Russian submarine, Knocker,' Hooky said. 'Thinks we're a spy-ship.'

'Like *Empire Clover* — d'you remember, Skip?'

Hooky recalled the ship, an oil-burning side trawler out of Hull. Her Majesty's Government had failed to inform the fishing industry that the Russians had designated restricted areas in which they were carrying out naval exercises. *Empire*

Clover was fishing in such an area, so the Russians held her in Vladimirskiy for five days while diplomatic negotiations took place for her release. Hugh Gunn had been on board at the time as a passenger, a fact which had made the incident more interesting. She'd been fishing off the White Sea when she had been arrested and taken into the Kola Inlet. The incident made any British skipper think twice before nearing any Russian twelve-mile limit. Hooky already felt uneasy, and the sooner he could catch a trip up here, the better. Then he'd get to hell out of it.

8: GINGER GREENO

After leaving Vardö astern, *Campion* stayed on the edge of the twelve-mile limit. Hooky had remembered to inform his insurers that he was now behind the Iron Curtain, so at least he could now concentrate on hunting the 'flatties'. A good trip and the anxiety about his future would slip from his mind. Kirkenes was astern now, and the Kola Inlet and Murmansk would soon be abeam. With the prevailing south-east wind sweeping off Siberia, the air was beginning to feel cold: the crew would be wrapping up now and the older men would begin flapping their arms to maintain circulation in their fingers. There'd be a difference tomorrow when they hauled: holding up the nets for mending was one of the coldest operations that had to be carried out on the working deck.

Campion left Cape Svyatoy Nos to the southward, then crossed the entrance to the White Sea which she could not fish because the twelve-mile limit successfully barred all-comers. With Archangel at its head, the inlet was inhospitable and cold, particularly for those men who still remembered the terrible wartime convoys.

Hooky was happy to press on to Cape Kanin, where he altered course northward for the fishing grounds. He was becoming used to the darkness, so he would 'shoot' at dawn tomorrow. If he made some good hauls, he would stay here for ten days to catch a trip. He'd work his way up towards Novaya Zemlya and hope to get into the fish.

They had been fishing for five days now. Hooky had slipped into the daily routine: shoot; three-and-a-half hours' trawling;

haul — day in, day out. The hands, too, were beginning to feel that they would 'catch a trip', for there were smiles and much chiakking on the working deck. Hooky, hands in pockets, in a woollen shirt which bulged open at the chest and belly, padded about in carpet slippers. He puffed contentedly at his cigar while regarding the mate's watch on deck. The oilskins glistened in the darkness, the steaming clouds of men's breaths rising like haloes above each yellow hood.

He had spotted a mark on the echo sounder and he immediately got into the plaice. He'd had a hunch that there were fish about, because of the two willet birds he'd seen: strange little black and white creatures in the grand design of nature. Swimming under water, they would surface suddenly to fly through the air for hundreds of yards before flopping back under water again, much like the flying fish. In a few million years, evolution would arrange for them to become airborne, like the puffin. The willets always returned to shore to roost at night after working thirty miles from land on their day's fishing. The skipper watched the mate undoing the cod-end knot: another ninety baskets, Hooky guessed. They were hooking on the wire to hoist up the net to the gentry head.

The last haul had produced some fine haddock, and the bosun had brought one up to the verandah for the skipper to see. Hooky gazed up into the night sky where, in this bitter cold, the stars sparkled like diamonds. How could a seaman not believe in his Creator? In these days, with the cynicism that accompanied the callous life ashore, men thought they could run their lives without God, but it never surprised Hooky when his crew talked sometimes of their belief in things other than the material. Take the haddock, for instance; for the fisherman, the tradition of God's fingerprint was not a legend: the evidence of the eyes was good enough for sailors.

Behind the neck of every haddock and Johnny Dory were the Lord's thumbprint on one side, and fingerprint on the other. The marks were in the precise position in which a fisherman would pick up a fish. The miracle of Jesus feeding the hungry crowd with two fishes and five loaves was not difficult to believe if you were a fisherman. There was so much at sea that was beyond human comprehension — perhaps that was why Hooky loved this life? He never ceased to be amazed by the instinct of the birds.

He had once steamed to Greenland from Iceland. The weather had been bad and the passage had taken a day and a half. One hundred and fifty miles off Greenland, he had shot the first trawl. The area was utterly desolate: no ships, nothing in sight. On the first haul, a solitary Molly bird had materialized. The catch was gutted, the guts floating astern in the sea. On the next haul, as the cod-end appeared on the surface, the sky became suddenly black with thousands of birds. How had they communicated and whence had they come?

It was damned cold out on deck. Black ice was forming along all the wet surfaces. It was as well that the wind was on *Campion*'s starboard quarter, or the slop over the bow would begin to cause icing up. Once the spray began to fly, a ship could grow about an inch of ice a minute — and then all hands had to move fast with the chipping.

Hooky watched the deckies on the slippery wooden deck beneath him. They should never walk across the net like that when the wires were being hauled — he remembered once when a net dragged a man straight down the ramp, when the winchman veered instead of hauled. The man had never been seen again — once overboard into the swirling wake, there was no hope.

Who *was* that, walking across the bulging belly of the net? By the size of the man and his short legs, it looked like the new deckie, Ginger Greeno. He'd done well as brassy and had been promoted to deckie in this ship. The mate had recommended him, and Hooky had always judged the lad to be a good 'un… Good God, what was happening?

Ginger Greeno was seventeen years and eight months old. He was enjoying himself working here on deck: at last, he was taking part in the haul. He had served his time as brassy, but he'd always been in the fish room: first as an axeman preparing the ice for the fish pounds; and then helping with the stowing of the fish. The previous mate had always kept a man in the same job if he was good at it; there was no swapping around, so a man could be in the fish room for life. Ginger would never work on deck with the nets, never keep a watch on the bridge. Even now, in this modern trawler with her autopilot, there was never a chance of taking the wheel and learning to steer. He'd have to leave *Campion*, even though he liked her, for a seaman's training in one of the side trawlers. Only by gaining a mate's ticket as soon as he could, could he progress to skipper — and that was why he'd joined: he wanted his own ship one day. Tommy Ballance, the temporary deckie, was beckoning to him from the port winch — he needed someone to back up the hoist wire on the drum. Ginger leaped across the net.

The ship took a roll as the toe of his boot tripped in the mesh. As he fell, he glimpsed the mate signalling to the winchman to hoist the belly of the net. Tommy's eyes were on the mate: Ginger's fall, concealed by the hump in the fish net, had not been noticed.

It took a moment for the young deckie to realize that he was in mortal danger. As he struggled to his feet, he felt the net jerk him sideways, overbalancing him again in a tangle of nylon and slippery fish. Swiftly he was rising into the air, head down and dangling crazily, while he swung like a pendulum across the ship's roll.

He yelled at the top of his voice. He heard his own cry, faint against the clatter of the haul and the howling of the wind. He shot upwards, the arcs of the gantry light blinding him as they swung to meet him; he heard the note of fear in the shouted orders; he glimpsed the confusion on the deck which was now receding rapidly beneath him: it spiralled, and began to swing dizzily in concentric circles, worlds away, miles below... Then, suddenly, as he hit the large leading block on the gantry head, he felt the agony in his foot. The gantry legs whirled before him; the Red Duster flashed before his eyes, a smear of red. The deck came tearing up towards him. He heard his own scream, drifting away on the wind...

9: THE WHITE SHADOW

It was the searing pain — scalding needles in his thigh — that was his first sensation of consciousness. Where the hell was he? The query revolved in his head, which ached as much as his body. He slowly opened his eyes: there above him was the deckhead — *Ginger Greeno: that's me, so I can't be dead.* He groaned with the pain, as he became faintly aware of a hand on his shoulder.

'You're okay, Ginger,' someone said. Was it Wild Bill's voice? He was a friendly, thoughtful bloke. 'I'll tell the mate you're round...' The voice faded.

He must have ebbed away again, for next he remembered the distant murmuring of another voice — and then he recognized the monosyllables of the mate's speech. Ginger was all right; nothing broken, they were saying. Tell that to the marines: he felt bloody awful.

They must have given him some drug because then he dozed off, half-conscious, his mind in a demi-world of grotesque images. Strangely, the details of his last run ashore came vividly to him, so that he held out his hand to touch her fingers; he knew that it was Belle taking his hand in hers.

Bella Dashwood had been in the same form at school. They'd gone steady for at least six months during their last year at school. She was a doe-eyed dolly, with long silky hair (honey-blonde, she called it) framing her pale face. Less than five feet tall, she had been his first serious girlfriend; even at sixteen, he'd loved her, and now, after their meeting again in Preston, she had told him that she wanted to marry him.

'You're too young, Ginger,' his father had said. 'Forget 'er. There's plenty more, at your age.'

But three months ago, up in the Lakes where they'd spent a weekend together, tramping the fells and making love in the heather, they'd pledged their lives to each other — and, last time in dock, she'd told him she was to have his baby. She had smiled when he'd nodded, disbelieving but proud of his manhood. 'Next trip,' he'd said, 'we'll get wed.'

He'd never told his mum and dad. He wanted time to think: these shot-gun marriages never worked, they all said. Bella was different: her mum was Italian and they were a Roman Catholic family. He'd love her, by God, he'd love her forever … and he sensed someone bending over him, prising open his lips and trying to pour some soup down his gullet.

On the morning of Ginger Greeno's accident, the fish disappeared. Hungry Mitch said that the mishap was a bad omen and that the trip would suffer. Soupy Ben agreed: Ginger was a Jonah. The skipper retired into his shell, humming to himself as he called upon his instinct to unravel the movement of the fish. After the sixth day, he gave up fishing across the banks where the other trawlers were working; he would lay his dan-buoy and fish methodically outwards from it, each haul a five-mile search outwards, like the spokes of a wheel. The wind freshened in the afternoons and the hauls were monotonous and unproductive: only twenty baskets in two days.

Hooky had been exercising his intelligence. There was little point in continuing here. Only another four days remained before he would have to steer for home. Why not try a haul off Bear Island on his way back? He yelled down from the verandah rail: 'Tell the mate to pick up the dan.'

'Right, Skip.' It was the pale face of Ginger Greeno that smiled up at him, waving an arm in acknowledgement. Hooky nodded: it was a miracle the lad had not been killed or badly hurt. The mate should never have allowed Ginger into the danger area — he tended to be too slack with the lads at times. To be a successful skipper, a man had to be hard: if he spent his time worrying about the safety and comfort of the crew, he'd never catch a trip. Hooky walked to the mic on the console and spoke through the mouthpiece.

'Shut the ramp doors — *steaming.*'

A garbled acknowledgement crackled in the speaker. He turned to the pitch control, set full speed, and altered course to 280 degrees on the autopilot. Then he slumped back in his chair, his stomach screwed up with apprehension: next stop, Bear Island.

Campion spent a day and a half fishing off Bear Island. Hooky trawled to within fifteen miles of the black mountain top that reared from the Arctic Ocean; only the crew of a weather station inhabited its inhospitable five-mile length. The hauls were desperately disappointing: with so many mixed bags of coleys, reds and mock halibut, *Campion* still had not caught a trip. So, on their sixteenth day, Hooky decided to make for the north-east of Iceland. Further to the north lay Spitzbergen, that mountainous land mass whence a man could walk, during ten months of the year, across the ice to Greenland and Canada.

Campion's skipper felt irritable and restless, his career possibly depending upon the success of his last two remaining days' fishing. He'd try Langanes, off the north-east corner: provided there were not too many other trawlers there, he might be lucky. At least they would be British, unlike the trawlers on the grounds he'd left: Russian, Portuguese, Poles, French and Spanish — all were there, an international fleet.

The passage to Iceland would last two days, twelve hours: eight hundred miles; but as only four hours (one haul) would be lost on the slight detour, Hooky thought it worth the risk. But, God, how he wished that his luck would turn, or he'd be sunk. When he returned to Iceland, the only risk, apart from the absence of fish, was having his gear chopped by *Hekla* or *Laki*, those bloody gunboats.

In the wheelhouse on the evening of the fourth day's steaming, they spent an amusing hour discussing world affairs. Hooky had lit his favourite cigar and with Langanes only eighty miles' distant, he felt he was at last bound to catch a bag of fish. Nothing depressed him more, after a bad haul, than the averted eyes of the crew when they passed him in the passageways.

They nicknamed him Kangaroo Hooky, and there was surely some grain of truth in their oblique reference to his character. This morning there was a real sense of disappointment; tomorrow's haul would be critical for morale.

How *could* a man remain depressed when he witnessed such a sunset as gleamed to the westward tonight? The dulcet tones of a mouth-organ were floating from the loudspeaker of his R/T set: that must be Bill Benson in *Sundown*; he must be within fifty miles. He always played his mouth-organ at this time of the evening, for the benefit of everyone in 'the Box': the sound was warm and welcoming, like the singing of country folk when a man came home on a winter's evening, with the lights glowing through the curtained windows of the pub. He glanced up at Peter Sinclair: he was talking to Ewan Massey, who for once was relaxing outside his radio office.

'Bill's at it again,' Sinclair said. 'He must have made his trip.'

Ewan laughed shortly. 'He doesn't mind whether he's out here or not,' he said. 'The taxman will take it all, anyway.'

Hooky felt grateful, for he knew what they were trying to say: that they didn't blame him. 'You never know how it will go, until the ball stops rolling,' was a favourite adage of trawlermen when they were fishing. Well, there were still forty-eight hours in which the ball could roll…

'We won't need a taxman at this rate,' Hooky said, the corners of his mouth turned down, his eyes doleful in his expressive face. Peter was listening to the R/T chatter between the skippers fishing off Langanes. The scene had been transformed by the warmth of comradeship, after the bleak loneliness of the White Sea. Even Hooky was chuckling as he listened to the baleful commentaries being exchanged over the air. Bill Cody was commiserating with Husky Tranto, skipper of *English Cowslip*.

'It's downright bloody robbery,' Bill was saying. 'How much did you make last trip, Husky?'

Knocker Wright was on watch and standing by the bridge chair while the skipper, mate and radio operator chatted amongst themselves in that hour before tea — this was the moment when, traditionally, trawlermen set the world to rights. Knocker enjoyed these interludes: for once, he would forget his miserable married life and ponder on the world outside. He smiled as he peered into the blackness ahead, to the seas smashing towards them, as rugged little *Campion* climbed the swell before slamming down again into the troughs. Knocker moved over to the radars and watched the screens. The mountains of Iceland were showing clearly now: soon the echoes of the trawlers ahead would be coming up. That small one, eight miles ahead, was clear enough: its blip showed at every few sweeps and the skipper must have seen it. Knocker raised his eyes from the visor and began rolling himself another cigarette. He glanced at the clock: five-thirty. Another hour and he'd be down for his tea.

'We made a good trip,' Husky was crackling away on the R/T. 'Good enough, Bill.' He snorted, the sound of disgust plainly audible over the air. 'Guess what the taxman left me to take home?' he said sadly. Knocker watched the three men grouped around the chart table as they listened to the discussion over the air: Husky, like the other good skippers, never reaped the rewards they merited — the taxman saw to that.

Knocker knew that poor old skip was worried, for they all knew the signs: he kept himself distant by humming tuneless ditties to himself while he pondered his next move. He had only another thirty-six hours' fishing time left in which to catch a trip — so that was why he had not yet betrayed his presence to the trawlers in the darkness ahead of him. He was gleaning all the information he could, before deciding where to fish.

To make a twenty-day trip pay, *Campion* had to catch a lot of fish a day. Over six hauls in twenty-four hours, *Campion* had to earn her keep — an average of forty baskets of cod a haul.

Knocker always calculated the economics on a trip. Because he kept his steaming watches with the skipper he shared, to an extent, his inner thoughts. On this trip, up to this evening, the ship had caught 1100 kit which, totalled with the mixed hauls and the prime cod, was nearing break-even point at today's market prices. To make the trip worthwhile, Skip had to get, in the next thirty-six hours, a few more good hauls. If only *Campion* could get into the cod now, Hooky would still do better than most.

Knocker glanced at the skipper. He was head and shoulders above the rest, a lion of a man. His tousled head was like the mane of the king of the beasts, but tonight he seemed subdued, isolated from the others: his mind was obsessed, feeling for the fish and where they might be. Though he was listening to Bill and Husky's moans on the R/T, his mind was working restlessly on hunting the fish.

Knocker peered ahead again for the lights of the approaching trawlers. They ought to be sighted soon. That echo ahead seemed to be stationary, an indication that the trawler was hauling and preparing to shoot again. Another few miles and they could call each other up, while *Campion* passed the trawler close to the southward. Hooky was steaming north to try his luck off Iceland — the trip would now be twenty-five days.

Bill Cody was whistling, the R/T loaded with anger: 'I'm staying off next trip, Bill,' Husky was saying. 'Why the hell should I be skipper of this ship and take home less than the mate? I might as well stay ashore because, by this time of the year, I will be able to draw my weekly tax rebate.'

'Makes you weep, this taxation system,' Bill was saying. 'We fish for three weeks and our earnings are put in on one day. If the date happens to be at the beginning of a financial year, we're taxed at millionaire's rates. Bloody scandalous.'

'We don't have to do this job,' Husky said.

Bill exploded in basic Anglo-Saxon.

I don't blame him, thought Knocker. The whole pay structure in the trawler industry needed rethinking, and that was the reason *English Lavender* had lain in dock for over three weeks. She was an older side trawler and, because she could not attract a crew, she was losing her owners and the country's economy a lot of cash. Admittedly, the skippers earned good money, but what sense was there in a system which made it more profitable for a skipper to make a small profit instead of a large one? Could anyone wonder at the bloody-mindedness that was creeping like a cancer through the islands?

Knocker was a passive man, anxious only to do his job as best he could. He had begun to detest the arrogance and the disruptive influence of the trade unions. He was not sorry that, in his calling, the strike weapon was almost unknown: it was difficult to act with solidarity, when half the fleet was at sea; and when those ashore wanted nothing but to be left alone to enjoy their three days with their families.

He had to admit that trawlermen probably endured the hardest of all callings: not only was there the separation from one's family, but there were moments of mortal danger: smashed skulls, broken bones, maimed bodies — any of these accidents could occur at any moment. The total loss of a trawler was not all that rare, particularly during the winters off Iceland when gales, icing up and black ice took their toll. 'So why the hell do we come to sea?' Knocker asked himself. 'We can do nought else, I suppose.' His patient acceptance was reflected in his face.

His thoughts were interrupted by the skipper who came over to glance at the ship's head.

'Okay, Knocker. I'll take her,' he said.

The winchman nodded and moved to the side; he leaned against the monitor panel, where he could keep his balance and still maintain his look-out through the bridge windows: these covered-in and heated bridges were a modern godsend. The skipper was crouched over the radar visor. He'd know about the echo ahead. It was stopped anyway, obvious to the skipper.

'She's hauling,' Hooky said, as he clambered into the chair. 'Could be Bill Cody, by the nearness of him.' The skipper's voice was rambling on in sympathy with Husky's tale of woe. *Cowslip* had had a good haul and the news had not been lost on

Hooky Walker who, to soothe his nerves, was lighting up a cigar. The mate and Ewan Massey were talking quietly by the chart table, while they waited for the hands of the clock to reach six o'clock. They were always hungry.

The trawler job bred many dangers, Knocker realized only too well. Had not the official enquiry stated that the deep-sea fisherman was twenty per cent higher risk than any other calling, including the miner? The hardship of the life bred a craving for the bottle, alcoholism claiming many victims. If a man, after a three-week trip, suddenly found himself ashore with one hundred and fifty quid in his pocket, the temptation to drink away much of it was too much for some.

What bugged Knocker most was the viciousness of the tax system. Where was the fairness, when you considered how some people in Britain earned their money? It was time this injustice was put right. The wives ashore worried themselves silly, too, not only for the safety of their men at sea, but because alone they were having to bring up the children.

It was no good the smoothies saying, 'You don't have to do the job.' Someone had to catch fish to feed the fifty million in Britain. The mass media and publicity had so drugged society, that the ordinary bloke never considered how fish-fingers reached the table, or coal filled the scuttle.

Take away the fish, and what was there left? Meat was too expensive, the rabbits had myxomatosis, and there weren't enough chickens to go around at a reasonable price, so fish was surely an essential part of the economy? The Italians had the right idea. It was said that they did not tax their fishermen or merchant service: that was how they compensated seamen for the hazards of the life. British trawlermen would not accept that system if it meant the nationalization of the fishing industry.

Knocker walked to the side of the bridge: it was a dark night, and the crests of the waves gleamed, white and ghostly, where they broke. He supposed he came to sea because he loved the elements and was happy to leave ashore his worries. At least the life was exciting, not only because of the danger, but because a man never knew how much he *could* earn if the ship made a record trip. Knocker would hate a fishing industry that was run by soulless civil servants, like the electricity people or British Rail. He relished the freebooter element of the fishing industry: the crew took a third of the trip; the remaining two-thirds went to *Campion* and her running.

Knocker always enjoyed the excitement of the hunt. Even now, after eighteen years of trawling, the thrill of a good bag of fish being hauled was a stimulating experience: from the skipper downwards, all shared in the wealth which those gleaming fish represented. He preferred the present set-up, but he'd like to see it improved.

A few gaffers still lived in the past, but most owners were beginning to look ahead and to realize that their prosperity depended upon a workable structure. Hooky sometimes spoke about how he would run the outfit, if he had the chance. Knocker smiled as he watched the skipper drawing contentedly on his cigar, his feet up on the console, his thoughts far away on the fish, while *Campion* pounded into the darkness.

Skip would run every trawler on a share basis: each man in the ship would earn one and a half per cent of the value of the catch caught. If the ship did not make a trip, the crew would earn nothing. He knew the system worked because of the experience of two skippers, now retired, who had worked this way: their ships always put to sea on time; they always made a trip and never suffered manning problems. Hooky also realized that it wasn't so easy for the owners — it was simple enough to be a sea-lawyer.

Knocker glanced across at the skipper. He was listening to the crackle on the R/T, away to the southward, a faint smile on his lips as he pondered his next move in the hunt for fish. He seemed happy now that he was on his own and rounding the North Cape of Iceland. Hooky was always one jump ahead — and Knocker knew it would not be long before he reached the ranks of the top skippers, whatever anyone else said.

Skip was a thinker. His solution to a proper reward for trawlermen was radical and simple: a tax concession should be made whereby, say, twenty-five per cent of a man's earnings after a trip was set aside for administration by the State. This percentage would not be taxed, but would be a contribution towards the man's old-age pension: the more a man earned, the larger his pension when he retired at fifty-five. Trawlermen were on the downhill run after fifty; they were old at fifty-five. Their faces reflected the hardships, a thirty-year-old resembling a man of forty ashore. Hooky's system would offer a man an incentive and a reward for a lifetime of hardship — a good trawlerman could then be happy for his son to follow in his footsteps.

'Knocker…'

'Yes, Skip?' The winchman pulled himself together, his thoughts reverting to his watch-keeping as the skipper addressed him from the depths of the bridge chair.

'Call the lads out for shooting.'

'Sure, Skip.' Knocker switched on the deck lights and disappeared down the bridge ladder to shake the watch below.

Hooky Walker was glad that the long steam was over; the passage from the White Sea had seemed unending. Now that he was round the corner and twenty-eight miles off Straumnes, he would be amongst the cod before any Icelanders realized it. The gunboats would be on the east side, and no one would suspect he was there. Three good hauls tonight and he'd be outside the area before noon tomorrow. He relit his Edward VII cigar and glanced aft to the gantry arc lights throwing their beams across the working deck. He turned again to peer for'ard through the windows — and then he froze, immobile in his chair. He felt his heart leap, as the horror before his eyes registered in his brain. Across the night sky a white shroud seemed to be stretched, hanging motionless, but growing larger every second, right ahead. There was a strange luminosity about its edges where it brooded over the little *Campion*. Then Hooky knew the terror for what it was.

The lights from the gantry were reflecting off an iceberg that lay directly in *Campion*'s course. It was a massive thing, a monstrous shadow gliding silently down upon the ship. Hooky's legs felt powerless as he tried to move towards the autopilot. For an interminable moment, his muscles would not move, cramped by terror.

His fingers twirled the knob. It flicked to starboard, but he felt physically sick when he realized that he had set the pilot control to move for rudder movements of only five degrees. He had fixed this setting earlier to reduce the ship's yawing, when the seas had worsened. Now, dear God, she was altering too slowly to avoid the mountain bearing down upon them. Gradually, desperately slowly, *Campion*'s bow began swinging to starboard.

Hooky moved suddenly, his reactions swift and sure from his years of seafaring. He lunged at the emergency alarm push-button, heard its clarion, and rushed to the port bridge door to wait for the inevitable collision.

The cliff of the iceberg towered a hundred feet above *Campion*, who was turning beneath the sheer of the ice overhang. Slowly she altered course, agonizingly sluggish with her live degrees of rudder. Hooky flung open the wheelhouse door.

It was the awful silence that was so unnerving; the hiss of the ship's way was all that he could hear as she slipped past the ghost-mountain.

'Searchlight...' Hooky yelled.

His hands were gripping the wheelhouse rail. Tensed and motionless, he was waiting for the scream of metal as she ripped out her bottom on the submerged outfall of the iceberg.

10: A SEAMAN'S CHOICE

A seaman — if his instinct is given free rein — will, in an emergency, turn to starboard, should there be no reason for turning one way in particular. Hooky reckoned afterwards that it was the Regulations for the Prevention of Collision at Sea that saved him. 'Starboard wheel and show your red,' was an adage that had saved countless ships and lives.

When finally he realized that *Campion* had miraculously escaped that silent monster, he took her slowly round the iceberg, her searchlight playing over the white mountain of ice. On the far side, a shallow outcrop of ice shimmered eerily a few feet below the surface of the sea. Here and there a jagged lump stuck up above the water, the swell breaking lazily across it. If he had turned to port, he would have torn the bottom out of his ship. She would have sunk in seconds — without trace. *Could the* Gaul *have gone this way?* he wondered.

Hooky remained silent, too shocked to speak. The hand of God — there was no other explanation — had saved them. 'Take her, Peter,' he said quietly. 'Let's get out of the damned place.' He sat down slowly and began to pull himself together.

This iceberg was *aground* on the Kögur bank in eighty fathoms of water. One fifth of the mass above water, four-fifths below was the Arctic Pilot's generalization on the sizes of icebergs. This monster must have drifted down from the Arctic to stick on the bank here — and Hooky Walker, Skipper of the stern trawler *English Campion*, had, through sheer neglect, nearly lost his ship on it.

He ought to be court-martialled and shot. Through inexcusable negligence, bad watch-keeping and over-confidence, he had mistaken that radar echo — he had assumed, through years of familiarity, that the blip on the radar was an Icelandic trawler stationary and fishing off Straumnes. He sighed, disgusted by his performance. He'd steam on for an hour and shoot on the western edge of the Kopanes bank — he'd be safe there until morning.

Away to the north-east, Hooky caught sight of a light, a trawler's masthead, probably, jigging in the swell. Apart from one sighting and the guttural conversation of the Icelandic trawlers on the R/T, he might still have been off inhospitable Russia. The one difference was that the white light was certainly not a shadowing Russian submarine. Hooky took *Campion* to the western edge of Kopanes and shot in ninety fathoms, on the edge of the continental shelf. There were fish marks on the echo-sounder trace and all his instincts told him that at last he was into a bag of fish. He needed only two good hauls to catch this trip. He'd be all right then — but the next eight hours were critical. He dared not think more about the problem; he was too exhausted and drained to worry any longer. He shot the trawl and waited for the mate to return to the wheelhouse.

'Peter,' he said, 'take her for a spell, will you? I've got to get my head down.' He hoisted himself from the chair and looked his mate squarely in the eye.

'Don't make such a balls-up of it as I have, Pete,' he said. 'Fish out to the edge of the bank and let me know before you haul.' He stood at the head of the bridge ladder and peered through the plate glass of the bridge window.

'Two good hauls should do it,' he said. 'Weather, icebergs or gunboats permitting.'

Peter Sinclair felt anxiety about his skipper. The continuous stress caused by his responsibilities, no exercise and his lack of self-control over food and the everlasting mugs of tea were making him grossly overweight: he must be at least eighteen stone, and there were no signs of abatement. If Hooky did not take himself rigorously in hand, he would drop with a coronary before he was forty-five. Obesity, unhappily, was an occupational disease caused entirely by this mode of life. Hooky Walker was not the only trawler skipper to have developed into a compulsive eater: anxiety and stress were the direct cause.

Peter glanced at Hungry Mitch, the reliable comedian of a winchman, who was still checking the trawl. The dark, unshaven face that peered from beneath the cap, through the window, wore a permanent air of amusement. The man's mind was concentrating on one duty only: seeing that all was properly secured before he left the winch cabinet. 550 fathoms were veered this time: the longer the warp, the wider the belly of the net.

Peter felt a genuine sympathy for Hooky — he was a bloody good skipper but, God, how he needed some luck now! So much could go wrong... *Campion* had no business to be fishing here. So long as nothing happened, there was no need for either the gunboats, the Icelanders or Gunns to know. But if Hooky was bowled out or had his gear chopped in this position, he'd be without a friend in the world: there was no other British ship out here. The gunboat's presence was also unlikely out here, unless *Campion* had been tracked to the westward by radar — difficult, with so many Icelandic trawlers off Straumnes. Arrest, imprisonment and suspension were all Hooky could expect if he were caught. He was gambling for high stakes, but did little to betray his worries.

Hooky could not forget that iceberg. He still felt the kick in his stomach when he thought about the near miss — it had been so horribly swift — *whoosh!* and they would all have been swimming for it in seconds. In those temperatures men lasted three minutes, so there was little joy in swimming: but were fishermen not fools when they did not learn to swim?

Peter moved over to the chart table and tapped the aneroid barometer: the pressure was dropping fast and was confirming the weather forecast. They were in for a gale, so it was essential to catch a couple of hauls before it blew too hard. Mercifully, the gale was south-westerly or they'd be in real trouble with icing up. If a storm blew up from the south-west, *English Campion* would have Isafjord under her lee — and the name still brought a twitch of fear into Peter's mind.

During 1955, a tragedy had been worked out here. *Lorella* and *Roderigo* had been caught out by a combination of high winds and low temperatures. It had been a race against time: they were well to the northward, away from the land and dodging into the wind where they iced up rapidly and became top-heavy. They had left the decision too late: when finally they turned, they broached and rolled over. Their farewell messages were heard over the R/T by the trawlers sheltering in the fjord. Then there was silence — nothing but the fury of the wind and sea.

However skilful a seaman the skipper might be, there were conditions in winter from which no human agency could save a trawler caught out off these hazardous shores. Not so long ago, a side trawler had struck the rocks on a lee shore under a high cliff about a quarter of a mile distant. Her bows had stuck fast, and reared up as her back broke. The after part of the ship broke away and sank, taking all those aft with her. The bosun and four others were left on the foc'sle head, where the freezing seas broke green over them.

The Icelandic Coastguards were magnificent and managed to pass a line to her. The bosun, just about dead from exposure, succeeded in securing one end of the jackstay to her foremast; the slack was then taken up by the rescuers ashore. They proceeded with the rescue, the distance being the greatest ever attempted in the history of the breeches-buoy. All five survivors were hauled to safety up the cliff, where they were looked after and restored to life.

Peter steadied himself from the motion of the bucketing ship. So long as they continued running before the wind, all would be well. He'd call the skipper now and start the haul before the weather deteriorated still further.

'Okay, Mitch,' he said, nodding at the winchman huddled in the starboard for'd corner of the wheelhouse. 'Call the hands, start the haul.' The next quarter of an hour was too long for both men: for the skipper whom Peter had called, and for himself, now struggling aft to work the haul. Peter looked for'd from the protective rail, where the remainder of the watch were huddled. The blizzard was sweeping across the ship, white curtains flailing across the flood-lit deck that swilled with water from the breaking seas. Peter could barely distinguish the pale faces peering from the winchman's window: one, the skipper's; the other, Hungry Mitch's. The floodlights bathed the ship in a ghostly luminosity: the yellow oilskins of the watch gleamed, the faces beneath the hoods glistening from the snow and seas that deluged the watch on deck.

Peter turned aft to catch the first glimpse of the cod-end, as it hustled to the surface: this was the moment of truth for this trip and, perhaps, for the skipper.

When Hooky was called by the mate for the haul, he was surprised how much the wind had freshened: he had known the weather had deteriorated because he'd been hurled about in his bunk. When he reached the bridge, they were hauling downwind. He sensed the customary quickening of his pulse when Hungry Much yelled, 'Short mark, Skip!'

Ah, there it was — the cod-end frothing white, astern of the two orange plastic buoys. He was expecting — as he had witnessed for the past ten days — a miserable apology of a bag; a scrape on the surface, a slight boil and disturbance, where the Molly birds wheeled. His heart leaped now — he had refused to believe that he could ever catch a good bag again — but there it was: a rounded white mound, a bulging belly of gleaming cod. Even Mitch took his eyes off the haul for a second to grin at his skipper.

'That's better,' was all that Hooky said. If he could keep this up for the next thirty-six hours, he would make a trip. The wires sang, the dan-lenos rattled as they rang up the fairways, the chains clattering merrily along the ramp; and, joyously stumbling to their work, the oilskinned men on the working deck worked with a frenzy to keep pace with the signals from the mate's gesticulating hands. Up went the belly of the net: out spewed the tons of cod, spilling from the burgeoned net and through the opened cod-end.

Hooky smiled: at last his instinct and initiative had been rewarded. One more haul — but he'd have to reverse course now, to trawl back into the fish — and that would mean bashing into the seas, taking them green and icing up. He noticed then that the wind had suddenly died.

He went out through the winch-room door and struggled to the starboard side of the verandah: he'd be in the lee where he could judge the strength of the gale. He glanced up at the scudding clouds — mushy black stuff, low and overpowering. Must be the eye of the storm — damn the thing, the wind would veer and he'd be forced to run before it, if *Campion* was to avoid icing up. As he watched the fish door subsiding on top of the fish shoot, he heard the coming of the wind.

The squall hit the after-end of the bridge, the force of the sudden shift heeling over the ship, so that she trembled in the confused seas which frothed and broke about her. Hooky was ready: he increased the propeller pitch to full ahead and altered course hard a-starboard.

The sudden manoeuvre surprised the men on deck but Peter had time to stop the shoot and move his men to the shelter of the rail. A deluge swamped the working deck, swilled to the leeward side and left a sheet of ice behind. *Campion* was round now, running safely before the astonishing shift of wind.

Hooky steadied her on the auto-pilot by using more rudder movement and by reducing speed. He glanced at the compass: course 095 degrees true. The wind was just south of west and must be gusting eleven. There was no question of heaving-to and stemming it: the spray would ice up in minutes. He picked up the mic but doubted whether they'd hear him on deck. 'Steaming,' he announced. 'Shut the ramp doors.'

The mate's arm waved in acknowledgement. A couple of the men staggered aft, while the remainder of the watch lashed down the net and the bobbins. This storm was routine, and there was no need to emphasize that they were now, once again, fighting for survival. He put Hungry Mitch on the wheel and moved over to the chart.

He glanced at the barometer: 962 millibars. Outside, the swell was sweeping past them, huge mountains down which *Campion* careered into the valleys between. It was snowing now, the white curtain drifting lazily in the floodlighting; the flakes were caught in the back-draught at the fore end of the bridge, the fo'c'sle head a white blur.

'Check the radars, Ewan,' Hooky called across to the operator who had emerged silently from his office. 'Make sure the de-icing gear's working.'

'It's okay,' Ewan shouted back against the shrieking of the wind. 'I've already checked it.'

Hooky nodded: radar would be vital to their safety tonight, because he was running for shelter onto a lee-shore. If he was faulty with his reckoning, there could be no turning round to make an offing: they'd ice up and broach. He switched on the chart table light and pored over chart 2976, *Snæfellsjökull to Straumnes*. The fifty-mile run to the coast appeared no distance on the chart. He must think straight. Their lives depended on his next decision: where to attempt a landfall.

Kopanes was the nearest land, at the outer extremity of Arnarfjord; there was a light on the point, visible at seven miles. The other good spot, Langanes, also lit, was at the end of the fjord, where there was a secure anchorage under the lee of Bíldudalur. He'd have to alter twenty degrees to starboard to make Kopanes: that would put the seas well on his starboard quarter and increase his chance of broaching while entering the next fjord to the north.

The southern headland of Dyrafjord was protected by the light of Selvogur, 171 feet high and visible, in good conditions, at a distance of eighteen miles. If he remained on his present course, he should hit the point directly on the nose. He could then make a choice: if the seas permitted, he could steam southward and enter Arnarfjord; if too dangerous, he could continue straight into Dyrafjord and round up beneath the lee of Hraun village. They'd be safe then, and he could find the anchorage at Haukadalur at his leisure. The fish were safely below and the fishing gear was stowed, so there could be no question of search and arrest — anyway, in these conditions the Icelanders had always played fair and allowed survival to take precedence over politics.

'Bring her round ten degrees to starboard, Ewan,' he called. 'We'll see how she likes that.' He'd play safe and set course in between Kopanes and Svalvogar — if his ship would allow him the liberty and not try to broach. He splayed his legs, so that he could better take his weight on the chart table while she heaved in the violent sheers. He'd better keep a good DR, in case the blizzard foxed the radar; up here the Decca stations were too distant for accurate fixing.

'She seems steady on 105 degrees, Skip,' Ewan called. 'George is just holding his own.'

Thank God for that, Hooky thought. A human helmsman would have his work cut out to cope with this. So long as the gyro did not jump off the board, they'd be all right. The magnetic compass would be hopeless tonight: there was a westerly variation of 28 degrees and, off the cliffs, crazy local magnetic anomalies. He walked over to his chair.

The blizzard was swirling around them, blanketing out the tumultuous seas that raged ahead of the ship. Hooky settled down in his chair to a four-hour plod: he dare not steam at more than six knots for fear of broaching-to. As it was, he reckoned the gale was pushing them along at another two knots. If Kopanes or Svalvogar did not show up by 0400, he would be in trouble. Whatever else happened, he was now committed and could not round up: the spray would ice up in minutes. That, added to the snow now piling up on the decks, would be unfortunate.

Hooky had never known time to drag like this. The motion of the ship was bearable but, strangely, with all this extra topweight caused by the hundreds of tons of snow she now carried, she was jumping about less than normally in these bad seas. She had tried to broach only once, sheering up to starboard and hanging there for a long moment, while men held their breaths. By increasing the rudder and sensitivity on the autopilot, Hooky seemed to have cured her dangerous tendencies. Then, at a quarter to four, as he was beginning to fret, the coast appeared on the radar: five headlands showing up clearly through the clutter of the seas, and stretching in a line NE to SW. Behind were the streaks of the mountains but, plainly, there was Arnarfjord and, to the north of it, Svalvogar and Dyrafjord. He wasn't far out, after all. The first flicker of the lighthouse showed dull and orange through the driving snow: the radar put it at eight miles, the lee shore being five miles on *Campion*'s starboard bow.

She must have made considerable leeway. The seas were now even more confused, with the lee shore so close. Hooky moved over to the chart table where, in silence, the bosun and Ewan were standing. The mate, propped up in the for'd starboard corner of the bridge, moved to the wheel. No one spoke now, each knowing that the skipper was drawing on his trust and understanding. He was poring over the chart which was now clipped to the table. He ran a parallel ruler across the paper. 'Steer 115 degrees,' he said. He was hauling himself back to the centre of the bridge, when the R/T loudspeaker crackled above the roar of the seas.

'MAYDAY — MAYDAY — MAYDAY...' a British voice was calling. 'This is trawler *Crescent Moon*, *Crescent Moon*, *Crescent Moon*, on 2182 — my position 320 degrees, Svalvogar four miles...'

11: THE SILENCE OF *CRESCENT MOON*

Doreen Clark was used to being on her own. As wife to the senior deckie in *English Campion*, she commanded respect amongst the trawler-women in Lilac Close, but that did not reduce her loneliness. She sat staring at the colour telly, drugged by its flickering screen. The weatherman had finished indicating the depression circulating around the coasts, when she realized that he had been pointing to Iceland. 'An intense depression,' he had said, 'is centred over Iceland.'

She was shocked by the thought that she did not care if it blew a gale or snowed off Iceland. Nobby was there, in that bloody trawler wallowing in the storm — and, sometimes, in the silence of the lonely hours while the remainder of Fleetwood slept, she confessed to herself that she would prefer it if, one day, Nobby did not return.

Down in the docks, they said, he was a good, trustworthy man: a good seaman. Ashore, no one ever mentioned his character. Once, she caught one of them winking across her shoulder; he'd been cupping his hands and jerking his wrist, in a drinking, right-arm motion. 'No, Doreen, he's not a plonky,' Margaret, her life-long friend and fellow filleter (and a widow, since her Fred had drowned off Tobermory) had tried to reassure her.

Doreen had decided long ago that he'd picked up his nasty habits when a national serviceman out in the Middle East. He was grey-bristled now, when unshaven as he usually was; but when she had met him on his return from demob, he'd been a real, handsome man. His eyes were very dark and they'd glowed when he was excited. His perfect teeth gleamed white when he smiled. Though his service days were long ago, he still wore his hair short. His hands were like hams — and she shuddered when she thought of them. She had always wondered, from the earliest days, whether he was normal. Their two children had arrived as routine and he was still proud of them, particularly now that Helen was filling out and growing into a beautiful young woman. She was his favourite, and Doreen chided him sometimes for not paying enough attention to Ronnie, their second child and only son.

She supposed she must be what was shamefully called a 'cold' woman: in Fleetwood, such a girl commanded no sympathy. There was little reticence as to what a trawlerman needed most when he reclaimed the marital bed after three weeks at sea. The sensible woman shared her love and understood, giving more than she received. But Doreen, particularly after those first weeks of marriage with Nobby, had realized that either she was different or he was obsessed with sex.

She peered dully at the telly screen, blind to the vacuous programme. God, how she wished she could put an end to it all. He'd told her twice, he'd kick her out — but she'd nowhere to go. Dick Truscott, the widowed grocer down the way, fancied her, but that didn't mean he'd marry her if she divorced Nobby.

The last few years had changed him. She had to grit her teeth now when he raped her (there was no other word for it), particularly the first night in dock. She was sure that for him, anyone, male or female, would satisfy his lust, if he could find a partner — and last time home, he'd told her he'd been with a boy. Now, they still shared the same bed, because there was no other room — but she told him then that it was finished, dead, stone dead.

The Legal Aid people had been very kind to her. They were starting proceedings now on her behalf. Nobby would have to be told either this time in dock, or the next, as soon as the case was prepared. But who was to tell him? He'd kill her, if he was on the booze.

Doreen Clark sighed and leaned over to snip off the telly switch. She rose from the old armchair, switched off the light, and slowly climbed the stairs: the youngsters were at a discotheque and wouldn't be home till late.

Outside, the wind was lashing against the windowpane. It was very dark and a gale was raging in the bay.

'SVALVOGUR…'

The name crackled over the R/T and made Hooky Walker's heart miss a beat. *Crescent Moon*'s distress call had sounded so loud and so clear that she could not have been far distant. A pale dawn was now breaking, a greyness suffusing the blizzard that was reducing visibility to zero. Even the window-wiper and clear viewer had seized up in the cold. Hooky was navigating blindly, their existence now dependent upon the two radar screens glowing beneath their black visors.

He plotted *Crescent Moon*'s position. If it was accurate, she should be within three miles of *Campion*, but what, in God's name, could he do for her in this appalling weather? He walked to the port door, pushed it open against the wind and peered into the white dawn.

The shrieking of the gale and the roar of broken water overwhelmed all else; he had to struggle for breath as his lungs sucked in the icy air. All about him was a mist in suspension, as if the sea had changed its state, half transmuted into another element. Here the seas were a different colour, a dirty yellowy-green where the breakers exploded upon the outlying rock-ledges off the coast. He ducked inside again, allowing the roll of the ship to slam the door behind him.

'Get in touch with her, Ewan,' he yelled to the operator who'd been up since the Mayday. 'See if we can do anything.' He turned to the mate. 'Have the line-throwing gear ready, Peter,' he said, 'and clear away the life-raft.'

Sinclair's face, usually brimming with cheerfulness, was tense, the lines at the corners of his mouth drawn tight. 'Better get a tow ready, hadn't I, Skip — just in case?'

'Reckon you had.' Each man knew, as their eyes met, that each was lying. Nothing could be done in this weather when they were so close to the lee shore.

'*Crescent Moon, Crescent Moon, Crescent Moon.*' Ewan's calm words broke into the tension on the bridge, clear, even against the background of the pounding engine and the banging of the wind on the windows. 'This is *English Campion, English Campion, English Campion.* My position three miles due south of you. I am proceeding to your assistance…'

Hooky called from the radar: 'I've got her!'

'Range two point six miles; due north.'

'…*Crescent Moon,*' the radio operator continued, 'we have you on radar and will stand by you. We should sight you at any moment.'

The skipper had regained his central position at the console. He flicked over the autopilot to alter course twenty degrees to port.

'I'll get to windward of her, Peter,' he said. 'Call all hands and let me know if anyone sights her.'

Hooky stared at the echo-sounder: nineteen fathoms — so he'd crossed the twenty-fathom line. Svalvogar light — must be 2.8 miles under his lee — everything added up. He was sure of this position and, as soon as Hafnarnes opened, on the northern edge of the headland, he'd be able to run into the fjord if he hadn't picked up *Crescent Moon* by then. It was now or never, because he wouldn't dare to round up in this maelstrom: she'd broach-to, even if she were not overwhelmed by the seas that would freeze upon her top hamper.

'*Campion, Campion, Campion.* This is the *Moon, Moon, Moon...*' The voice seemed weary, devoid of hope. 'Hullo, Hooky. Can you hear me?'

Hooky grabbed the instrument from Ewan's grasp: 'Yeah, Colin. Go ahead.'

'I'm trying to make Dyrafjord. I took a sea down my funnel and my engine rooms swamped. I'm drifting downwind before this bastard...'

Hooky could imagine the chaos, the sense the terror in Colin Brooke's mind. They'd enjoyed a jar together when last they'd met, when *Campion* had docked in Hull.

'We're full up with snow,' Colin called. 'Rolling on our beam-ends: there's nowt you can do, thanks Hooky, but pray for us.' The transmission was weaker now, distorted and difficult to hear. 'We'll try to anchor once we get inside...' The tired voice failed. Then suddenly there was a shout: 'I can see you, Hooky — up to windward of us.'

Hooky jumped to the leeward door and squinted across the for'd edge of the bridge screen. He felt the breath knocked from him, as he cupped his hands to shield his eyes from the cutting wind — and then he realized that the snow had eased. From the corner of his eye, he watched the huddle of men peering out through the windows from which Joe had cleared the frozen snow. There, lying beam-on to the surging seas, wallowed the old diesel side-winder, *Crescent Moon*. Her grey hull, rearing out of the water as she rode across the crest of the foaming waves, was rust-streaked. She lay a-hull, her starboard side towards *Campion*. She was rolling on her beam-ends and, when she emerged from the terrible seas, she seemed to be low in the water, with no freeboard in sight. She would lie there a moment, poised on the crest of a wave: as she rolled slowly towards *Campion*, she would hang there interminably, her working deck exposed to view. The gallows were thick with ice; the derrick was slashing backwards and forwards and was flailing murderously — but what caused Hooky to catch his breath was the terrible thickness of ice — mountains of it enveloping the bridge structure, the fo'c'sle head, the masts and rigging.

She must be carrying hundreds of tons of topweight. Her stability had gone; her metacentric height was nil. He could see the orange-clad figures of her men hacking away at the chocks of the lifeboat. On the roof of her bridge, someone was frenziedly chipping at the ice on the radar aerial.

12: BEYOND UNDERSTANDING

Tom Routledge had been bosun of *Crescent Moon* for two years. Under the command of Colin Brooke, a small, rumbustious man of fifty, he'd been tolerably happy. Though Routledge was already twenty-five, he was still trying for his mate's ticket and his time in the *Moon* had given him plenty of experience: now they were in this mess, iced up, snowed up and frigging about at the entrance to Dyrafjord. Colin Brooke cared too much for his owners' condemnation if he got mixed up in this Cod War: otherwise, he would have run for shelter, instead of plugging up and down out here for hours. Now they were caught out: a freak wave had smashed into them, wrecking everything and flooding the engine room through the funnel and air intakes. The diesel had stopped and was now a useless hunk of metal.

'Keep that radar aerial clear,' the skipper had ordered him a few moments ago. 'Might as well have something working while we've still got the auxiliary generator.'

Tom slung on his heavy anorak which he had dumped on the settee by the chart table. He turned down the flaps of his Russian hat, pushed on his canvas gloves and leaned against the leeward door. As he opened it, he heard the skipper talking to *English Campion*, Gunn's latest stern trawler that was drifting down towards them from seaward. She was a reassuring sight, blue and white as she lay comfortably in the seaway; she was iced up, it was true, but not unstable because of the absence of top hamper.

Tom allowed the door to slam behind him. Clambering up the steel ladder, he subconsciously noted the feverish, but pathetically inadequate, efforts of the chipping party as they hacked away at the ice. What use were their puny efforts, when the whole fore-deck was a mountain of snow and ice? Then, as he lunged towards the radar on the bridge roof, he saw the gigantic seas rolling down upon them, the horizon blotted out by the foaming maelstrom. He clung to the pedestal with both hands while the old trawler slithered down the slopes of the oceanic mountain, into the abyss below. When she reached the trough, he felt her roll, sluggishly at first, then further and further, as if pushed over by a giant's hand.

She lay on her beam-ends for a few interminable seconds. The strength of the shock prised Tom's forearms from the radar pedestal, and he was hurled from the roof to slither over the edge to the verandah below. He hauled himself upright; through the window, he glimpsed the skipper shouting into the mic. Tom heard his words through the open doorway.

'We're going, Hooky,' the man was yelling. 'Remember us to our wives and families.' And then, as an afterthought: 'We're laying over. *God help us...*'

Routledge gasped when the icy sea clutched him. He struck out in terror as the ship sank beneath him, rolling away from under his feet.

He never knew who hauled him on board the inflatable raft. It must have been the mate, that tough thirty-year-old who'd served on board *Moon* for twelve years; the only other survivor was the brassy, a seventeen-year-old boy who'd been climbing out of his deck clothes as the ship rolled over. He shook himself, felt again the power to think and, with it, the will to live.

The raft was the right way up with its protective spray hood already automatically raised. The three of them cowered in the water swirling along the bottom slats. Tom was astonished that the raft did not blow upside down when it reached the crests. The air temperature was, he knew, -12 degrees centigrade and the mate, whose speech was slurred, was ashen-grey from exposure. The brassy, a slightly built and thin lad, seemed in even worse straits: he was clad only in a pair of jeans and a singlet.

'Buck up, lad,' Tom Routledge growled. 'Slap your arms and hands together: you've got to keep warm.' He roughly shook the boy, whose teeth were chattering with cold.

'Where are your clothes?' Tom continued angrily. 'You'll die if you don't keep your circulation going.'

'I was just rolling into my berth when she went,' the brassy said quietly, his words slurring as he opened his eyes. 'Never had no time for me clothes.'

Tom felt the water freezing through his flesh and entering his bones. His brain was becoming numb: he couldn't think rationally. He couldn't make the effort to save the survival gear and the bailer: when a wave sluiced them over the rounded sides of the raft, he watched them, with listless eyes, bobbing up to windward while the raft sailed crazily downwind.

'Hi, Jack,' he yelled to the mate. 'We've got to get some clothes on the brassy.' He turned and shook the other motionless figure slumped in the swilling water at the bottom of the raft. There was no response. The man was dead.

Anger swept over Tom Routledge, rage at his impotence in this crisis. The fury he felt with himself made his blood course through his veins: he hung on grimly when the next wave flung the raft sideways. For a split second it hung like a sail, teetering between being blown over or flopping back to float the right way up. When the raft slapped down again, it was empty save for the brassy and himself. It was now too late to strip off the mate's clothes in order to clothe the brassy.

He did not know how long he sat there, staring out across the greyness of breaking combers. His glazed eyes watched impassively as the brassy grew colder with every second, literally freezing to death before his eyes. Tom's brain refused to work, but he struggled to consciousness and forced it to function: there must be, dear God, there must be a solution…

If the brassy was not clothed immediately, he would die, if it wasn't too late already… What clothes were there, other than his own, Tom Routledge's? They'd both die, then…

'Better, surely,' a distant voice was prodding, 'to keep your own clothes? At least one of you might live.'

His fingers had lost all feeling, but he watched them fumbling, searching for the zip on his anorak. Slowly he peeled off the coat. He held it a moment, gripped between his frozen fingers as he fought the wind tearing it from his grasp. Crouched above the boy, he lifted the shoulders and began to lever the arms through the sleeves of the anorak.

The brassy's eyes opened: they were glazed but there was sensibility there. He nodded, then grunted, as if in gratitude. With trembling fingers, Tom zipped up the coat but he could not prevent the terrible cold from piercing the lad's thighs, legs and feet. He struck the brassy's cheeks, banged his head on the rubber sides of the raft, yelled obscenities at him.

'Wake up, for God's sake — pull yourself together…'

Tom was screaming now; he heard the hysteria in his own voice, as his words mocked him from the bottom of the raft.

Tom Routledge kept the brassy alive for over an hour. Then, at five minutes past eight, the lad died. The bosun watched the life ebbing rapidly away, but the natural order of things shocked him not at all. It was his turn next.

Then he remembered the anorak. He began slowly to undress the brassy, peeling the sleeves from the dead boy's arms which were already stiff. Tom was talking incoherently to himself, keeping himself awake, as in a dream, he struggled back into his life-saving anorak. All about him was the grey, green world of foaming spume and icy spray — a white hell, a driving blizzard and always, always the roar of the seas…

From far off, from another world, he heard the mewing of a sea bird. Plainly he heard it. He was certain of it… Then, between the gusts of wind, he heard the lapping of wavelets on a pebble beach — there was a grating noise and his rubber platform came suddenly to rest.

He opened his eyes. He rolled across the stiff and sodden body of the brassy. He hauled himself over the rounded rubber of the raft: it was aground at the head of a small bay, the wavelets of the fiord lapping against it. He glanced at his watch, which had misted inside the glass. Eleven-thirty: he'd been adrift for four and a half hours.

His body ached in every joint as he flopped out of the raft. He attempted to haul himself to his feet, but his knees gave way under him. 'I must get away — *get away…*' He began crawling, like a frenzied land-crab, up the beach towards the brown moss that was the edge of Iceland's vegetation. When he reached it, he slowly turned his head to glance back at the derelict raft. The motionless body lay in the bottom: Tom turned his back on it.

There was a survivor's stone hut three hundred yards away, one of those shelters which the Icelanders provided around their coasts for the succour of shipwrecked seamen. If he could only reach it, he would be shielded from the wind and might survive the night if it came to that. Someone might find him there… Surely God wouldn't bring him this far just to desert him? The argument forced him on, up, up, towards the hut, hand over hand…

When finally he reached the door of the hut, his lungs were bursting. He stretched upwards to the door-latch, but his fingers couldn't reach it. He was unable to stand, his legs collapsing beneath him however much will he exerted. He felt bitterly cheated. Dry sobs rasped his chest as he realized that he would now die, if no one found him before the night fell…

He crawled round to the leeward wall. There, inch by inch, his groping fingers hoisted his slumped body to a sitting position. With his back propped against the wall, he might waken if his head slipped…

An old fisherman and his wife were gathering the precious sticks and flotsam that the seashore always provided. As darkness was falling, they worked their way down to the survivor's hut. They found there an Englishman: his eyes were staring, and he was grunting incoherently.

The old man stayed with the exhausted survivor, while his wife hurried back to the farm. Half an hour later, Tom Routledge was being nursed back to life.

13: A MATTER OF CHOICE

The Minister of Agriculture and Fisheries had convened the meeting at Whitehall Place. His deliberations with the British Trawlers' Federation had been so important that he had persuaded the Prime Minister to see them all at Downing Street; being the man he was, the PM had summoned his full team and had insisted upon the meeting as early as possible.

Hugh Gunn found it difficult to realize that he was a member of this conference which had been so hurriedly assembled at Number Ten. He had been summoned from Fleetwood and had caught the first plane to Heathrow, where he had been met and whisked into Whitehall by an official car — and here he was, watching history in the making. Sir Andrew, Chairman of the Trawler Owners' Federation, was sitting on his right, so that the Owners' representatives were facing the Prime Minister, who was positioned on the opposite side of the long table.

Hugh, just forty, was used to these circles. He'd been born into this world but had taken pains never to allow his privileged position to breed arrogance in himself. He was careful to heed the trammels of power, and this was his strength with those who worked for him. They respected him for his common touch, but they also enjoyed the touches of flamboyance expected of a tycoon trawler owner: the Silver Shadow, the game-shooting fortnight, the salmon on the Dee. Yet, beneath the image of a sporting gentleman and in spite of the air of pseudo-vagueness which he cultivated by wearing a permanent homburg on top of his straggly locks, he was a very shrewd and hard-working businessman. The company's trouble-shooter because of his charm and instinct in handling people, he had returned only two days ago from sorting out a problem in one of his trawlers fishing off the Falkland Islands.

Hugh Gunn yawned: the pace of life was getting him down. He tapped his pencil on the sheet of paper before him. He'd better keep his wits about him — the Prime, Minister was opening the proceedings.

Before the great man had begun to describe his visit earlier that week to the trawlers (one a side-trawler, the other *English Campion*, who had returned from Iceland after the tragedy), he expressed his sympathy for the *Crescent Moon* disaster. He was addressing the chairman of the Owners' Federation: 'Would Sir Andrew please convey the condolences of Parliament to the people of Fleetwood?'

Hugh Gunn felt humbled by his own role in this conference. Though *Crescent Moon*'s loss had cast a note of sadness upon the gathering around this table, the incident would help to accentuate the hardship and dangers to which the trawlermen were exposed for every day of the year. Hugh was glad that the Prime Minister had thus opened the conference. The PM was a strange character: the more carefully Hugh studied him, the more of an enigma he seemed to be.

Thank God that the nation had at this moment thrown up this man as its leader. He knew something about the sea and could speak with authority about the element. He had even taken the trouble to visit Fleetwood to obtain at first hand the views and opinions of the skippers: how best was the nation to cope with this, the Third Cod War?

Hugh Gunn had accompanied Sir Andrew on the Prime Minister's tour of the fish docks. All three had been impressed by the good sense and loyalty of the skippers who had, entirely on their own, borne the brunt of these potentially explosive disputes. Men like that Gunn's skipper, Hooky Walker, had by their own common sense stopped the Icelandic politicians in their tracks: this truth was evident from the Prime Minister's opening precis of the present position.

The heavy face, with its searching blue eyes meeting, in turn, each face around the table, was decidedly in control, Hugh noted. After three years of office, the Prime Minister had found his confidence.

The sagging jowl and the gleaming smile were deceptively disarming. Behind this joviality was a man of strength and integrity: the two qualities for which true Britons of all political hues had been yearning for so long.

'That man, Skipper Walker,' the Prime Minister was saying, 'accurately described this dispute to me. "It's different this time," Walker said to me when he took me round his ship. "The Russians are on *their* side."'

Walker was, of course, referring to the First and Second Cod Wars of '56 and '73: the disputes ended with the two-year agreement between Iceland and Britain. Hugh felt a certain pride, though, God only knew, he had the easiest part in it: he wasn't out in those winters, risking fifteen people's necks and his own.

'That '73 dispute was highly political,' the Prime Minister went on, 'but, because trawler skippers and owners were so disciplined and behaved with such tenacity, the Icelanders never managed to arrest a British ship.' He stopped and smiled sadly at them all. 'It seems so long ago now, doesn't it, gentlemen?' He sipped a glass of water before continuing, 'By remaining in the boxes and by keeping the Navy within hailing distance, we underlined that we were not going to be hustled out of international fishing waters — to the fifty-mile limit as the Icelanders demanded — or anywhere else.'

'Their gunboats chopped too many of our trawlers' gear,' Sir Andrew growled. 'The Navy ought to have been called in earlier, sir.'

'The government of the day was attempting to reduce the tension.' The Foreign Secretary, a distinguished-looking man with an easy manner, administered his mild rebuke. 'Iceland was endeavouring to show us up to the world as the big bully: they desperately needed an incident to underline their argument.' He smiled, the crow's feet wrinkling at the corners of his eyes. 'But no one gave them the chance — not a single British trawler was arrested during the whole of those two years, in spite of all the efforts of their gunboats.'

'We felt safe when the Royal Navy was called in,' Sir Andrew said. 'The skippers would not have continued fishing without the protection of Her Majesty's ships.'

The Prime Minister drummed his fingers on the table; he waited for Sir Andrew to finish, then, with a touch of impatience, continued his soliloquy: 'We all realize that the Second Cod War ended in compromise: we would restrict the number of ships and the areas in which we would fish, based on a figure of 130,000 tons of fish. The Icelanders required that their spawning grounds be left alone — and we continue to fish up to the twelve-mile limit except in those designated areas.'

The Prime Minister's face was solemn; he had begun to wrestle with the contemporary situation. 'That we succeeded in compromise was due, apart from the patience and tenacity of the trawlermen, to two important factors which are absent in this present dispute, the Third Cod War: first, that Iceland's Communist Prime Minister had to heed the democratic voice; second, that the Russians disagreed strongly with Iceland, even though they shared her political creed. Russia shared the same fishing problem as us: her own fishing grounds were still bountiful, but she needed to conserve them. Far better for her to fish other nation's grounds throughout the world. She was dispatching her ocean-going fishing fleets to all corners of the globe: as early as 1973, she was busily fishing out New Zealand's grounds. She realized then that soon the world would be short of fish; when the inevitable disaster came, she would be able to retire to her own waters which had been saved through her own conservation.'

'The Japanese were the same,' the Foreign Secretary said. 'They fished out West Africa, while they prevented anyone from fishing their own waters which they were conserving for themselves. That was the position in 1973.'

An earnest, slightly built man in a dark grey suit raised his balding head and peered around the table. 'We warned the world after the failure of the UN Conference at Caracas on the Law of the Sea,' said the Minister of Agriculture and Fisheries. 'The White Fish Authority continually warned of the disaster facing us.' He spread his hands wide. 'It was like the pathetic efforts we put up for the preservation of the whale. However piously the human race agreed to stop hunting that superb animal, the Russians, Japanese and Norwegians cynically continued to slaughter our planet's greatest mammal to extinction.' He glared at the assembly, his pale eyes angry behind the rimless lenses. 'Do we want to follow suit with the cod and halibut: the haddock, salmon and herring?'

His impassioned words imposed a silence on the conference. *We all know this*, thought Hugh Gunn, *but how can we translate our genuine desires into action?*

'Of course we don't.'

Hugh peered across the table at the man in the pepper-and-salt suit. He seemed younger than the others and there was a saltiness about the grey eyes: an unusual man for the Royal Navy's First Sea Lord. 'And, if I may make a suggestion, sir —' and he looked at the Prime Minister — 'the whole problem of conservation ultimately falls on the efficiency of policing the fishing areas.'

There were murmurs of assent from all quarters of the room: sailors were practical men.

'You will all realize, gentlemen,' said the Prime Minister, quietly reasserting his position as chairman, 'that today's Third Cod War is vastly different. Russia is most definitely *not* on our side.'

He allowed the well-worn fact to sink into the minds of all present. The Foreign Secretary took up the spiel: 'Now that Russia and Japan *have* exhausted everyone else's fishing grounds; and now that world hunger and the exhaustion of the planet's capital and energy resources are the obvious threats to the future, those lucky enough to have a seaboard are jealously guarding their fishing waters — and Russia not the least. She claims a fifty-mile limit, so she will support to the brink Iceland's claim for a fifty-mile limit.'

'...and even beyond the brink,' the First Sea Lord said, 'if my intelligence serves me right.'

'Thank you, Admiral...' The Prime Minister glanced at his Service Chief. Sabre rattling was discouraged at any time, but particularly at this juncture: the sinister undertones had left no one in doubt as to the grave issues involved in this present fishing crisis.

'It seems to me that the supply of the world's fish should be regarded as a world matter — an international crisis, not a nationalistic crisis.' The Minister of Agriculture and Fisheries was pouring oil on waters which were beginning to undulate, like the warning of bad weather given by the long swell that suddenly appears upon a glassy calm. He peered at his next-door neighbour. 'I know that Mr Dalbridge, the Fishing Secretary, would like to say something on this matter, if you wish, Prime Minister?'

The scientist's distinguished head inclined in acknowledgement. Hugh watched as Clive Dalbridge, a gentle man with a sensitive face, pondered his reply. He was one of the world's authorities on fish and knew what he was talking about.

'I cannot see,' he began, 'how any nation can claim that a fish belongs solely —' and he smiled sweetly at his own terrible pun — 'to that country. Surely a fish belongs to many nations…?' He looked innocently round the room.

The Prime Minister had extracted his pipe and was enjoying the ritual of filling it, Hugh noted. He wondered what Mrs PM was like — did she nag him about his filthy habit, or was she one of those who, supposedly, reclined in the shadow of the strong man and the aroma of his baccy?

Dalbridge was well away now: 'The oceans circulate round the globe; the Gulf Stream is the obvious example, but whose water is it when it sweeps past continents and islands? Why should these inhabitants claim the right to fish the real genesis of which may have been thousands of miles distant? The world's fish, in the same way as oil, should belong the world community.'

Hugh sensed an irritation in those close to him: here was the intellectual dreamer airing his platitudes. Couldn't Dalbridge face to up the realities, accept facts as they were?

The Fishing Secretary had noted the cynicism. He flushed angrily as he continued: 'Those of us who are fortunate enough to fish the continental shelves, are reaping the harvest while it is still there; some of us call this greed. The world will starve when there are no more fish — and time is very much against us, gentlemen.' He looked round, ready for a fight — ah, there was the Foreign Secretary, a sceptic, if ever there was one…

'How do you know, Mr Dalbridge?' the urbane Secretary asked mildly.

'Less than ten years ago,' the scientist continued, 'our skippers were reporting good trips of prime fish from the Labrador grounds, from Newfoundland and Greenland. They're fished out now — all killed off. The White Sea will be finished in a year or two. Years ago, we were all fishing to within the three-mile limit off Iceland. The Icelanders ignored conservation and murdered their young fish by dubious fishing methods; through sheer greed, they fished themselves out. They then pushed us to a twelve-mile limit, the British who have been fishing Icelandic waters for three hundred years: we're the most disciplined and conscientious of all the nations with regard to conservation.' The Fishing Secretary was in full spate now. There was no stopping him. 'The 1973 Cod War was the inevitable result of Iceland's continuing policy of selfish greed: after the twelve-mile limit, they meant to push us out to fifty miles, so that they could rape those grounds too. They didn't succeed, thank God, and they haven't succeeded yet.'

He was addressing the Prime Minister who, in return, asked bluntly: 'What would you forbid, Fishing Secretary?'

'Three methods of fishing, sir, which are morally indefensible as regards conservancy. Through disgusting greed, the young fish and fish stocks are being massacred every hour, every day of the week. Modern detecting methods can locate the fish and the exact depth of the shoal; modern trawling techniques can enclose the shoal which, as you know, can be at any density layer because fish are highly sensitive to temperature.'

The civil servants are looking bored, thought Hugh Gunn — *but, good on yer, Dalbridge, give 'em socks...*

'The fish may therefore swim up to ten or fifteen fathoms off the bottom, with these changes of temperature. The bottom trawl, which fishes only, say, seven to eight feet from the bottom, will miss that shoal. Along comes the pelagic trawl, adjusted precisely for the depth, and complete with sounders on the headline of the net: when ruthless operators use the small-mesh nets, every fish in that shoal is gobbled up, the baby fish as well. The fish have no chance. When the net is hauled, out of a haul of one thousand baskets, seven hundred are thrown back, as uneconomical, into the sea. Those thousands of fish will die because they cannot survive the pressure changes from the deep: they will then pollute the sea. The fish are not being allowed to reproduce their own species... This mass murder is continuing every moment of the day, gentlemen. How long can the world allow it to continue?'

No one spoke. Then the Fishing Secretary quietly continued: 'Industrial fishing is the second technique of fishing I would ban. This is genocidal murder, gentlemen. Huge factory ships, either with pelagic nets or purse-seining, scrape up everything that swims. Every living organism they catch is pulped into fish meal for use as agricultural fertilizers. Nothing escapes, nothing reproduces its species. This nauseating practice continues day in, day out.

'The third crime, in my opinion, is purse-seining. By this means, the food of all fish, that miraculous fish, the herring, is being methodically annihilated. Herring is the most hunted fish in the sea. All fish hunt the herring; if the fish don't eat them, the fishermen will net them. This is essentiality a world problem, for without herring, the prime fish stocks will die, as they are doing so rapidly.

'As you know, gentlemen, the herring is a remarkable fish: the shoal behaves like a colony of bees, having its mysterious communication system. If a purse-seiner, which for a short spell keeps its haul dangling in the net below the swell, is not quick, the millions of herring that there are in the one haul may act suddenly with one will. They will dive as one for the bottom. If the boat is small and happens to be overloaded, the sudden shift of weight can overset the craft.'

Hugh saw that Dalbridge was angry as he glanced at his listeners and said, 'I don't feel sorry for those fishermen.'

The Foreign Secretary coughed and glanced at the Prime Minister before the scientist went on.

'There used to be an abundance of herring round the Iceland coast — and particularly off the east coast in October and November. That's gone. Our own fisheries are being cleaned out now: the Norwegians are purse-seining for our herring; the Icelanders are off the Scottish coasts and hauling up our herring by the ton. Everyone is going for herring. The fish will soon have no herring and neither will you, gentlemen, on your breakfast tables.' He looked belligerently around the room.

'No kippers either?' The questioner was the Foreign Secretary, but no one laughed.

'With modern sonar pinging around the shoal, with modern echo sounders and with the purse-seiners ringing around the fish, the herring do not stand a chance — a lot of those herring are now being used for fish meal.

'With respect, gentlemen, all governments seem to believe that the seas are limitless and the fish will always be there... If we continue as we are, by neither conserving our fish stocks, nor halting pollution, we're committing world suicide. The writing is on the wall.' The Fishing Secretary sat down. There was an uncomfortable silence.

'Thank you, Mr Dalbridge,' said the Prime Minister. 'Most helpful.' He looked across to his Foreign Secretary. 'Have you anything to add, Sir David?'

The formidable chief of the Foreign Office removed his Dickensian spectacles and nodded towards his senior colleague. 'The issues now are entirely different to the 1970s, Prime Minister,' he began, and Hugh Gunn felt like a schoolboy listening to his headmaster's address. 'In those days, we Westerners were never hungry. If there was no meat, because it was too expensive when we joined Europe, there was always fish. Then came the oil crisis. Sadly, many of us had forgotten the lesson of appeasement and we gave in to political blackmail. So when the Arab world's demands became unbearable, we had to go to the brink of a third world war to start the oil flowing again. You won't forget that, eh, gentlemen?' He looked around at them with amused disdain. 'Wouldn't it have been better if, at the time, we had allowed the Admiral and the Air Marshal to solve the problem for us?'

Hugh Gunn felt uncomfortable. This had been a hot political potato for years, just as Suez had been in the fifties.

'By being weak, then, we now have a much bigger challenge: Russia and Japan — and probably China — are prepared to risk the Third World War to safeguard their people's fish diet. Without it, they'd starve.'

'Are you serious, Foreign Secretary?' asked the Minister of Agriculture and Fisheries. 'You don't mean that?'

'Of course he's right. Empty bellies mumble the loudest.' The last observation originated from the First Sea Lord, whose far-seeing eyes were, for once, serious. 'Yes, gentlemen, that is my opinion. Why else has Russia moved a considerable number of heavy units from her Baltic Fleet to Icelandic waters? Why has she maintained the world's largest navy for years?'

The First Sea Lord was peering straight at his political master: the Navy estimates had been pruned again last year.

'D'you really mean the Russians would go to war?' Sir Andrew asked. 'Accept the incineration of our planet, just for fish?'

The Foreign Secretary nodded. 'I do,' he said. 'They said they would and they announced it to their own people, who are already suffering near-starvation.'

'The situation is uncomfortably similar to 1939,' the Prime Minister added quietly. 'Hitler miscalculated then: he thought we were a demoralized lot without the guts to say, "Enough is enough".'

'Have we the guts now, sir?'

The First Sea Lord was sticking his neck out, thought Hugh. A fine man; too straightforward for politicians.

'Is there no alternative to war, Prime Minister?' asked the Minister for Agriculture and Fisheries. 'It never solves anything.'

'You don't want fish if you're dead,' Sir Andrew muttered.

'There's only one alternative,' the Prime Minister said, smiling sadly. He waited for his pronouncement to have its effect. 'World government.'

'Fish would bring world government?' chided the Foreign Secretary. 'I could think of more likely causes, sir.'

'Is not hunger the greatest spur in human behaviour?' The questioner was again the Fishing Secretary; he commanded more than usual attention. 'If the United Nations are now learning to police the world and its squabbles, why can't they act as policemen for the nations who catch the oceans' fish?'

Some laughed politely; others fiddled with their blotters, determined not to be drawn. Then Hugh Gunn felt the intense gaze of the Prime Minister resting on Sir Andrew.

'Granting that the world cannot risk ultimate war, how would you organize the planet's policy, Sir Andrew?' The Prime Minister's face was serious. He was directing his question at those who were closest to the fish.

Sir Andrew cleared his throat. 'With respect, sir, I haven't been to sea for many years. My colleague and neighbour, Mr Hugh Gunn, has strong views of his own: I know he could contribute much to the discussion.' He glanced at his younger colleague. 'With your permission, Prime Minister?'

Hugh felt a moment of dread. He was the boy here, years younger than the other. Sir Andrew was rushing him — but there was the Prime Minister, nodding and smiling. 'Please, Mr Gunn…'

The courtesy broke down all barriers. Hugh took a deep breath and found himself spilling out the ideas he had kept for so many years in his head — never again would he have such an opportunity to help bring sanity to the fishing industry or be able to use such an influential platform. He inclined his head towards the Prime Minister and began. 'The main cause of dispute seems to me to be the unfairness that exists between those countries which have ocean around their seaboards, and those countries that are landlocked and have none. The situation is very like the world's energy problem: why should a few states hold up the rest of the planet to ransom? The world situation seems to me to be identical to the internal problems of the free nations during this century: how to resolve the blackmail of a minority section holding to ransom the majority? The answer seems to me to be so simple that presumably it will never materialize.' He grinned at the Prime Minister, who smiled back at him and nodded.

'Go on, Mr Gunn,' he exhorted. 'Tell me how you propose to run the world's fishing.'

Hugh took the point. He braced himself and went on: 'Each maritime country would declare a fifty- or a two-hundred-mile limit. Where a seaway of less than a hundred miles is shared between two countries, the limit would divide down the middle. I am against the two-hundred-mile limit for the reason I'll suggest in a moment.'

'Each maritime nation — by that, I mean a country lucky enough to own a seaboard — would be responsible to the World Fishing Organization for its fifty-mile areas. Each state would take care of its own conservation policy: all the ground service; the control of fishing areas by opening and closing them as required for conservation — and, most important of all, by re-stocking its fishing grounds from its own fish farms.' He looked around, surprised to see every face was turned towards him. 'For us, this last requirement would be relatively simple, with so many sea lochs available to us.'

'Who would provide the money?' The Chancellor had not yet opened his mouth. His lugubrious voice was matched only by his dispirited eyes.

'The organization would be financed entirely by the charge on licences issued to each fishing vessel: an annual licence could well cost fifty to sixty thousand pounds. It might be more sensible also to offer ten-year licences, so that countries and owners could plan ahead for their shipbuilding programmes.' Hugh felt well away now, confident as he warmed to his theme. 'A licence would be sold to each ship of any nationality, so that a land-locked nation like Switzerland, relatively rich in industrial wealth, could well afford to pay for the privilege of catching fish for her own markets — and a licence would cover specific areas, however each maritime nation wished to play it, but all in concert with the World Fishing Organization.' He paused to sip his glass of water and was surprised to hear the Foreign Secretary's voice.

'But this is the beginning of world government, Mr Gunn...'

'Better than a Third World War, isn't it?' The First Sea Lord was staring across the table at the Secretary. 'Wouldn't you say so, Foreign Secretary?' he repeated.

The wise head nodded in silence. There could be no argument.

Hugh Gunn, feeling that the opportunity was slipping through his fingers, continued quickly. 'Surely it is in the interest of every nation to support some such scheme? Why should it be impossible, with the planet's existence at stake?'

'With respect, Mr Gunn,' the Prime Minister interjected, 'you are lucky enough to be still young. World co-operation is also young, but it is rapidly developing.'

'Not fast enough, sir,' Hugh said. 'There is so little time left. Consider the wretched whale. The world wishes to preserve this beautiful creature, yet the whale is being slaughtered to extinction by a few nations. How can majority opinion stop these selfish interests, short of going to war?' He felt the anger rising inside him. 'It's quite possible for rational controls to be exercised, sir. Even industrial fishing could be licensed in certain areas for controlled periods, if the fishing grounds would stand it. After all, this is the practice in South Africa.'

'How do they manage it?' the Foreign Minister asked curtly. The Minister for Fisheries was pleased to supply the answer; the Foreign Office should have better briefed its master.

'The South African government have a controlled fish meal policy, I believe. Is that not so, Mr Gunn?'

'Yes, sir,' Hugh replied. 'I have recently visited the country; I was very impressed with the South Africans' attitude. A ship may fish industrially for perhaps only a limited period in the year: the canning factory in Walvis Bay is open for only three months in some years. It's the same with their crayfish catch: both industries are ruthlessly controlled. Bottom trawling is allowed much more freely, because South Africa desperately needs the friendship of many nations because of its geographical position. South Africa is therefore reluctant to act unilaterally over its own fishing limits. There has recently been some measure of agreement internationally on the size of the mesh.'

The voice of the First Sea Lord grated on Hugh's right; a gale of wind was springing up from that quarter. 'Surely, Mr Prime Minister, this is the nub of the problem — how do you police such utopian ideas? You know that even our present Icelandic squabble is stretching our frigates to the limit.'

Hugh met the Prime Minister's gaze: his blue eyes were uncomfortably penetrating.

'How would you ensure compliance with your scheme, Mr Gunn?' the great man asked.

'The licence income would go a long way in financing the protection service, Prime Minister. As I hinted earlier, this is the reason why I would advocate only a fifty-mile limit: without a huge fishery protection fleet, the two-hundred-mile limit would be unenforceable. We should start with a fifty-mile limit and see how it goes.'

'What sort of fishing protection do you envisage, Mr Gunn?' There was no hint of sarcasm behind the First Sea Lord's question, but Hugh could sense his hostility. This man was a professional seaman. He knew what it felt like to be stretched to the limit when patrolling the Arctic oceans in winter-time.

'The World Fishing Organization,' Hugh replied, 'would provide fast sea-going ships manned by the maritime nations whose waters were being fished. Some vessels would be service ships, some protection gunboats, others support vessels. I wouldn't solely rely on the physical presence of ships for policing.'

'Explain, please, Mr Gunn.' The First Sea Lord was probing again. 'How would you dissuade a belligerent Russian trawler skipper from breaking the rules?'

'I'd tear up his licence for life,' Hugh said. 'Better still, the World Fishing Organization would tear it up, so that the offender could never again fish — and nor could his ship.'

'That should do it,' the Prime Minister said. Hugh thought he heard a faint whistle from somewhere on his left.

'The Icelanders will do that now,' Hugh said, 'to any offending skipper. Makes sense to me.' He sat down. He'd said enough.

To his embarrassment, a spontaneous but discreet clapping emanated from the Fisheries Minister's corner. This unusual display was discreetly taken up around the table until the Prime Minister, smiling appreciatively, raised his hand.

'Thank you, Mr Gunn,' he said. 'I've taken note, serious note, of all that you have said. Would anyone like to add anything, gentlemen?'

There was a long silence, while each regarded the other. It was almost with relief, it seemed to Hugh Gunn, that the Prime Minister closed the proceedings. He rose from his chair, placed his outspread fingers upon the polished mahogany table and looked slowly round the assembly.

'I have listened, gentlemen, with great interest to our deliberations,' he said quietly. 'I will report to my full cabinet and, I promise you, I will speedily take this matter to the highest international level. Of course, I need time to reflect, but I want to assure you all that I do appreciate the gravity of the situation and the extreme urgency.' He looked round at them all before he went on, selecting his words carefully. 'The naval confrontation off Iceland, between the Russians and her Icelandic friends, and our ships of the Royal Navy, remains an explosive situation. The Russians have committed themselves publicly and cannot back down, not only for face-saving but for their own food requirements. Their people are hungry and hunger crumbles political systems. The Russian navy will shoot it out, gentlemen, if it comes to the crunch in Iceland.' His glance flickered across to the rugged face of his First Sea Lord.

'I thank you for coming to this meeting, gentlemen, but remember that the next three weeks are vital for this country. I am about to have talks in London with the Icelandic Prime Minister. It is imperative that I am not embarrassed by any provocative actions by our trawler skippers during this period.'

Hugh Gunn rose to his feet as the Prime Minister left the room. It was one thing for the government and trawler owners to give orders; it was another for frustrated, harassed and angry skippers to accept them.

14: THE EAVESDROPPER

The tragedy of *Crescent Moon* detracted somewhat from the fact that *English Campion* had brought home only a very average catch. In spite of that one good haul, Hooky had only just made a trip. Now, after only sixty hours in port, the little ship was out again and making her first haul on Hari-Kari bank off the east coast of Iceland. Nobby Clark slapped his yellow oilskinned arms about him to keep the circulation in his fingers.

It was bloody cold. He swore to himself and watched the vapour cloudlets of his breath wisping away to Leeward. This first haul had been a disaster: one half of the cod-end had been torn by the huge boulders which had been dragged up in the net. When they hosed the mud off it, they identified the offending object as a whale's vertebra: these bones originated from whaling days and were a menace to the trawls, as were the old coal buckets which also snagged the nets.

Nobby talked only in monosyllables when working on deck. The cold numbed his brain, so that he could think only of fish and his wretched non-life ashore. He disliked 'holding up' for the others to mend the nets — his hands were motionless for long spells at a time while the others' darted in and out with the needles and kept themselves warm. He was always given the job of 'holding up' because he seldom spoke and accepted his lot. 'Like a stoopid ox,' he murmured to himself. 'I'm just thick.'

He wished he could stay out here forever, fishing and being part of a crew that asked no questions. Trawlermen were tolerant people: so long as a man pulled his weight, that was all that was asked of him — but on shore, hell's teeth, he was swallowed up in a morass of misery.

They all blamed him, he knew that — Doreen's mum and dad; the uncle, cousins, aunts: Nobby was no good, they said — not to his face, mind you; they were all smiles and shifty eyes then, but once his back was turned, they tore him to pieces. What did they know of the misery of being married to an ice-cold woman?

He dreaded the first meeting with the kids: their accusing eyes, now that they were almost grown up, the contempt in their minds so obviously implanted by Doreen and the family, while he was flogging his guts off Iceland.

'C'mon, Nobby — gorn ter sleep, 'ave yer?'

His mouth twitched and he slid his numbed fingers along the next length of bolt rope. The yarn and the needles flew as the lads pressed on with the mending.

When the ship docked in the afternoon and after he had drawn his money, it was usually opening time. The Star, his favourite pub, lay on his route home — a dram would give him the courage he needed to face up to the family. When he pushed open the door of the public bar, he always knew that he was taking the first step to oblivion. But, God, this time it had been a king-sized disaster...

Doreen had been waiting up for him. The pub had thrown him out at closing time: he could feel, even now, the cold of that winter's night which sent his mind spinning. He'd collapsed in a dark corner at the end of Dock Lane and thrown up. When he came to, a bitter resentment against the injustice of it all had captured his reasoning. He remembered staggering home to 19 Lilac Close, and banging on his own front door. He recalled Doreen's blazing eyes when she looked down at him as he collapsed again inside the hall. It had been her contemptuous silence that sent him berserk.

'Wake yer bloody self up, Nobby,' the bosun was shouting. 'What d'yer want us ter do? Freeze 'ere till Christmas?'

Nobby shook his head and moved further down the bolt rope. He didn't want to remember the next few minutes of that terrible home-coming: for the rest of his life, he'd try to scrub clean from his mind those shameful moments.

He never tried to kid himself about always wanting a woman — what kind of a man was it who didn't feel randy after three weeks away and with no proper exercise? When he came home to Doreen, he wanted, he so desperately needed, a woman's warmth and passion. But on this last time, the devil had taken hold of him: with the whisky and the anger simmering inside him, her taunt — 'You're disgustingly drunk! Get out!' — had caused something to snap inside him: he hadn't even waited to take her upstairs.

He remembered struggling with her while he forced her into the parlour of which she was so proud. That bloody picture of the 'Stag in the Fells' had crashed to the floor as he splayed her on the settee — but it was the horror on his son's face as he stood in the doorway looking down at them that had scarred itself into Nobby's memory. The pain of that moment overshadowed the remainder of that bloody night: the calls for help to the neighbours, the shouts of disbelief echoing through the banging doors down the street; his own fury and stream of obscenities when they slung him out and he had to walk the length of the Close. He would have walked over the side of the dock and allowed the black waters to put an end to it all, if he hadn't run into Slippery Sal: her warmth and understanding had saved him that night. He hadn't gone home again that spell, because he'd been told by the firm's runner that Doreen was suing for divorce — well, thank God, there were nearly three weeks to go before having to face that lot again.

Nobby heard the clanking and rattle of the winch drums: they were hauling again. *Better luck this time, eh?* He looked aft and watched the warps trundling remorselessly through the bollards, those huge snatch-leading blocks swinging in tandem from the gantries on each quarter.

Ah! There was the cod-end — and a huge swollen blister of white and grey broke surface in the seas astern. There was an air of excitement amongst the lads as they completed the haul: up went the belly and down slithered the haul through the fish doors.

The effect on morale was instantaneous — laughter and rumbustiousness he had not noticed before. A hundred-basket haul of prime cod was worth good money.

Nobby watched carefully as the heavy wires thrashed about; a man had to be quick as well as strong to survive this game. A moment's carelessness and someone's skull could be pulped by the swinging bollards or the trawler doors. With this heavy gear, limbs could be sliced off like bacon fat.

Only this morning, Tommy I parted the port overhaul, the wire that hove up the main warp into the bollard. The wire had to be manhandled in order to lift it through the snatch and on to the sheave.

As soon as the fish doors were lowered, hissing as they closed, the hands hurled themselves into preparing the trawl for the next shoot. The skipper, watching from the bridge, had already increased to thirteen knots: he was opening out to turn on a reciprocal course so that he could trawl again along the same line of soundings. Nobby heard the wind beginning to whistle in the rigging, and the seas slapping against the sides. The old girl took on a list as she turned under full rudder, her red ensign streaming horizontally from the strength of her own wind.

On the working deck, they were swiftly inspecting the net, before each man went to his own side. The brassy had, at last, some colour in his cheeks; there seemed to be a new eagerness about him as he made ready the needles. Nobby smiled as he thought of his own youth. Wee Willy spent much time aping his seniors: he deliberately affected the 'couldn't-care-less, I've seen-all-this-before' act. He smoked continually to keep up with the rest, but he was a good youngster who needed guidance. He had come to sea because he had collected no O-levels: in Fleetwood, the trawlerman's life had ensnared him before he needed even to shave.

Nobby shared a berth with Wee Willy, a double berth, with curtained bunks one above the other. There was no scuttle but the berth was snug, clean and well furnished. Willy either slept continually or read the semi-porn trash and the comics that circulated throughout the berths.

Nobby leaned against the rail and peered up at the bridge.

'Ready, Skip,' Knocker was shouting from the winch control panel. *He's a good and steady lad*, thought Nobby. *He must be going through the same sort of hell as I am*. But it was amazing how Knocker appeared not to know about his own missus having it off with most of the town…

'Let her go,' called the skipper, his huge head jerking towards the working deck.

'Right-o!'

Knocker opened the door and yelled aft into the wind, a grin creasing the grey stubble of his unshaven face. The bosun waved an acknowledgement from the deck and the next 'shoot' had begun — but not before the important ritual of tying the cod-end had been enacted. Using a length of manila, the bosun wound it round and round into the shape of a cone, taking pains to leave a bight sticking out halfway up the knot. At the top of the tie, he made a reef knot; then, taking one end, he passed it through the protruding bight to make it up on its own part, before tucking it under one strand. Then he kissed the knot. If the cod-end tie came adrift, four hours' fishing and thousands of pounds could be wasted.

This, Nobby knew, was what made the fishing game what it was: for this was no mere job. This was a way of life, because men risked their lives in the cruellest of oceans to hunt for fish. This contract was common to everyone on board. The instinct was elemental, but very real. If fortune was with them when they shot, then there was compensation for the absence of a soft life ashore: they would be taking home real money — if that was a satisfying purpose for life. Nobby dragged deep on his cigarette.

The cod-end went out first, eased on its way by the yo-yo, the derrick which protruded over the stern. The elliptical floats were banging on the steel deck as they began to trundle aft and then the clatter of the bobbins announced the beginnings of another shoot: the cod-end was streaming out through the ramp and into the water, for the skipper had eased *Campion* down to four knots.

For an instant, the mass of gear remained suspended, motionless as the creamy-coloured cod-end streamed slowly aft, lolloping up and down in the slow swirl of the wash. Imperceptibly almost, the gear began to slide down the ramp: the trawl went slowly at first then, after being tripped by a stopper from the outhauls, with a rush, to the zany accompaniment of bobbins, shackles and chain. The great green net, with its two splashes of orange fluorescence — the two marker buoys — had returned to the element in which it belonged.

High up in his winchman's cabinet, Knocker, the unflappable winchman with the executive horn-rimmed spectacles, watched attentively as the bosun waved both arms, his green gloves protruding from his yellow oilskins like a batsman's on a flight deck: the winch rumbled, the great drum revolved and both warps began to veer.

The outhauls were then hooked on to the dan-lenos, the wires being backed up round the drums of the quarter winches: the ground chains rattled and the headline leg shivered as the trawl sped on its way, to the music of hope that rang from the iron deck as the chains snaked over the lip of the ramp, steam smouldering from the friction where the links bit deeply into the steel. There was now a rhythm about the work, each man knowing his job and tuned to his highest pitch.

The bridle chain sank beneath the wake, the long wire bridle following smoothly after it. All eyes were now on the bridle, for each deckie was anticipating his own move in the game. The Kelly's eyes, one each side, streamed next, those forged-steel double shackles which took the weight of the whole trawl; as they slid along the deck, they were grabbed by two men standing behind the fore-end of the combing, one on each side. They held the shackles, while the bridle, chain and wire ran through them until the Kelly's eye was reached.

The wires stopped: the bosun was moving both hands, the movement being seen immediately by Knocker, on whom the lives of all those on the working deck depended. Knocker's eyes never left the man in charge, bosun or mate, whatever the rest of the lads shouted or signalled to him.

The back-strap, which took the weight from the two pendants on the back of the doors, was shackled on — the tow was then veered gently until the weight came directly onto the doors which were hanging by a chain from the lower gantries. It was now the turn of the big stuff, the heavy gear...

The jimpsy was hooked on to the figure-of-eight shackle at the end of the warp; the auxiliary winch whined and the wire tautened to hoist the bight of the main warp up through the snatch of the bollards and into the sheaves. This was always a moment of danger because two men had to wait by each door, while the bridge winchman hove in to take the weight of both doors, plus the added weight of the whole trawl, directly on to the warps.

The doors banged home, hard on to the diagonally-grooved transom on the stern of the ship; the two deckies moved in, silent, concentrating now on their own safety as they wrestled beneath the doors, the heavy links and the swinging bollards. One man unshackled the securing chain from the front side of the door; the other slung the bight of the independent wire across the inboard cheek of the door and, tucking the bight over the triangular steel bracket, hitched the end to a retaining hook. Their hands flew upwards to signal to the hawk-eyed bosun, as they moved into the safety of the gantry shelter and of the ship's rail.

The green gloves spiralled slowly: Knocker on the bridge eased his control wheel and the warps began to move, silently now, as the doors descended to the waiting sea. Down they threshed, weaving in the blue-green wake, until they assumed their silent slant from the pressure of water acting on their front faces: only because of the precise siting of the towing-brackets did they plane outwards, as did the others in the Oropesa sweeps, to spread the trawl and to open as wide as possible the mouth of the net that swirled below.

All the watch, save the rock-like figure of the bosun, had gone now, down to the gutting room below, to begin once again the treadmill work of gutting another haul. The bosun remained motionless amidships, until he was satisfied that the doors had glided safely to adopt their proper angles. A snarl-up now and one door would tip the other, to bring disaster to the trawl.

The bosun swung his arms in a movement of finality. The big winch raised its voice and veered the warps, precisely symmetrical, streaming out their five hundred and fifty fathoms. For the next three hours, the trawl would work invisibly, churning up the ocean fields to harvest the fruits of the sea.

Nobby often dreamed of the depths. Down there in the blackness of the deeps, the trawl, trundling along the bottom, carved up clouds of dirt that formed towering hedges on either side. Along the undisturbed highway between the hedges, but fearful of the commotion on either side, the cod, coleys and the bergylts, all the feeding fish, jostled together for mutual protection. Then, darting upwards, they turned away, in flight from this fearful holocaust. Still the square of the green nylon net advanced towards them, barely seven feet above the ocean field.

Faster they swam, away, away, into the narrowing lane that diminished instant by instant, as they panicked in their legions. The grey trap opened and they were swirled into one side or the other of the cod-end, which now sealed their fate.

Nobby turned away as the winchman pushed over the brake levers. The next trawl had begun.

Knocker Wright, the forenoon winchman, snapped back the control levers, heard the hiss of the hydraulics, and slammed on the brakes. Towing with 550 fathoms out, *Campion* bumbled on happily at four knots, her trawl rolling across the bottom of Hari-Kari bank. Dusk was drawing in and he could have an hour or two's peace now, enjoying a smoke while he kept watch through the wheelhouse windows. Skip was on the bridge: they felt secure when he was in the chair. The weather had got up and the ship was slamming, even at this speed, into the breaking seas ahead. It was always bloody here, with the prevailing north-easter blowing against the current of the Gulf Stream which ran across the banks: no wonder the seas were always confused — some of the most unpleasant in which a man could ever fish.

What was Hooky up to? As Knocker watched through the for'd windows, he caught sight of the white light on the horizon. It showed intermittently and was blinking, like a road works' warning light, from the masthead of a ship.

One advantage, thought Knocker, had accrued from the Cod War: the Icelanders had forced Britain to organize its trawling fleets. The Dutch and Germans had paved the way, and now even British owners were providing service ships for their trawlermen off Iceland. In communication on VHF and on 2182, the service ship was constantly standing by to help with engineering breakdowns, spares and medical assistance. When she and the RFA oiler, *Petrolido*, where in the offing, thought Knocker, somehow life did not seem so lonely. The Dutchmen even provided church services, but then the Dutch observed the Lord's Day and did not fish on Sundays. He stubbed out his cigarette and turned towards his skipper who, slouched back in his chair, was staring through the port window. A natural leader, thought Knocker: no flannel about him. He knew his job better than anyone else on board the ship, that was all…

The R/T was hammering away in the background, every word between the various skippers being listened to, deciphered and considered by Skipper Walker. All *Campion*'s wheelhouse personnel knew the signs now: when he was silent, chewing his cigar and tapping the arms of the chair with the tips of his fingers, his intelligent brain was working overtime. Knocker was certain that skip was wrestling with something, was unravelling the intricacies of the hunt so that, if the next hauls were bad, he'd be off to fresh grounds. Knocker stiffened — why was that warp alarm bell ringing?

The insistent clamour caused the skipper to hurry to the winch control panel where, in the corner, the handle of the brass safety release was sited. Knocker glanced at the warp tension-meters above the chart table: over eight tons was registering on the port warp. The trawl must be snarled on the bottom.

The skipper waited a moment, silently watching the pointer. As he reached for the safety lever, the alarm bell ceased and the tension-meter resumed its two-to-three-ton indication. The warp had cleared.

The skipper returned to his chair to be alone with his thoughts. The R/T ship-to-ship was chiakking away from the receiver behind him, when he pricked up his ears. A trawler skipper, Ron Burger, was nattering away to another, the conversation being peppered with *effing* this and *effing* that.

'D'ye hear the *effing* news at *effing* twelve o'clock?'

'*Effing* 'ell! What's oop, then?'

'They're *effing* well taking the *effing* navy out tomorrow, Ron.'

'*Effing* 'ell. That's *effing* charmin', ern't it? What time then, Bill?'

'Three o'clock. *Effing* 'ell.'

'Any fish, Ron? Nowt here.'

'Not much 'ere, Bill — only a mixed bag, but as long as it's got *effing* fins and it *effing* swims, I'm not particular.'

Hooky's fingers drummed on the arm of the bridge chair rhythmically, in slow time. That craggy face seemed carved out of granite. His face was shrouded by his rusty, fuzzy hair, the sideburns running nearly to his chin — and all the while he was listening to Skipper Ron rambling on about his difficulties in dock. Hooky remained silent, his face a study in concentration. No snap decisions for him: he'd see how things developed before shifting his ground.

'I feel let down,' he said quietly. 'Scandalous, I call it. They must have known weeks ago, when Iceland said she'd break off diplomatic relations if the Navy didn't get out. Our politicians *must* have decided a week ago, but they couldn't even be bothered to tell us.'

Peter felt the bitterness in the skipper's voice. *They*, the people ashore who hadn't the faintest idea what it was like out here, had not even informed the skippers what had been decided.

'The Navy'll hate it,' Hooky continued. 'They're doing a grand job at the moment; they've just about got the hang of things — got it sorted out.'

'How d'you mean?' Peter said.

'They lie outside the twelve-mile limit and pick up the gunboats on their radar. They wait for the contact and then shadow the gunboat wherever it goes. The Navy's got the hang of it all right — and just when things are buttoned up, the Government is calling them off. Poor bastards, they won't like leaving us.'

Peter knew, too, that the Navy had done a good job. The skippers felt safe when the grey ships with the White Ensigns steamed up out of the mists.

'We'll see what tomorrow brings,' said the skipper. 'If there's harassment, we'll have a vote amongst the skippers. If we've no protection, we'll give the Government only six hours this time. Then we'll stop fishing — all of us. We've had enough.'

'Who'll organize it, then?'

'I will,' Hooky Walker said. 'If there's harassment, I will — we'll see.'

Peter felt a certain pity for the Icelanders. Skippers like Walker would take a lot of beating: for sheer, dogged determination, there could be no equal — that rugged chin and the Norseman's blue eyes boded stubborn cussedness, if ever characteristics did.

A garbled six o'clock news confused the announcement. Atmospherics distorted the familiar voice of the Prime Minister, but even up here the pretentious voice was unmistakable. All smooth and matter-of-fact from No. 10 Downing Street. A pity, thought Peter, that some of these politicians weren't rolling their guts out up here.

Peter walked out on to the verandah a moment, to catch a breath of air. As he stood there, his eyes were drawn to the Red Duster streaming proudly in the wind. Beneath the working lights on the gantry, the hessian was blood-red and defiant.

The radio crackled that the frigates would be withdrawn at three o'clock that afternoon. *Campion* shot once more on the Hari-Kari bank, fifty miles from Iceland: after three and half hours, she hauled only thirty baskets.

During that evening, Hooky began to talk about the Icelanders: a sure sign that he was distressed and thinking hard about the fishing. 'I've no time for them at all: a dreary lot, without humour,' he told Peter Sinclair, who was with him in the wheelhouse.

Peter was again worried about his skipper. If Hooky's luck failed, he might as well pack up because, however hard he tried, he would not necessarily find the fish. A successful skipper had to feel by instinct where the 'holes' were and where the fish lay.

A private company like Gunn's, Peter appreciated, as he watched the lights of a side-winder gliding past them to starboard, was run by men who understood what the sea was all about. Gunn's were unusual in that they realized that a seaman's life was a different world, with different values and sensibilities, with ways and traditions which a landman could never understand. The lubbers ashore, intent only on making money, could never begin to enter the basically honest and simple, in the real sense of the word, world of the seaman: very rarely did a man afloat steal from his messmates. Peter felt secretly proud of the life he was following.

Hooky was moving fast up the coast now, some thirty miles off Iceland. He'd shot the trawl twice but caught only ten baskets — disastrous — and now the Navy had been called off.

'You know, Peter,' Hooky was saying, thinking aloud, 'now that there can be no "boxes" with the Navy gone, some of my crafty skipper friends will try to sneak off to the northwest of Iceland — which is the best side for cod at this time of year.'

Peter saw the roguish grin twitching at the corners of his mouth.

'I can always say that I'm on my way to Greenland,' Hooky said with a wink. 'Ted Bayley would accept that. We'll try another night here, and if it's still NBG, I'll phone Gunn's office in the morning.'

Peter took over the watch at dusk. The evening was still windless, but there was a vicious nip in the December air. Peter walked to the port door and stepped outside for a moment. There were ridges of silver mares' tails in the sky and long bands of cirrus stretching from horizon to horizon. Green-tinged cerulean; blues and greys; the chill colours predominated. The feeling persisted in his thoughts that this sinister sky could be nowhere but above Iceland. The sky boded ill, and the glass was falling.

Peter stared towards the snow-covered mountains. There was probably more bitterness in Iceland against Britain, their former ally, than there had been in those far off wartime days of which his father had sometimes spoken. He was sure that there existed, even now, a pro-British party in Iceland.

Even this morning the skipper of *Ocean Flood* had been closed by *Hekla* and ordered to shove off outside the fifty-mile limit — otherwise his gear would be chopped. The trawler had weakly complied. If only, Peter thought, pursing his lips, the skipper had been Hooky and the ship, *Campion*.

Hooky would have stood firm to test whether the gunboat was bluffing during the period of these impending talks between the two Prime Ministers. If *Hekla* was serious and *had* cut *Campion*'s gear, then Hooky would have summoned the Navy, and telephoned the owners to tell 'em to inform Press.

The gunboat had been seen earlier that morning, but she had remained six miles off. She was obviously shadowing, but

Hooky was sure that, if she had been *Hekla*, she would have recognized *Campion*. If there were to be any fireworks, Peter agreed with the skipper, they would probably be sooner rather than later.

By the time dawn broke on the following day, the weather had truly followed the portents. It was blowing hard, and the discomfort had not given relief to the frustration in the wheelhouse of *English Campion*. What was the sense in remaining inside a 'box' with thirty-six other trawlers, once the cod had been frightened off? Hooky was restless, even after his good breakfast of eggs and bacon. It was already nine o'clock and he was wasting time. He knew where the cod were, and he meant to go after them.

To hell with politics and those bloody Icelanders! He felt expansive now that his mind was made up, but he would have to be cunning: Ted Bayley could often see through Skipper Walker's more crafty moves. The ship was rolling like hell, but fortunately she was fishing downwind, so he did not have to slam into the seas like that oiler off the starboard bow.

'Get me through to the office, please, Ewan.' The radio operator put down the megger with which he was checking a fault on the track recorder and disappeared into the radio office.

'Should get through right away this morning, Skip. Reception's good.'

Three minutes later, Hooky was sitting in the radio office chair and chatting to Ted Bayley through the GPO link at Portishead.

'I got your "sched" okay, Hooky.' Ted's voice was distinct; he could have been in the wheelhouse, he seemed so close. He must already have received this forenoon's daily reports from all the company ships. The 'scheds' would tell the same story: to fish too many ships in such a small area was a frustrating and fishless task for skipper and owner alike.

'Oh, aye,' Hooky said. 'You know the Navy's out, don't you, Ted?'

'Yeah — Government told the owners yesterday. How's things up there?'

There was an imperceptible pause, as Hooky remembered that the conversation was not private: anyone on this frequency could overhear. 'Not so bad, Ted. There's no fish about here, off Bullnose — too many ships.'

'Any interference from the gunboats?' Ted Bayley's voice was guarded, playing down the tension.

'Someone was threatened yesterday morning. The gunboat threatened to chop his gear if he didn't clear off outside the fifty-mile limit.'

'Did he haul and go?'

'Oh, aye,' Hooky said. 'He did.'

Peter grinned. The contempt in the words could have been interpreted from Iceland to China.

'What are you going to do, Hooky?'

Peter could visualize the manager, sitting in his office, quietly sympathetic and sharing a mutual trust between himself and one of his most promising skippers.

'Well, Ted, if there's nowt doing off the north-east box, I'm thinking of packing up and trying Greenland. Can't be worse than here.'

The air went silent except for the crackling of the atmospherics. Hooky thought he could catch the sounds of other voices in the background.

'When will you be steaming there?' The voice was Ted's again, anxious not to betray the information to the rest of the world fleet. Neither of them wanted the whole trawling fleet to trail after *English Campion* to Greenland. There were too many sheep about.

'Tomorrow night, if Langanes is no good.'

'Will you be going on your own?'

Hooky did not reply at once, his mind racing. While on passage in these waters during the winter, trawlers had been steaming in pairs, not only for protection against the gunboats but for mutual support in bad weather. Instead, Skipper Walker asked his own question: 'Same day docking, Ted?'

Again, that slight pause before the manager replied. It was important that the world did not know the docking arrangements: chaos reigned if too many trawlers returned to discharge at Fleetwood on the same day. Ships would be held anchored outside on a lee-shore; and a glut of discharged fish would flood the market — and for the following day or two, the docks would be empty.

'Aye, same day, Hooky,' Ted Bayley replied. 'Have you any important defects for the marine superintendent?'

'No, not yet, Ted.' The conversation was at an end.

'Good luck, Hooky. Let us know when you reach Greenland.'

'Aye, I will. So long, Ted.'

Hooky heard the *click!* at the Fleetwood end. He passed the handset to Ewan. 'Thanks,' he said and, as he returned to his bridge chair, he heard the radio operator signing off with Portishead.

'Thanks, old man. Seven and a half minutes for *English Campion*…'

Hooky felt pleased. They hadn't rumbled him at the office. He'd haul now and nip up to Langanes for a nominal shoot. The passage would be uncomfortable in these seas, but at least if his plan succeeded he'd soon be on his way to Greenland: what he did on the passage would be no one's affair except his. It was then that the R/T on 2182 began crackling again…

'Pan-Pan-Pan. Iceland Coastguard, Iceland Coastguard, Iceland Coastguard…'

Hooky pricked up his ears. What was coming now?

'…this is *Petrolido*, *Petrolido*, *Petrolido*. My position 130 — Ingolfshofdi — thirty-five miles — I require immediate medical assistance.'

'Iceland Coastguard, Iceland Coastguard, Iceland Coastguard…' The reply was immediate. 'Come in, please, *Petrolido*.'

'This is *Petrolido*. I have a man with a suspected fracture of the skull. He requires immediate treatment. I can transfer casualty by helicopter. Can you help, please?'

Hooky stood by the loudspeaker, his glance meeting Peter Sinclair's. There was no need to speak: each knew of the gravity of the emergency. Some seaman or mechanic had been thrown in these seas and had fallen to the iron deck below; or some gear had broken adrift and smashed in a skull…

'Iceland Coastguard calling *Petrolido*. Wait, please. I will call you back.'

Hooky was always impressed by the Icelandic coastguard. They were efficient, courageous and resourceful. When it came to saving life at sea, politics were forgotten. In the background, Hungry Mitch had started the haul and the winch was drumming again as the wires were hove in.

Several minutes elapsed before the R/T crackled again: '*Petrolido*, this is Iceland Coastguard. Please land your casualty at Skarsfjord, I repeat, Skarsfjord. Ambulance will be waiting. What will be your ETA, please?'

'Coastguard, this is *Petrolido*. Thank you very much, Coastguard. Wait please...' Then two minutes later: '...Coastguard, this is *Petrolido*. My helicopter can be at lighthouse in ninety minutes' time, if weather does not worsen. Please confirm that RACON is operative.'

'Understand your ETA is 0700,' the Icelander replied. 'Affirmative RACON. We will be waiting for you and will have landing pad illuminated. Coastguard ships are standing by... OUT.'

'Thank you, Iceland Coastguard.'

The slamming of the seas against *Campion*'s bow emphasized the appalling conditions in which those selfless pilots operated. But, a fractured skull... The man's chances must be slender — and yet others were risking their lives for him.

'Not much chance,' Hooky said. 'Better get on with the haul, Peter.'

As suspected, when the cod-end appeared, it was almost empty.

'Shut the gates,' Hooky ordered through the internal broadcast system. 'Steaming...' A yellow sleeve waved in acknowledgement. Hooky rang on full speed, off to Langanes and then...

'Iceland Coastguard, this is *Petrolido*.' The R/T was crackling again.

'*Petrolido*, come in, please.' The guttural syllables seemed impersonal, yet, by their efficiency, strangely reassuring.

'Regret to report,' the calm British voice continued, 'the man has died.'

There was a short silence. Then the coastguard spoke again. 'We are very sorry to hear that. Is there any more we can do?'

'Thank you very much, Coastguard. There is no more you can do… OUT.'

'Goodbye, *Petrolido*. We are very sorry. I will cancel the emergency… OUT.'

Hooky sat back in the bridge chair. No one spoke on the bridge. The man was dead. All part of the job. *Petrolido*, their oiler, would have to return to the UK now: no more help from her.

A thought crossed his mind: if *Hekla* was duty Emergency Coastguard ship, would she have overheard *Campion*'s talk with her owners in Fleetwood? Ted Bayley may not have bowled him out, but what about *Hekla*, if she'd been listening? Her captain wasn't a thought-reader. And yet, and yet…?

15: CRI DE COEUR

Gunn Brothers' manager slumped down in his chair behind the oak desk that had served the central intelligence system of the firm ever since Samuel Gunn, the founder of the original Gunn Steam Trawler Fishing Company, had waved his first ship off to sea. Ted Bayley caught Samuel's eye, looking down at him from that faded sepia photograph on the oak-panelled wall opposite. Ted smiled back, as he did secretly every morning, at the strong, whiskered face with the gleam of devilment in the eyes.

Ted Bayley started the second half of his morning's work at between nine-thirty and ten, but he was finding that this second heave was becoming more difficult. He always started the day at six, shaved, and drove down to the fish dock to be there by seven o'clock when the market opened and the selling began: he liked to be around when one of his Gunn's ships was unloading.

Twenty-three years he'd been with Gunn's, since he had first pushed his way through those forbidding swing doors on the floor below. Reliability and hard work had hoisted him to the top, so that when Hugh and Geoffrey Gunn had summoned him before them on that February day a lifetime ago, there were few people in the Company who did not wish him well as their manager.

The fish market had been pretty good this morning. *English Cowslip* had docked on the morning tide; her skipper, Husky Tranto, a broad-shouldered, front-row type, was hoping for good earnings from this trip. He was breathing down *Campion*'s neck and it needed only a record catch for him to pass Hooky in the annual stakes.

Husky had smiled when they shook hands in the freezing cold of the fish market. Now that the Navy had been withdrawn, Husky guessed, Hooky would be up to his old tricks if the trawlers were allowed out of their boxes. 'That'll give him a head start on me,' Husky had said, shaking his balding head. 'I'd like to get in amongst the cod off Hindenberg bank.'

Ted nodded thoughtfully: the Hindenberg bank was off the north-west coast of Iceland...

'That's where all the Icelanders will be,' Husky added. 'No wonder they're laughing while we're all boxed up on the east coast.'

'Hooky rang me yesterday,' Ted said. 'He's off to Greenland.'

'Oh, aye...' Husky turned to watch the final unloading of his ship. He stamped his feet on the cold concrete of the fish dock: the slushy ice that had been unloaded from *Cowslip* inches thick on the dock and floating in sheets around the ship. Ice was a nuisance to unload, but it was essential for all trawlers except the factory ships. It was cheap, but chopping it was laborious work at sea; it was also uneconomical when lumpers had to unload baskets 40 per cent full of ice. Whatever the disadvantages of ice, no one had thought of a better solution for a twenty-day trip — and at least the lads could work better in fish rooms which were not so cold as the -20 degrees Fahrenheit temperatures in the freezer trawlers.

The unloading of a ship always fascinated Ted, even after all these years. Though the lumpers were a voracious breed of union men, ruthless and selfish in achieving their demands, they had worked damned well this morning: on some days, they laboured with a will, singing as they worked. The 'down-below' men in the fish room loaded the fish into baskets. Then up they were jerked, hoisted by the 'swingers' on the whips; these hoists led through leading blocks rove on the jackstay which was rigged high up between the gantry mast and the funnel hold-fast.

Clad in their orange waistcoats and wearing their black, shiny hats, the 'draggers', with their hooks, pulled the baskets down the sodden planks that spanned the distance between the ship's rail and the platform erected over the hatches. At the dock-end of the plants, the 'catches' received the baskets and took them to the packers, who arranged the various species of fish in neat, rectangular batches along the dock. The number of lumpers employed on unloading was decided by an agreed scale which was based on the size of the catch.

The one operation that Ted always watched carefully was the final washing down. Powered by three mobile pumps worked by operators on the dockside, the fish room was pressure-hosed down with a germicidal solution: this precaution ensured bacteria-free and sweet-smelling ships when they put to sea again seventy-two hours later.

The market had opened promptly at seven, with Gunn's auctioneers starting the bidding. When they had finished selling for their owners, the other sales panel, also dressed in immaculate white coats, would complete the sales for the remainder of the port. The big buyers had been there this morning, all except Arctic Circle, one of the fish-finger people, whose working force was again on strike.

Wearing clogs protected by cut-off Wellington boots to reduce the icy wetness, many of the buyers stood on the boxes to obtain a better view. Forming a semi-circle round the open boxes of fish, the white coated and voluble auctioneer was conducting the bidding. The buyers, longstanding friends amongst themselves, some using walkie-talkies, represented all sections of the fish industries, from the small fish supplier in Fleetwood to the giant fish wholesalers with fish markets throughout the world. Famous names in the industry: Rutter, Ascot, Chadwick, Beale, JWM and Lancaster — their tallies were there, each claiming the boxes for their own company.

Surprisingly, the salting business was doing very well this morning. Bert Stock had been there, buying for the Fleetwood wholesaler who salted his fish; he then packed them in sacks for onward transport by boat around our coasts and across to the Continent. Bert was tallying up and seemed very content with developments when Ted had chatted to him.

The bergylts, 'reds' or 'soldiers' as they were called, had fetched a record price this morning. The Germans considered them prime fish and a delicacy, though they had never caught on in Britain, probably because, with their bulging eyes and lungs, they had a somewhat grotesque appearance. Their beautiful pink colour and spiney fins made them unique but, for the British palate, they were too oily.

There was a time when soldiers and coleys could not be sold in Britain; they were thrown back into the sea. Now, with world hunger, everything which swam was kept and sold. Even coleys or saithe (rock-cod, as they were known by southern fishmongers) were rising in price every day. Vast numbers were sent by lorry to Grimsby and Hull where they were salted and shipped across to Europe.

King Cod was still monarch of the fish kingdom. Ted Bayley had not seen for some time such a fine sample of shelved cod: shining and fresh, they gleamed green and white where they lay head-to-tail in their boxes, uncrushed by ice for the past nine days. They had been well looked after by *Cowslip*'s crew and the trouble they had taken was rewarded by a record price: well over twenty quid a box. With twenty-five boxes to a loaded trolley, considerable numbers were being trundled off to the refrigerated lorries, some of them belonging to Gunn's subsidiary transport and storage company, Frozen North.

Husky, hands stuffed into his serge jacket, tieless, unshaven and his hair hanging about his ears, had been a happy man this morning. Joking and chatting wherever he went as he toured his boxes of fish, he puffed joyously at his cigar, his laughter ringing loud amongst the babble of voices.

He never missed the market and always enjoyed watching the buyers gathering round his boxes of shelved cod, which they felt and admired while they pondered their strategy. He secretly relished the knowledge that, at the back of everyone's mind while he strolled amongst them, was the realization that without the skippers' skill and cunning, all of them would be out of work. He had once told Ted that he enjoyed the aura of his reputation, but he was realist enough to know that, once he started to slip, there would be few helping hands.

Ted lit a cigarette: it helped him to concentrate his thoughts. He needed one this morning for, apart from this unique event of having four Gunn ships all in from Iceland and docked on the same tide, an ugly suspicion was niggling at the back of his mind. He was worried about *English Campion*.

The Prime Minister's Private Secretary had been adamant: during the waiting period for the talks between the British and Icelandic Prime Minister, there must on no account be any incident either of poaching or arrest inside the Icelandic fifty-mile limit, let alone the twelve-mile. As Ted understood it, the Icelanders had tacitly agreed not to harass British trawlers during this vital waiting period — but Hooky Walker knew nothing of this yet, because he'd sailed before the government's announcement had been made.

Hooky had always been a 'goer', a loner who used his initiative. Ted was worried about him, because he had seemed under stress after their last interview. The skipper had certainly regained his poise, but he seemed obsessive about his fishing and his rivalry with Husky. His professional pride may have been wounded by the brothers' admonishment; Ted had been wondering for some time whether they'd been pushing Skipper Walker too hard. Ted sighed: it was not easy being a manager. He'd feel better when he'd discussed his doubts with the brothers Gunn in half an hour or so.

The owners sat themselves down in their respective chairs on either side of Ted's desk. They usually begun the day thus: a quick ten-minute policy discussion and then they were off — Geoffrey perhaps to Hull and, too often now, Hugh having to fly out to South Africa. On this morning, to Ted's bewilderment, Geoffrey was scowling: the brewing storm must be concerned with expenses. The signs were only too apparent — scowling forehead, knitted brows and restless, angry eyes in that determined face. For a man of thirty-five, Geoffrey was a formidable character.

'You remember Green Banner's cashier, Ted — Stephen Bland?' he snapped.

'The chap who ran a newspaper and a glove factory on the side?'

'That's the chap — Banner knew for years that he'd been fiddling the books. When they came to sack him, their managing director, who was livid with Bland's dishonesty, told him that he would take him to court. "I'll prosecute you too, then," Bland had retorted. So the man was sacked, with no questions asked. Can you beat that?' Geoffrey's face was a study of outraged incredulity.

'You don't realize the amount of fiddling that goes on, Mr Geoffrey,' Ted said. 'Stealing used to be the name for it, but now it's an accepted practice.'

'It's difficult to stop in this amoral climate, Ted,' Hugh said, 'and in the end, it all comes out of the crew's pockets as well as the owners'. How would you stop it, Ted? You're our manager.'

'You can't change man's standards, Mr Hugh. If we prosecuted every offender, we'd never sail a ship to sea — but anyway, most of the pilfering is carried out by landsmen. How'd you check the disappearance of fish, for instance? Impossible.'

'Ship's stores, engine room spares, food and even meat out of the fridges.' Geoffrey gave the catalogue. 'What can we do about it?'

'The practice wouldn't be so bad,' Hugh said, shrugging his shoulders, 'if they were just helping themselves. What gets me is when they re-sell ashore what is the firm's property.'

Ted looked out of the window to where a huge container lorry ground its way down the Dock Road. 'Half a lorry disappeared the other day,' he reminisced. 'They found the driver's fridge at home was full of meat. They fined him a hundred quid.'

'Bloody ridiculous — wish I had time to be a magistrate,' Geoffrey growled.

'The gutters would be running with blood if you were,' Hugh said.

This is the moment, Ted thought. 'I'm bothered about *English Campion*, Mr Hugh,' he said. 'I had a link call from Hooky Walker yesterday.'

Both partners were watching him as they waited for him to continue.

'He's not found cod off the east coast; he says it's hopeless, with over forty ships fishing in a single box. He's off to Greenland.'

'What's so odd about that?' Geoffrey asked. 'He's always off to that part of the world at this time of year, isn't he?'

Then Ted told the brothers of his fears: he was uneasy lest Hooky might be up to something foolish, in order to catch a really good trip. 'There's something driving him, Mr Hugh: it's almost an obsession,' he concluded.

'He won't have had the Federation's instructions yet, will he, Ted?'

'No — I understand that London is making this announcement this afternoon through the BBC.'

'What d'you reckon Hooky might do?' Geoffrey snapped, staring directly at his manager.

'Reckon he might break off on passage and nip down to the west coast — before these disputes, that was always his favourite hunting ground in the winter.'

'D'you honestly believe he'd do that?' Hugh asked incredulously. 'And risk the breakdown of the talks if he was clobbered?'

'Reckon he might,' Geoffrey said. 'Particularly if he hadn't received orders. He's obstinate enough to go off on his own if he's that stressed.'

'Don't forget,' Ted reminded them, 'he doesn't yet know the seriousness of the situation. Didn't you say the Russian note was only delivered this morning?'

'First thing this morning, the BTF told us. The Prime Minister would blow his top,' Geoffrey blurted angrily. 'He'd never trust the Federation again. He'd say we weren't capable of running our own affairs.'

'And he'd be right,' Hugh said. 'We've got to warn Hooky that he mustn't deviate from Greenland.'

There was a pause, each man with his thoughts.

'I'd prefer not to put through a link call,' Geoffrey said. 'It would be interfering and I don't want the whole world to know our problem.'

'It's a hell of a risk, though,' the elder brother complained. 'Suppose he *is* off to the western side…'

Geoffrey groaned. They were in a dilemma and did not care for it.

'Wish we could use the Nimrod,' Geoffrey went on. 'Our troubles would be over.'

Every day the RAF sent a Nimrod reconnaissance aircraft on its circuit around Iceland, her objective to check on the British trawlers. One of the heartening incidents of this Cod War had been when the Icelandic Air Control had refused to comply with their own government's order not to help the Nimrod with navigational and communication information.

'That gives me an idea,' Ted said, stubbing out his cigarette. 'Why don't we ask the one person who would know Hooky's mind?'

'Mrs Walker?' Hugh raised his eyebrows. 'Sure. She'd know — but is it fair to ask her?'

'The stakes are so high, Mr Hugh,' Ted emphasized. 'Most of all for Hooky himself: if he *has* made up his mind to risk the north-west corner, we should try to save him for his own sake — they'd jail him for years.'

'And he'd become another Captain Jenkins…? In this climate, an incident like this could start a shoot-out with the Russians.' Geoffrey's harsh words sounded alarmist, but too accurate for comfort.

'Ted,' Hugh said, 'go straight round to Molly Walker and ask her frankly whether Hooky intends to fish off the west coast. It'll come better from you.'

Ted didn't relish the idea; he'd no desire to ask Molly to betray a confidence. She was his own wife's best friend, and he wanted no part in pressuring her — but Geoffrey was nodding emphatically.

'It's all yours, Ted. You won't be gone long; we'll draft out a message while waiting for you to get back. *"Please remain in boxes or fish only off Greenland. Imperative no incidents occur whilst waiting for impending talks"* — or something like that.'

'Shan't be long,' Ted said, picking up his overcoat. 'I hope she'll play.'

'Even if she does, Ted, we may be too late,' Geoffrey snapped. 'Get cracking.'

Molly Walker, though not enjoying housework, was thankful that the demands of their new home managed, in a small way, to distract her mind from the continuous worry she endured over her beloved but infuriating husband. She loved him dearly: they had survived together the many difficult years when he'd first been a skipper.

She flicked a duster over the new coffee table he had bought her last week. 'Got to be good now, love,' he had chided her. 'No sense in buying you a top-class house, if you don't furnish it properly, is there?' She had pecked him on the cheek (she hated displays of affection in public) and he'd bought it there and then, no questions asked.

Her movements were brisk, efficient; she was houseproud, particularly now that their boy had followed his father's career. Mark was away working as a brassy, but she sensed he was hating the life, though he hadn't told his dad. Seventeen was young enough, surely, for the sea to take him from her? So little time ago, she'd held him to her breast, her very own first-born. 'Every inch a trawlerman,' Harry had said (why did they call him Hooky?). 'Look at his shoulders…' and he had pinched the little mite's arms.

Mark was as obstinate as his father: if there was an easy or a hard way to do something, he'd choose the difficult path, just to be different from his successful father. 'Contrariwise,' the family called him, when they teased him amongst themselves. Even little Sue, their nine-year-old, tormented him — and Molly smiled to herself when she thought of their second and last child. How Sue adored Harry, and he, the soppy thing, loved the little nipper. He spoiled her dreadfully — and Molly Walker stamped her foot in annoyance.

Harry, she knew from their last night together, was very tensed up at the moment. He was concerned about Mark who had, very foolishly, rebelled against being ticked off continually in *English Foxglove*. Without referring to his father, he'd left the ship on returning to Fleetwood. He insisted on going his own way and was now at sea in the old side trawler, *Noontide*. He was determined to make good without his father's influence. Molly was secretly proud of him, but Harry was furious, as well as anxious. 'I'm worrying more about *Noontide* now than my own ship,' he'd confided to her before they'd fallen asleep. He would have enjoyed helping his son into the skipper stream, as had so many other skipper fathers.

It was Harry's obsession with catching more fish than anyone else that really concerned her. Molly knew that she was incapable of not worrying: with other women, it might be the change of life, a husband's infidelity or making ends meet, but with her, it was her man's health and his peace of mind.

Getting that new Gunn ship meant everything to him. 'It's my professional reputation at stake,' he'd said. 'That means a lot to a seaman, Moll.' He would go on trying to catch more fish, always more until he packed up. 'It's the hunting instinct,' he'd told her. 'Or pure greed,' she had replied, not entirely mocking. He seemed unbalanced recently by his hatred of the Icelandic gunboats: *Hekla*, wasn't it? 'My worst enemy,' he'd said, and she'd been frightened by the cold fury aroused in him when he was talking about the gunboat. She had never known that he could hate.

She sensed that he was beginning to worry about his health, but he would never talk to her about it. She didn't want to be left alone — and she caught her breath as she realized the enormity of her thoughts. She glanced in the oval mirror above the sideboard: there were lines about her eyes and hard creases now, like crescents, at the corners of her mouth caused by pursing her lips in self-discipline. Her red hair, once her crowning glory, was greying now — but, and she was glad to witness the phenomenon every time, her striking steel-grey eyes, the colour of the mountain lochs, had not lost their piercing intensity. She was still a beautiful woman, Harry said, and he loved her dearly. A shadow crossed the mirror. She slipped off her flowered pinny and hurried towards the hall: the chimes of the doorbell would sound at any second.

They finished their first cup of tea before Ted, after coasting round the whole horizon, finally came to the point. How many times had that handsome and likeable man apologized to her for intruding into their personal lives? For Harry's safety and career, Ted asked her for the umpteenth time, could she possibly help them with information? Did he intend to fish off the west coast of Iceland? Could the idea even be in his mind?

She had, at first, been deeply offended. What right had the manager to pry into their private lives? But, then, her heart racing, she had realized the importance of their knowing. It was for Harry's own safety…

'Yes, Ted,' she said calmly, 'he has been worried of late.' She had begun diffidently, looking out of the window to the paved garden of which he was so proud. 'His talk with Mr Gunn in the office did upset him.' She paused to watch Ted Bayley, but he was saying nothing. 'He's been worried about the bad luck he's had recently, not so much because of trying to reach the top, but because of his professional pride. The restrictions of the box system are getting him down when he knows the cod are off the west coast.'

'Yes, Molly, I know, but has he said anything about his intentions for this trip?'

She looked down at her tiny feet. She waited, teacup in hand, trying to put into words the conversation they had shared only five nights ago. 'He was going to give the impression he'd be steaming for Greenland,' she said, her words barely audible. 'He said that he'd break off on passage and fish close inshore, where the cod were. "No one will know," he said. "I'll get into the fish there. They'll never find me at this time of the year." Those were his words, Ted. I tried to dissuade him until eventually we quarrelled about it. But you know Hooky, Ted — he's the boss.'

The manager was already on his feet. 'May I use your phone?' he asked. 'Hugh and Geoffrey Gunn are waiting in the office. We daren't lose any time, Molly.'

16: THE HUNT

Jane Victoria Dalby worked as a barmaid in The Manx Inn, at the foot of the hill in Ramsey. She had lived on the Isle of Man since her parents had moved there on their retirement, so now she considered herself part of the landscape of that beautiful island. She was nearing her thirties; no one dared hazard a guess at her age, but who cared when she shared such zest and happiness with those who demanded happiness of her? She was plump, with an inviting, roly-poly figure. Beneath her chestnut hair, her eyes laughed, taunting any man within reach and particularly those fishermen who put in for shelter in the lee of her island. They loved her, those who knew her; they loved their Come-Again-Jane.

Jane was proud of her nickname, for she knew there was no viciousness in their fun. Fishermen laughed knowingly when they mentioned her amongst themselves, but they were not unkind. Why should they be — with her so warm, so loving and kind? For kindness was Come-Again-Jane's besetting weakness.

From Morecombe Bay, from Over-Wyre; from Fleetwood and from Douglas, at one time or another, the fishing boats would round-up under the lee of Ramsey, their chains rattling as their anchors plunged to the bottom — for Jane, this unmistakable tocsin was the heralding of another joyous night. She made men happy and lonely men less lonely.

Tonight she felt wistful, yearning for her Wild Bill, with a longing which she had not experienced in years. At last, since that first time with that boy from the grammar school, she was in love; dying of rollicking, ecstatic love.

She looked slowly around the bar, the bottles glinting in the firelight. The customers were a dull lot tonight: either boys with no experience, or old men with no steam — the night promised little joy. She felt relieved. Bill was hers and she'd wait, for the first time in her life, for his homecoming.

William Mason, Wild Bill they called him, was away off Iceland in that little boat, *English Campion*. He'd joined for his first trip in her because they were short of one deckie. She was a top-earning ship, he'd told her, and a good 'un. Good money, and he'd smiled as he looked down at her again, his eyes shining with delight at her inexhaustible reciprocation. Together they were an ebullient, overflowing, perfectly matched pair of lovers: they could never have enough of one another. She clasped her hands about her, enfolding herself, dreaming of him, her eyes closed.

'Half a mild, Jane.'

She came to her senses and smiled across at old Fred. He'd given up trawling now and used only a line boat for daily fishing.

'There y' are, Fred.'

He smiled sadly at her, his eyes passing the old, old signal. 'Wish oi were younger, luv,' he said and slowly moved back to the settle by the fire.

The trouble was, Jane thought, that she was supposed to feel degraded and a sinner. She couldn't see it that way, when all her adult life she'd been giving comfort to fishermen and enjoying the work, so to speak, at the same time. She had married once, but both of them had known from the start that they were set for the rocks. They were together for three weeks and then he returned to the mainland. She never saw him again. Marriage wasn't worth it, she'd learned.

The pill had, for her, changed everything. Careful, she was, selective, jealous of her health, so her reputation had grown with the years. And now came Wild Bill, twice married, badly bruised from his present nisi-wife, but needing her services as hotly as any man had ever craved for her. But this time, for both of them, it was love.

He was coarse, he was tough, he was brutal. 'Feel 'em — forget 'em. That's wot we lads want, Janie,' he'd whispered the first time. 'But it's not that with you. I love you, Janie.' She'd cried then, into his shoulder, and from then on they'd begun to share their lives.

I needed my brains tested, she thought, as she wiped down the bar top. *Here I am, ready at last to marry the man I've been searching for all my life, and what do I settle for? A man with two ex-wives, two kids and enough alimony costs around his neck to sink a battleship...*

'I suppose I'll have to work for the rest of my life, darling,' she'd said, smiling down at him this time. She loved him, she loved him, God, she did; forever and ever ... but he was a hell of a long way away, off Iceland in that little boat. And it was blowing tonight and very dark. *Goodnight, my love — God keep you safe...*

She snapped off all the switches save one.

'Time, gentlemen, please,' she called, smiling dreamily at them all. 'Drinking up time, me sweethearts.'

Hooky Walker had certainly tried: he'd steamed flat out from the south to Langanes. He'd threaded his way through the myriads of lights bucking from the upperworks of over thirty trawlers; and he'd shot in a patch of shallower water, on the inshore side of the fleet nearest to Iceland where the cod had been reported. He'd caught damn-all.

At three in the morning, he shot again; at dawn he hauled: ten baskets of mixed — reds, coleys and mock halibut.

'Shut the gates,' he shouted down at the watch on deck. 'Steaming to Greenland.' He could hear the groans.

The Icelandic twilight gently merged into daylight, the coast of the island slowly breaking through the haze. Though still twenty-five miles distant, the string of snow-capped peaks reared like jagged needles into the silver sky. A primordial convulsion of the earth in its birth pangs had flung up this volcanic excrescence of an island, through the crust of which volcanoes still erupted.

On the south-eastern corner, islets jutted out to the southward and merged again into the horizon. The land then reared upwards, stretching away to the northward, steely-blue and white, with its identifiable granite strata showing as white bands across the mountain sides. There were vast fjords where, during the war, the ships of the Home Fleet sheltered while waiting for the Russian convoys to assemble. The steep sides of the mountains slid into the fjords which stretched back into the depths of the island where the glaciers, rivers of green ice, drifted down into the sea.

The chain of toothed mountains stretched away to the north-west corner which ended in the sheer cliff of Digranes and Thorshofn. The low-lying finger of Langanes was still invisible below the horizon.

To the eastward, the sun was well into the ascendant before its ghostly circle gleamed silver behind the gauze of stratonimbus. Hooky shivered inside himself — the whole place breathed hostility and, without being dramatic, he felt a deathly coldness about the place.

He crouched over the chart table, drawing out his course: 275 degrees true, for Greenland. This would take him nearer to the fifty-mile limit, so a small error could easily bring him where, in his own mind secretly, he had already decided to go. He snipped off his distance to Point Skagata. When the light was abeam to port, he'd break off if nothing untoward had occurred. He whistled softly to himself, longing to tell the mate, but much could happen yet. He peered through the windows to enjoy the silver seas breaking fitfully ahead of the dipping bows — at least the weather was fair but, if the temperature rose, he was bound to meet fog before nightfall. He turned towards the northern horizon where the visibility was sharp and too clear — a bad sign: there'd be rain about. Then he saw them, those two sleek silhouettes, hull down but standing out starkly as they creamed up from below the horizon.

He whistled and called across to Ewan, who was servicing the echo sounder. 'Slinky-looking beasts, aren't they, Skip?' Ewan said. 'So the reports were right, then…'

'Yeah — and there's not much doubt about the situation now. If the Russians are here, our boys can't be far behind.'

Hooky focused his binoculars on the two grey shapes; their silhouettes came up to meet him, sharp in every detail. He was surprised by their size: they must be the latest class of Soviet cruiser, by the look of them. He'd enjoyed his recognition course when he'd been in the RNR — he'd thoroughly benefited by his training in the Services; he'd left as a senior lieutenant and only because he could no longer, as a skipper, spare the time for his annual drill. He had a soft spot for the Royal Navy and valued the discipline it had given him.

'Powerful-looking ships,' he observed, handing the binoculars to his radio operator, 'and doing all of thirty knots.' Their sterns were down, their wakes frothing white; their bow-waves slashed the surface and there was a valley abreast their bridges where the dark red antifouling showed; and abaft of that, another constant wave that broke abreast the funnel, keeping pace all the while … thirty-five knots, he'd bet.

'Why are they steaming westward?' Ewan asked. 'Ah…' His voice was suddenly elated. 'Look, Skip: the Navy's back…'

Hooky grabbed the binoculars. There she was, a frigate of the Royal Navy, with only her high fo'c'sle, funnel and cross-trees showing — and further away still, another crosstrees. They were all steaming fast.

'Two of theirs, two of ours,' Hooky said. 'Wonder what they're at?'

'Shadowing, I suppose,' Ewan said. 'Bloody dangerous situation, isn't it, though?'

Hooky nodded. He looked serious, but there was a light in his eyes. 'Hardly the time for poaching,' he said.

The radio operator laughed. Skipper Walker was not near the top by fair means only; Ewan was used to Hooky's sudden urges to poach the proscribed fishing areas, when the uncontrollable impulse hit him. Though he may have fished illegally — there was that dreadful time when that suspicious dog woke up the whole village at two o'clock in the morning as they were shooting only a cable off shore — he never used a small-meshed net.

Ewan was watching the Russian cruisers hastening below the horizon, their wakes boiling after them. He had an uneasy feeling at the back of his mind that Hooky was up to no good, even though *Campion*'s course was set for Cape Gustav Holm, a Godforsaken neck of land halfway down the eastern coast of that remote and unhappy land. So desperate was the decline in population of the settlements in the remoter fjords of Greenland that the elders still sent off their daughters in the dories for servicing by the trawlermen. The Greenland run was popular with fishermen of many nations: Poles, French, Spaniards, Portuguese and British.

Ewan was re-entering the door of his radio office when he recognized *Campion*'s call-sign stuttering through the ether: *dot-dot-dash-dot* and so it went until, with a sigh, he took down the message:

To English Campion from Manager, Gunns, Fleetwood. It is IMPERATIVE, repeat IMPERATIVE, that, pending negotiations between Prime Ministers of Britain and Iceland, British trawlers remain in east coast boxes. On no account should they expose themselves to the risk of boarding or arrest.

There was little ambiguity about that message. He held it before the skipper's eyes. There was a momentary pause.

'Oh, aye,' he said. 'Thanks, Ewan. Now pull the main wireless fuses, will you? I don't want any more messages.'

Ewan nodded and returned to his office. With a tug at the switches, he broke the link between themselves and England. He would refuse to break H/F communications; that was a safety measure and vital for local communications. Anyway, the skipper could never do without H/F: it was too valuable as an information gatherer.

As Ewan turned round for the 1233 traffic list, he saw the two aircraft, flying up from the horizon. They seemed huge, long, flying pencils, like gigantic gliders. Their incredible speed was accentuated by the silence with which they moved — and then, between the Russian 'Bear' reconnaissance planes, for as such he recognized them, the familiar silhouettes of the RAF Nimrod flashed past, barely five miles north of *Campion*. She was travelling, and as she sped by she dipped her port wing in friendly greeting to the little trawler whose ensign streamed in the wind. Ewan suddenly felt safer: at least our lads knew what was going on. But those sleek Russian cruisers were too damn big and too close for his…

Ewan had pricked off the distance to Greenland — a couple of days should do the trick. He couldn't understand why the skipper was fixing the ship so regularly — Walker knew the coastline so well that he knew instinctively where he was and didn't bother with visual fixes, so long as he was within range of the coast by radar. Today he was fixing every hour: the Decca chain was unreliable at these long ranges so, with the coast only thirty miles distant, he was fixing by radar range and bearing. Grimsey island had just come up on the port bow. How foreboding it looked, with the seas spurting white in leaping spumes where they hurled themselves against Eyjarfótur. But once past the forbidding cliff, Húnaflói would open out. Skagata should be an easy point on which to fix.

The radio operator snatched an hour in which to get his head down after the midday meal — Soupy Ben had managed that steak again. The cold had made Ewan hungry and his stomach could accept the heavy food now. With beans, roast spuds, carrots and a fresh cabbage, there wasn't much that anyone could moan about. The cook was an important man in a trawler — and Soupy Ben was excellent.

Benjamin Steel, *Campion*'s cook, turned out of his bunk, restless from the violent bucketing of the ship. Slammed from side to side, he bumped monotonously between the ship's side and his bunk board — he was losing a night's sleep and that made him irritable. He'd be rolling out in a couple of hours, because he liked to be well ahead for breakfast, for the bread and for the preparation of the day's meals. *That's why I'm a good trawler cook*, he thought to himself. *The lads are good to me because I keep 'em happy with four-course meals and plenty of choice.* It was a far call from the days of the steam-trawlers when Balm-Cake Billy, Dry-Ash Jimmy, Cow-Pie Golly and One-Slice Jack held sway in the galley. Fill their bellies and you've got a happy ship, they always said. Ah, God, but he was tired of it all — fifty-four years old and still going to sea ... but it was especially important for him that this trip should be successful. His life had changed suddenly and now there was hope.

Ben was father confessor to them all: with sleepy brown eyes and a lugubrious appearance, he was a kind man who had been hammered by life. His first wife, Hilly, had been flighty: when he was at sea, she had soon found that life without male attention was little fun. She had borne his first child and then left him. Disillusioned, Ben had been knocked sideways. The bottle had become his palliative and, with the three-week trips across the oceans, the passage of time had gradually healed the wound. Rough language and alcohol deadened the pain, until one day in Fleetwood, whence he had moved to digs, he met a widow who changed his life. Janet was as lonely as he was, and they fell in love, so it was not long before they shared their bed. Time passed, but it was three years before they married. She, a companion for him; he, a friend to her. They both admitted that life together was pleasant enough, but neither of them could set the other on fire.

For fifteen years, every three weeks, Ben had put to sea. As everyone said, the trawlerman was always the last to know: after a long February trip to the White Sea, he returned one day to his semi-detached house. The curtains were drawn. Before he opened the door, he knew that she had flitted. On the hall table was a note: that was all. So Ben, once again, found himself alone with the bottle beckoning him. He stayed ashore and was drunk for a month; when he realized he was killing himself, he forswore the booze and put to sea again.

One nostalgic day, he returned to Liverpool. The past drew him and he found himself walking down Littlewood Avenue, where his first wife and he had lived. He paused for a moment outside the semi-detached villa, then he pushed open the green gate. He knocked on the door; there was a shuffling inside and a grey-faced old man peered out. 'What do you want?' he asked suspiciously.

'This was my home once,' Ben said. 'Can you tell me where Mrs Steel has gone?'

'She's not here — left two years ago.'

'Do you know where she is?'

The old man canted his head, his eyes shrewd and questioning. 'Who are yer?' he asked. 'Maybe she doesn't want me to tell you.'

'An old friend,' Ben said. 'I'm trying to find her again.' His voice trembled: he knew that now he must find her.

'She's moved to the dales,' the old man said. 'Don't know where, exactly.'

Bernard knew then that a power greater than him was calling: he must try, just once, to see Hilly again and try to explain. He enquired after her at the shop and in the newsagent's, but it was the milkman who finally gave him the clue. Thornton-le-Willows, a village in Graswater Dale. He had returned to Fleetwood but for the whole of the next trip, his heart pulled to that Lancashire dale.

He had now reached fifty-four and the end of the road was in sight. He felt, before the sea or the bottle hooked him, that he wanted to make his peace with the girl-wife he had married thirty years ago. He never blamed her for what had happened: they had been too young and the war had swallowed them up.

The marriage had lasted only two years, as had so many others which had failed. They had known nothing of complete lovemaking: only frenzied one-night stays in seedy hotels, wherever his ship had been. Resentment, misunderstanding and incompetence were the main ingredients that had broken the marriage; and now, looking back, after thirty years of maturity, he held no bitterness: he wanted to tell her this before he died. After the last trip, he decided to hire a car and to try and find her.

On an August afternoon, a visitor stopped outside the grey-walled cottage in Thornton-le-Willows. Hands in his anorak pockets, Ben savoured the pink ramblers sprawling across the grey stone: his heart was pounding as he tapped gently on the green door. He heard a movement in the hall and then the door opened. 'What d'you want?' asked a dark-haired girl in her middle teens.

'Is your mother in?' he asked quietly.

'Yes,' she said. 'Who shall I say?'

He hesitated. 'Just a friend,' he said. 'An old friend.'

She showed him into the little parlour. He stood there, gazing out of the window. Then he heard her talking: 'Who is it, Nellie?' The sound of her soft voice, more mellow than he remembered, re-awakened his excitement.

'A man,' Nellie replied irritably. 'Said he was a friend.'

'I know, but who?'

They were whispering, and then he heard the girl being pushed into the kitchen. 'You stay there,' Hilly said — and then she came through the door. They stood there a moment: slowly, the joy of recognition softened the hard lines in her face. They faced each other, saying nothing.

'Ben,' she said, 'what are you doing here?' She smiled, her eyes suddenly alight.

'I've come a long way to see you, Hilly,' he said. 'How are you?'

'I'm fine. You look … you look…' She couldn't find the words for which he knew she was searching.

'I'm not a plonky, Hilly — but I've had it hard, you know.'

'Sit down, Ben.' She bustled about, fluffing up the cushion on the chair. She pushed him gently down and touched his shoulder. 'I'll get some tea,' she said.

Five minutes later they sat down, the young girl with them.

'Nellie's my second husband's girl,' Hilly said. She couldn't bring herself to speak his name.

'Ah, she's a lovely girl,' Ben said.

The girl blushed and left the room to top up the hot water.

'Hilly,' he said, 'come out on to the moor with me: I want to talk to you.'

She hesitated before replying. 'I'll be with you in a shake,' she said, tossing her head as she gathered up the tea things. She hurried from the room, a spring in her step.

Ben slipped on his anorak and left the house. Hands in his pockets, he looked across the dry-stone wall of the little garden. Then he strolled up the hill, to wait for her while he gathered his thoughts. *This is where we used to walk*, he thought, as he looked across to the other side of the dale; *there we courted, thirty years ago. It has not changed: the village is the same, desolate and almost uninhabited.* He heard her rustling behind him: she was buttoning up her raincoat and tucking the hood over her head.

'Shan't be long, lass,' she called over her shoulder. 'Back for supper.' She led the way down the lane and past the bend in the road which wound up to the dale. Ben strode beside her, his thoughts racing.

'You don't mind, do you, Hilly?' he asked. 'I wanted to see you.'

She did not speak. She took his hand in hers and enfolded it for a moment.

They walked for half an hour until their conversation gradually became natural. They reached the gate where they used to make their tryst. No vaulting now, but he opened the latch for her and led her up the hill, past the only holly tree to where the rowan berries were ripening. He spread his anorak for her and helped her to the ground.

They sat in silence, watching the clouds sweeping behind the crest of the hill. Already, the evening sun was bringing a sense of finality to the day. A dark, azure sky was sweeping up behind the silver and then, quite suddenly, they picked up where they had left off, thirty years ago. They poured out their hearts and whispered the truths they had never dared mention before. 'If only we hadn't been so young,' she said, 'I would never have let you go.'

'I don't suppose it would have worked,' Ben said, 'but I want to tell you something.' He put his arm around her and drew her closer.

She kissed him, gently at first; but then, no longer a girl, she allowed her passion to engulf them both. He pushed her gently away from him, his eyes absorbing the tenderness reflected in her face.

'I've never kissed like that,' he said.

'What a lot you have to learn,' she whispered. Her eyes were smiling, but there was sadness in their depths.

He took her hand and looked directly into the dark pupils. 'What would happen if we took up again?'

'I would make you happy,' she said. 'I've learned a lot, but I'm still as lazy. You'd be good for me, Ben. I'd come tomorrow, if you asked me.'

He turned her to him. 'Would you, my dear?' He searched then, into the depths of her.

She said nothing, but spoke through the fire in those charcoal eyes. 'Take me now,' she whispered.

Ben felt the longing, sensed the pain of refusal. 'No, dear; not now,' he said, surprised at his own strength. 'I've found you again to tell you one thing: you may see me again, but I want to tell you before I die that I have blamed myself for the past. Not you, Hilly: I'll always have the love I first had for you. I tried once to hate you; there were times when I did my best to snuff you from my life.'

'I'll come back with you tonight,' she whispered, 'and make you happy — as never before you've known.'

He pushed her gently from him. 'Come on,' he said roughly. 'Let's go.'

She reluctantly stood up when he pulled her to her feet. As they walked back down the hill, he could not think logically: he longed to make love to her, craved her warmth and friendship, but he was too mixed up to surrender at this moment. If she had been a different woman, he would have stayed with her that night. He'd have to think it out... Had she changed at all...?

He accompanied her back to the cottage, where he kissed her gently on the lips. He stood for a long moment, as the tears streamed down her cheeks.

'Goodbye,' he said. 'I'm off to sea again.' He closed the gate behind him and strode down the hill.

The cook of *English Campion* turned on his back. He switched on the light above his bunk — good God, it was 0545. Ben rolled out and slipped into his white shirt, his chef's cap and the chequered trousers. He'd need to hustle now — in fifteen minutes, the watch would be in for breakfast.

Ewan rolled out from his bunk and, bad-tempered and frowsty, he hauled himself up the bridge ladder to the wheelhouse. The skipper was in the chair, staring out into the dark of the early arctic afternoon. Ewan glanced at the compass: course 265 degrees. *We must have altered to the southward for an echo ahead*, he thought. He went over to the radar and peered into the visor. There was nothing ahead on the screen: only the coastline to the south and south-westward. He looked up and found the skipper fixing him with his steely blue eyes.

'Would you fetch the mate and bosun, please?' he said, stroking his bristly chin with a huge hand. 'I've got something to tell you all.'

Hooky had expected a sign of disapproval from one of them, but Peter had grinned; the bosun had pursed his lips and muttered something about hell reproducing itself; and Ewan had merely inclined his head and peered into the radar screen — the operator understood now why he'd been ordered to break the main receiver switch.

'When will you be altering for the northern tip of Kolkugrunn?' Peter asked. 'I'll check the trawl: I don't want to foul you up.'

'I'll sack you if you do.' Hooky was grinning. 'It'll be a case of a quick haul — in and out — and another two during the night if we're lucky.'

Peter felt the tension. They would be right on the edge of the twelve-mile limit. The Icelanders were jealous of these grounds, because the cod were always here in December. It needed only a gunboat to dispute *Campion*'s position... The next twenty-four hours should be interesting.

'I'll be hauling at dawn,' Hooky continued, 'and will push off northward to try the Horn bank. It's not so good as really close in, but we might as well be seen to be honest...' He was still grinning broadly.

'Then to Greenland?' the mate asked.

Hooky felt irritated by the question. If he was into the cod and his luck held, he'd make another attempt on the following night. By ensuring that he was sighted well to northward and steaming to westward, there could be only one assumption: *Campion* was a British trawler on passage to the Greenland banks.

'All right,' he said, looking directly at the mate. 'Yes, to Greenland, but I'll alter course now for Kolkugrunn. That should make it drier on deck.'

'I'll give you a hand,' the bosun said, nodding at Pete. 'It could be a long night.'

Hooky felt the warmth of comradeship. No wonder the ship was reasonably happy, with men like these three. They'd support him through the worst that fate could chuck at them, providing they were hunting the cod. He'd be amongst the fish in three hours' time if the weather did not worsen: it was almost force seven now, from the north-east. Surely he couldn't suffer such bad luck? He'd fish however bad the seas, so long as they could still work on deck.

It was nearly nine when Hooky picked up the first echoes: a cluster of blips right ahead, where he wanted to be — four miles north of the Odhinsbodhi Shoal. He did not dare to nip in there — they couldn't fail to arrest him if they bowled him out. He'd resist the temptation and settle for Kolkugrunn; he could always slip off half a mile northward, and then no one could prove he'd been inside the twelve-mile limit.

An hour and a half later, he watched the mate shooting the trawl in ninety fathoms — on the edge of Kolkugrunn. If he drew a blank, he'd have one try in the middle of the Icelanders; and if that was fruitless, he'd steam north to the Horn bank before pushing on for Greenland. If he'd fished quietly now on Kolkugrunn, the Icelanders ahead would soon lose interest and assume that he was one of them — he'd merge with them and become lost in the crowd. He picked up the deck broadcast mic: 'I'm switching off the main lights,' he announced. 'You'll have to do the best you can.'

The only lights down on the working deck now were the police lights, spaced out inside the rail and on each quarter. From outboard, only *Campion*'s navigation and fishing lights — the green and white all-round — would be visible. He turned down the rheostat and the lights dimmed: in this visibility, she would not be visible much over three miles.

Hooky heard the hiss of the winchman's levers — good; the trawl was veered now to 450 fathoms and all was well, with *Campion* towing comfortably downwind, even in this half gale. Suddenly he felt elated — he knew he'd get into the cod now — those Icelanders a few miles to the westward were crackling on the R/T. He'd haul in two hours' time. He needed three hauls tonight, before first light.

At 2320, precisely, the cod-end surfaced. Hooky swore beneath his breath: damn all. He felt bitterly disappointed: a rotten haul. Then, hardly crediting his ears, he heard on the R/T a Lancashire voice he recognized clearly: Digger Greaves in *Noontide* calling up *Shower* — and nattering away like hell. Interspersed with the unintelligible guttural of the Icelandic trawler skippers, Rod's speech was like an ambulance siren in Canterbury cathedral.

What was *Noontide* doing over there? And, for that matter, why was *Shower* here, though her skipper, Dick Pennel, was always a sheep? He must have followed Digger, but why the devil did *Noontide* come here to complicate matters? Mark, his own son up here, in a ship that was sticking her neck out? Bloody hell! Hadn't he, Hooky, enough to worry about? He picked up the H/F mic, paused a moment, then replaced it in its socket. He'd be crazy to break silence. He wanted that cod and, by God, he was going to get it.

'I'm going in amongst that lot off Odhinsbodhi,' he said, as the mate clambered up to the wheelhouse. 'Stand by to shoot the trawl when I get there, Peter.' The yellow-oilskinned figure disappeared, his boots clumping on the rungs of the ladder.

I'll heave-to northward of them, he mused to himself. *Then drift down amongst 'em from windward; I won't get too close, and in this darkness they won't be able to identify my silhouette. As long as there's no gunboat around, I'll get away with it — but why the hell should any gunboat be here, amongst its own kith and kin?*

The three o'clock haul was fruitful. Hooky couldn't believe his eyes: the net was burgeoned — he even wondered whether the hoist might part with the weight. There were tons of rounded, shining fish, prime cod right up into the belly of the net. That was one of the largest hauls he'd ever seen — his heart was hammering against his ribs. He let out an involuntary cheer — and his elation was echoed by the lads down in the darkness of the working deck. The risk had paid off — they were into the cod.

As Hooky turned the ship, he saw the frenzy with which the watch was preparing the net for the next shoot. By the time *Campion* was turned and slamming head-on into the breaking seas, they were ready. He nodded at Knocker.

'Right-o…' the familiar cry was blown away on the wind. Out clattered the bobbins; the kelly's eyes sang — and the trawl was shot again. *By God, we'll make it yet*, thought Hooky. *Shoot, haul; shoot haul — I'll worry later about quitting the area — I'll call all the hands if need be…* How marvellous this was! He couldn't wait for the next haul… If he could finish the last haul before first light, he could be away and out of this dangerous situation before anyone could tumble to it — and he would have made a good trip. That would confound his critics, damn 'em all… Ole 'Ooky's luck was back. Who said he wouldn't make good?

He'd bloody well show 'em now… He'd fill the ship to her gunwales with prime cod — young Husky couldn't touch him now…

He lit his fifth cigar: this was one of the best moments of his life. Dare he come back again tomorrow night? The weather might worsen even more and that would decide it; he was only just able to prevent the spray from flying even now: if he had to steam any faster, he'd have to use the axes. Roll on five-thirty — he'd not turn in tonight. He'd catch every cod there was, right underneath the Icelanders' noses — and to hell with those instructions from the idiots ashore. He'd show 'em what a professional seaman and trawlerman could do…

First light was already stealing like a thief into the eastern horizon. Barely perceptible, but to a seaman like Hooky this was always the moment for which he'd been yearning during the long night. There it was, a pale fringe of green, a sliver of steely grey in the towering sky. Then he saw the cod-end breaking surface a cable astern of the frothing wake — like a whale, bulbous and wallowing in the long, undulating swell. He heard the yell of triumph from the lads who were clustered by the ramp on the deck below. If anything, the haul was quicker and even better than before: tons of shining prime cod.

'Close the gates, lads,' Hooky yelled exultantly into the mic. 'Steaming.' The mate's arm lifted in acknowledgement: the drams would be issued today. The skipper leaned over the autopilot and set the course to the northward. He moved the pitch control to full ahead: thank God, the wind had moderated. Now to get to hell out of it...

Hungry Mitch had come on watch, his humorous face creased in a wider grin than ever. 'Cup of tea, Skip?' The man was happy and Hooky felt good: there was no better feeling than a winning hunch. Mitch was turning round to the ladder when he paused in his tracks; he retraced a step and peered out through the port doorway. Then it was that Hooky sighted also the outlines of the three ships.

There was little difficulty in identifying the first silhouette that detached itself from the twilight dawn. It was the sidewinder, *Shower*, the first of the oil-burners built after the war. Smoke was belching from her funnel; the seas were breaking and freezing in fronds of ice crystals on the superstructure. Her traditional lines were part of the element in which she lived, a superb seaboat — and very unlike the sleek silhouette that was plugging up from the southward, the spray leaping upwards in cascades of flying water. Unmistakable — she could be no other than *Hekla*, that ubiquitous gunboat ... and, to the westward of her, another trawler, British by the look of her, steaming like a bat out of hell away from the area — must be *Noontide*, skipper Walker thought... Hooky threw open the door. The wind hit him hard and the cold made him gasp for breath.

Yes, that was *Hekla*: there were her squat, athwartship grey funnels; the mast on the foredeck ... and that vicious 57 mm.

He could see the gun's crew sheltering abaft the gun-deck screen. When the gunboat eased down, they'd man the gun which they had already uncovered.

Hooky picked up the H/F transmitter: '*Shower, Shower* — this is *Campion*,' he broadcast crisply. 'Make towards me, Dick. I'm closing you at full speed.'

As the loudspeaker crackled, Hooky saw the rust-splotched trawler keel over crazily in the running seas, as she turned towards, under full rudder.

'...glad to see you, *Campion*,' the phlegmatic voice of the Yorkshireman drawled across the air. 'The bugger's loaded one up the spout. He's bloody berserk. Watch out, Hooky.'

Hooky Walker felt a fury mounting inside him. Here was the bully again, armed with a lethal gun and prepared to shoot in international waters at an unarmed fishing vessel committing no crime. 'Call the watch below,' he yelled down to the working deck. 'I'm going in to help *Shower*. Get out the hoses, Peter — you may have to repel boarders.'

17: CONFRONTATION

Maria Karlsen drove slowly through the green gates of their house. It was already dark, so she was glad that Sven had thoughtfully left the outside light burning. She never liked returning in the dark to an empty house, particularly now, with these violent and unruly mobs that were touring the streets at night. She slid out of their Mini, opened the sliding door and eased the car into the garage until the bumper nudged the bicycles at the far end.

Carefully locking the car, she rolled down the garage door, to the ringing of the weights knocking against each other in the wind. She always enjoyed their welcome, particularly when they sang on their own, impelled by the gusts pummelling up from Reykjavik. She threaded the latch key into the kitchen door and pushed her way inside. On went the lights; it was good to be home, even though a house without Sven was lonely for her. With the children away at school, she found herself worrying much more about her swashbuckling sailor husband than she used to when they were first married.

It was too long a drive along the Americans' highway to Isafjordhur, so Sven always used the plane. Maria relished these journeys with him to the airport: she felt needed, though she served merely as a chauffeuse for returning the car to home base. At her time of life, things like this were important to her. The children, like all youth, were too interested in themselves to worry about her feelings, so it was all the more gratifying when Sven needed her for the practical things in his life.

The partings were brief — but, recently, much more frequent. The pattern was always the same: the drive against time, his mind already obsessed with the problems of command; the baleful lights of fishing villages in the fjords; the wet and greasy jetties where the black waters lapped against the iced-up piles; the quick kiss and the *thunk!* of the car door; and the loom of his presence at the window as he saluted her briefly. Then he was away, hurrying towards the control tower, his steaming bag swinging from his left hand.

Maria would slide across into the driving seat then, and move off before the sadness hit her. She could no longer, as she once did, wait to watch the little aircraft taking off into the twilight. Her imagination was too vivid: she hated the mountains and the mists through which he had to fly to join his *Hekla*.

She moved into the living room where she turned on the television. The usual unction would soon be spilling from the obese Icelandic faces of their Communist politicians — and now she endured a new feeling, one that she had never before experienced in Iceland: the eroding influence of cynicism as she watched the leaders of the proletariat exhorting their comrades to fight against the appalling conditions in which they were all supposed to be living — why couldn't men live peaceably amongst themselves? Surely God provided enough bounty for all in the world, if only men would share it out fairly?

Maria leaned forward and switched on the electric fire — and even that was rationed now, so it was cold in the house. She had not yet discarded her sealskin coat — and, pulling it more tightly around her, she snuggled into its warmth.

The upper bar of the fire began to glow feebly, but *she* was lucky — Sven and his men were now fighting their way round the north-west corner at Straumnes. She worried when Sven was up there, but she thanked God he was such a fine seaman.

Dreamily she watched the electric bar, which was now glowing redly — her Sven was like one of his Viking ancestors, with his vitality and drive. He had been particularly silent this morning, his mind over-burdened from his flying visit to Reykjavik and from his meeting with the Minister of Justice, the political head of the Icelandic coastguard. She felt fear deep within her and she closed her eyes. Though the Russians were supporting Iceland this time, she felt a terrible unease. Those grey ships lurking below the horizon — and calling in regularly at Reykjavik for repairs and fuel — were not suffering the hardships of an Icelandic winter merely to show the hammer and sickle. She wished they'd go away — she'd prefer the British to have the fish, than see the world incinerated.

She turned to the puffy face twitching on the television screen. She was sick of the Minister of Justice, who was always over-dramatizing the situation. It was men like him who could spark off the Third World War. She turned the knob and, to her relief, the face faded...

Straumnes, the captain of *Hekla* decided, was the worst cape on the whole coastline of his beloved island. The weather was so bad today that he had decided not to risk making the inshore passage between the races. Instead, he steamed fifteen miles outside, doubling the distance but avoiding the fight through the mountainous seas off Straumnes, where half a gale was blowing from the north-east against the Gulf Stream.

Sven Karlsen had been up for most of the night but he had snatched an hour's sleep before dawn, after he had altered to the south-eastward when Hornbjarg light was broad on his starboard beam. He had been able to turn in with a serene mind: every half-minute the three yellow flashes blinked comfortably to the south-west; and the pounding in the eyes of the ship been replaced by the usual corkscrew motion *Hekla* always adopted in a quartering sea. He was happy to hand his ship over to Olaf Hagander, his Number One, that tall and enigmatic Dane who now preferred to live in Iceland.

Sleep, which usually came so naturally to him, eluded him for a while this morning: he lay on the captain's bunk, his eyes riveted on the scuttle where the faint circle of light swung crazily across his vision between sea and sky — that leaping horizon below which lusted the sea-power and might of the Soviet Union.

He sighed, the stress of responsibility refusing his mind the rest it craved. It was all very well for Bjarni Vedel, their present Minister of Justice, to harangue him in his office yesterday, but the politician was safely ensconced behind a desk in the capital city. When the crunch of decision came, it would fall on one of only a few men, naval officers in their early forties who could be said, without being dramatic, to be able to affect the fate of the planet. The Russians, below the horizon there, were waiting only for a cast-iron incident before they moved in. And Vedel had ordered him, Sven Karlsen, to become the pawn in the game if circumstances warranted it. 'Even using live ammunition?' Karlsen had asked.

'So,' the Minister had affirmed, nodding his head. Karlsen, who was not now as naive as he had been in the previous Cod War, had insisted on his orders being confirmed on paper. Vedel caught the innuendo, but he nevertheless signed the type-written sheet which had been quickly disgorged by the secretariat. Sven had then left, a cloud of depression hanging over him. He loathed being used as a political instrument. He hated politicians and their knaveries, and found that having to obey his political masters was becoming more obnoxious to him as he grew older. He was a seaman who understood the sea.

He turned in his bunk, wondering whether Maria would be up… He felt drowsier now; at least he'd enjoy a peaceful forenoon amongst his own trawlermen. Those stubborn British were still pinned down off Langanes and the east coast — the unwritten truce between them all was a relief while the peace talks went on. It afforded the men at sea a break anyhow, but the Icelanders would never give up their claim for a fifty-mile limit, now that the Russians were openly showing the mailed fist.

As he drifted into sleep, he realized why the Russians had been building up their navy to become the second most powerful naval force in the world — and no one had lifted a finger to stop them…

'Captain, sir…'

The whistle blew shrilly next to his ear; Sven Karlsen was immediately awake, alert…

'Two darkened ships to port of us — look like trawlers, sir.'

'Are they fishing?' Sven was already out of his bunk and pulling on the sheepskin boots Maria had given him last Christmas.

'Can't tell yet, sir…' Number One's voice boomed down the voicepipe. 'Shall I alter to investigate?'

'Bring her round. I'll be up.'

Sven felt exhilarated but angry. Surely *Laki* and he had taught foreign trawlermen that it didn't pay to ignore the orders of the Icelandic Coastguard? Those British were so stubborn and infuriatingly determined. Not one of them had yet been boarded or arrested, though many of them had their gear chopped by *Laki* and himself. This dispute had started a year ago now, but still the British fishermen couldn't get it into their thick skulls that this Third Cod War was different... They still dreamed of Dunkirk and the Battle of Britain, but they couldn't even run themselves now. Sven took the bridge steps two at a time and moved straight to the captain's command position.

'Where are they?'

Olaf Hagander withdrew his head from the radar visor. 'Red four-o and red six-o, sir — four miles. I can't see their nav lights yet.'

Hekla had settled on a collision course and was butting hard into the advancing seas which were breaking over her entire fo'c'sle and smothering the bridge in clouds of flying spray.

'Ease down,' Karlsen snapped. 'Can't afford to ice up.'

He heard the telegraph ring, felt the vibration diminish. Ah! There were the two echoes, bearing 060 degrees and 040 degrees — and there was another, faint, showing only intermittently in the clutter: it was away to the south-east on the edge of his own trawling fleet — probably a stranger.

'Go to action stations, First Lieutenant.'

Olaf Hagander saluted and turned to the alarm buzzer.

'Don't uncover the gun until I've eased down,' the captain added. 'I don't want a man washed overboard.'

6,000 metres at first contact; now 5,000 and still no lights. It was improbable that two trawlers should have navigation light failures simultaneously — and why hadn't they set oil lanterns? Ah, there was a glimmer — faint and yellow, a string of lights on the working deck of one of the trawlers. Karlsen's eyes ached as he peered into the gloom of the cold dawn.

Both were side trawlers by the look at them, with their sweet lines that merged so naturally into the contours of the sea...

Then he saw the dim red light of the nearer trawler, her bridge squat as she rolled in the swell. Her steaming lights snapped on: then he saw the dark outlines of men working on the fore-deck while they worked the nets over the side. They were hauling and they were in a hurry. Sven Karlsen swore beneath his breath. They had sighted him.

'Starboard ten,' he ordered. 'I'll round up her windward side, Number One. Stand by the gun's crew and the cutting gear.'

'Aye, aye, sir.'

Karlsen could depend on his officers and men. They had so much experience of this game behind them, that he need no longer worry about their efficiency. All he had to do was to lay his ship alongside if she was hostile — or to swoop up astern of her, nip in and cut her wires with his explosive sweep.

'You're right, First Lieutenant,' he shouted above the clatter of the gun's crew mustering by the mounting on the gun deck below. 'They're British.' The two ships were communicating on H/F between themselves.

'Okay,' a Liverpudlian voice was saying, with a note of anxiety. 'I've hauled. I'm off westward. Good luck, Digger.'

Karlsen stood close to the loudspeaker, trying to identify the ships. They must have been fishing on the edge of the twelve-mile limit. He'd move straight in and stop the nearer of the two, the older by the look of her: she was silhouetted against the eastern horizon, on the edge of that rain squall that was sweeping down between her and her fellow conspirator.

'I'm away too, Dick,' an older voice replied. 'The bastard's coming up fast.' By the harsh twang, the skipper sounded Australian. 'Want any help?' he added.

'No — you bugger off. We'd best separate. So long, Digger.'

There was a *snick!* and the air went dead. The radar showed 4,000 metres now: the distances seemed much less. Karlsen thrust his head down to the visor again and … ah! There was that third echo; no doubt about it now — and less than two thousand metres away. As he looked up, the squall thrashed against the bridge window in a flurry of snow. *Hekla* was blind now and racing in towards her invisible target, the mysterious stranger who was so close.

The huge seas were smothering the gunboat and the spray was enveloping her in a blanket of ice. The clear-view screen whined in the windows but visibility was nil, even the fo'c'sle being obliterated. The gunboat captain swore beneath his breath — that damned trawler would be well outside the limit if *Hekla* reduced speed to avoid icing up. Karlsen decided to hold on and to risk the icing.

'Look, sir, right ahead…' The starboard lookout was shouting, his hand pointing to the northern edge of the squall drifting like a sombre curtain across the sea. 'Stern trawler, sir…'

Karlsen spun round. There she was, a small stern trawler, with a large yellow gantry aft, a white bridge cocked forward, and with white upperworks and a blue hull. She was smart and must be one of the Gunn fleet. From the staff on her port quarter, the Red Ensign, that Red Duster of the British marine, streamed provocatively. He'd recognize that ship anywhere, his private and personal adversary, that bastard in *English Campion*… In that brief moment, he felt hate, a new emotion for him, rising within.

Recognition decided the issue in Karlsen's mind. He'd maintain his speed and risk the icing: that damned stern trawler was already edging into a position between *Hekla* and the gunboat's original quarry, the old side-winder. The squall suddenly dispersed to reveal Karlsen's first enemy, but now her rusty transom was towards him and dipping every few moments into her foaming wake as she ran at full speed northward.

'Stand by to close-up,' Karlsen shouted. 'I shan't be able to get between them, Number One, but I'll lay off and stop 'em with the gun.'

'Live ammunition, sir?'

'No, not yet. They'll see sense, I hope.'

He turned round to sight the more modern trawler of the original pair, but she was almost out of sight and steaming like a bat out of hell into the western horizon. The British were, as usual, fine seamen, but *Hekla* had them this time — so long as that bastard in *English Campion* didn't interfere — a forlorn hope, because the hatred was, Karlsen knew, mutual. He picked up the H/F transmitter.

'Give me 2182,' he snapped. Then he spoke into the mic, distinctly and slowly: he had not been to Cambridge for nothing.

'Keep out of my way, *English Campion*, or I shall arrest you too, for interfering with the coastguard.'

He heard the muffled sounds of bridge movement and then a snort as the English skipper picked up the mouthpiece of his microphone (Walker, wasn't he? Reykjavik intelligence had supplied the names of all the British skippers).

'If you get in my way, *Hekla*,' the steady voice boomed over the air, 'I'll ram you, so help me God...'

Karlsen paused, measuring the distance with his seaman's eye. The stern trawler had succeeded in coming between *Hekla* and the side trawler, now almost abeam: *Shower*, of Fleetwood, by the registration on her stern; FD 186 in smudged white paint, barely visible across the port bow. He would take *Hekla* up further, before ordering them to heave-to.

'I warn you, *English Campion*,' he shouted through the mic, 'I'm arresting the trawler *Shower*. If you interfere or resist, I shall arrest you too.' He felt the anger boiling inside him. The impertinence of these swine... 'It is forbidden for you to fish in these waters.'

'Who said so?' The reply was immediate, and Sven could sense the anger in the British skipper's voice. 'The British Government does not acknowledge Icelandic jurisdiction outside twelve miles. In the eyes of my Government, I am doing nothing illegal. These are international waters and if you molest *Shower*, I'll call the Royal Navy.'

'You do that, you English bastard.' Sven knew that his own fury was uncontrollable. 'I've already reported you to my Government. Keep clear. I repeat, *keep clear*...' He turned to his First Lieutenant. 'Uncover the gun,' he ordered briskly. 'I'm rounding up.'

He took *Hekla* to within two cables of the bucking side trawler *Shower*, who, her funnel pouring filthy black smoke, was steaming at full speed to the north. Karlsen could see the red-faced, middle-aged skipper sheltering behind his open bridge door, while the icy seas swept across his old ship. The man's mouth opened and shut, but his invective was carried away on the wind.

'Stop your ship or I'll open fire,' Sven Karlsen ordered; he spoke clearly in perfect middle-class English. He held the mic in his hand and waited for the old skipper to stumble back inside his wheelhouse to pick up his R/T microphone.

'Go on, then, you bastard,' the Lancashire voice yelled. 'Open fire on a defenceless ship.'

The insolence stung the gunboat captain.

'Open fire with practice ammunition,' he ordered. 'Put a shot across her bow.'

He watched the helmeted gunlayer lay his sights, saw the loading number ram home the shell. In this sea, accuracy was going to be difficult.

'Point of aim, fifty yards ahead of her stern.' Karlsen heard the gunnery officer's orders, yelled and garbled in this wind. 'Ready to open fire, sir...' and the captain saw the pale, young face turned towards him, the eyes bright with excitement.

'Shoot,' Karlsen commanded.

The tension of expectation; the shock; the *bang!* — and then the splash on the other side of the old trawler's bows; the British seamen sheltering behind the steel wheelhouse: all this was routine now.

'All right,' the raucous voice from the trawler growled. 'I've stopped.'

Karlsen watched the way coming off the old ship. 'Stop both engines,' he ordered. 'Keep station on her, Number One.' Then he picked up the mic. 'Tell your friend *Campion* to keep clear, or I'll sink you both,' he ordered over the H/F. His words sounded unemotional. He did not relish having to make good his threat. 'Muster every man on deck. Send them aft where I can see them.'

There was a delay while the three ships wallowed in the seas, all three slowly drifting beam-on as the way came off them. They lay a-hull and Karlsen could hear the slip-slapping and hissing of the seas breaking against the rusty sides of the trawler. Karlsen watched from the corner of his eye, as the flared bows of Walker's ship nudged up between him and the side trawler.

'Hurry up,' Karlsen yelled at *Shower.* 'I'll give you one more minute.'

He watched her crew, some still in their vests and trousers, others in their oilskins, go scrambling through the break and up onto the stern deck.

'They're all aft,' *Shower*'s skipper shouted. 'What do you want now?'

'Follow me,' *Hekla*'s captain ordered. 'I'm arresting you for illegal fishing inside the twelve-mile limit.'

A bitter laugh crossed the space of water between the two ships. The skipper was shouting from his wheelhouse: 'Get stuffed, you bastard — just you try.'

Karlsen saw the old man winding away on his telegraph handles. There was a kick of white at *Shower*'s stern.

'Put three rounds into her fo'c'sle head,' *Hekla*'s captain ordered calmly. 'Above the water-line.'

He was watching *Shower* when the gun barked again — once, this time, with a deliberately aimed shot. He saw the whiff of rusty flakes flying where the shell drove a neat hole through the black-painted plates.

'Send a man for'd to inspect the damage,' Karlsen commanded. He'd play with the old skipper, until he broke his nerve: then he'd arrest his ship.

Karlsen watched as a deckhand clambered into the fore peak. Seconds later, he emerged, shaking his head. The damage was not lethal, provided they plugged the hole. The shell had passed through and out of the other side.

There was a shocked silence in the British trawler. Then the old man walked slowly over to the bridge door. He opened it and for a moment stood there, arms spread wide on the rail and staring across with disbelief. He raised his fist then and shouted, but his invective was drowned by the roar of the seas that jumped between them, and the whistling of the wind.

'Open fire,' Karlsen commanded. Twice more the gun barked: two more holes slammed through the trawler's bows.

'*Watch out, sir!*' The First Lieutenant was shouting from the starboard side of the wheelhouse. He was pointing aft. Karlsen spun round.

All he could see were the flared bows, blue, and topped with white, tearing down towards him. In the centre window of the bridge, he caught sight of Walker's face — large, grim and utterly determined. The gunboat captain saw the bow wave breaking, watched the flukes of the lethal anchor protruding from the flare. *English Campion* was only fifty metres off and closing fast.

'Full ahead together,' Karlsen snapped. 'Hard a-port.' *Hekla* was over-endowed with power. Her turbo jets exploded into life and, with a swirl foaming at her stern, she spun off to port, away from the menacing trawler intent on destroying her.

'Come on, you Icelandic bastard,' an English voice was shouting. 'Why don't you open fire? Sink me — come on, you...' Karlsen couldn't catch the remainder for, as he took his ship free of those maddened skippers, the first banks of swirling fog suddenly enfolded them all, blotting out everything from sight.

18: PLAYING HOOKY

Madge Gledholme was well known in the supermarket. She knew she was large and shapeless, but at forty-eight and having borne her drunken husband twelve children, what else could a woman expect to be? The girls at the cash desks were always kind to her. She had to have two trolleys to carry all the provisions, and she always brought their Ada to help push the loads around. Ada was their tenth, just fifteen and already causing trouble with the boys. Mother Gledholme smiled when she looked down at her youngest daughter — and when the placid mother smiled, there was a light about her face which transfigured her.

'Why you 'appy, Mum?'

The pretty blonde girl was already almost a woman — Ada's face was so like her dad's when Madge had first met him after Korea. Stan had been a rip-roarin' lad then, and when she took him for her husband, she should have known what was in store for her. Life was hard sometimes, particularly when her hubby was on the booze. He'd always been a deckie and would be nothing else, so at least all she had to contend with was his alcoholism and his randiness. She hated the first and enjoyed the second, so there was comfort in her brood of children. But, Mother of God, she did miss her last little 'un, young Willy, out there as brassy in *English Campion*.

'Hullo, Mrs Gledholme…'

She turned round towards the kindly voice behind her. There was Mrs Walker, of all people, the wife of Willy's skipper.

'I was just thinking about your husband's ship, Mrs Walker,' she said, happy with the warmth and comradeship shared. 'Our Willy's his brassy, you know?'

'Aye, but we do miss 'em, don't we?' Mrs Walker sighed as she rearranged the goods in her trolley. She was looking anxious and peaky, Madge thought, but perhaps it was the cold. 'Your lad's at sea, too, isn't he, Mrs Walker?' she went on. 'Followed his father too, didn't he?' She did not mention Stan, though Mrs Walker probably knew all about him: there were few secrets amongst the women of Fleetwood.

'Aye — but he's not in his dad's ship now. He's in *Noontide* with Digger Greaves. He's been out seven days now — the brassy, you know.'

There was no need to cover up, Madge thought. Everyone accepted that a skipper's son had the edge on the others: it was a way of life in Fleetwood, from generation to generation.

'How's your family, Mrs Gledholme?' the skipper's wife was asking her as they moved one up in the queue. If only that couple in front would stop giggling and get on with the job… Once their children came along, it would be a different matter then. No time, never no bleedin' time…

'We're all very well, Mrs Walker, thanks ever so…' replied Madge, 'but I'll be glad when our Willy's back. Seems too young, don't 'e, to be out there with them 'ard men? 'E's still a nipper at sixteen, ain't he?'

Mrs Walker was biting her lip.

'Bleedin awful,' Madge went on, 'Worse for us women than the men… When's 'e coming back, then?'

'They ought to be back for Christmas, Mrs Gledholme. Won't it be wonderful?' The skipper's wife was smiling now — they both had the love of their sons to share between them.

Impulsively, Madge stretched out her plump arm. The worn fingers took the younger woman's hand. 'Wonderful, missus,' she said, her haggard face vibrant with the joy of anticipation. 'We'll drink your 'ealths, that we will!' She turned and squeezed her way into the bottleneck of the cash desk. She hadn't deliberately meant to hold up the queue.

Brenda Dodds was waving at her: that cheeky dolly-bird, shouting across at her from the other gate. ''Ere, Maggie, 'ave you 'eard?' she called, excitement in her high-pitched voice. '*Campion*'s been on telly. She's in trouble or somefink.'

Hooky Walker had never before blessed the oncoming of fog. Now, with that bloody gunboat breaking off the chase, for the first time in his life he felt delayed shock. He held out his hands and extended his fingers — they were still trembling, and he could not stop them.

'Near one…' It was Sinclair, quietly reassuring him, as he lifted his head from the radar visor. '*Hekla*'s disappeared now: 245 degrees — sixteen miles,' he reported.

The skipper nodded. 'No one but an idiot would have stuck with us in this fog,' he said. 'Not even that Mad Axeman.' He frowned, then asked, 'How far ahead is *Shower* now?'

'About seven miles, skipper.'

Hooky Walker stared directly into the mate's eyes. 'I'm going back,' he said, 'to catch some fish.'

Sinclair stood transfixed. Then he moved towards the bridge chair; he stood close to his skipper and faced him squarely. 'Are you serious?' he asked softly, so that the watch-keeper, Knocker Wright, could not hear from the charthouse settee.

'Yeah — deadly serious.'

'They'll crucify you, if they arrest you.'

'I'll not be arrested. I'll only be steaming through the twelve-mile limit. I'll be fishing only in international waters, outside the twelve, but inside the fifty-mile limit.'

'*Hekla* will be waiting,' Sinclair persisted. 'All they want is a cut-and-dried incident. You haven't heard the BBC?'

Hooky's rusty eyebrows became two crescent moons.

'America has placed her forces in the first stage of a nuclear alert,' the mate went on. 'And you're already in the news…'

Hooky's gust of laughter was like the rumble of summer thunder. 'Who, me? What the hell have I done?'

'According to the Icelandic Government, you and *Shower* have caused an international incident. The Navy's sending in reinforcements.'

'Are you serious, Pete? It's as bad as that?' Hooky was smiling broadly. At least he'd stuck to his principles, and no one was going to drive him from the sea. 'All the more reason for going back to Hornbjarg. There are fish there and I'm going to get 'em. I'm fed up with being pushed around by these bloody Icelanders.'

He could see that Sinclair disapproved: the man's jaw was set as, saying nothing, he continued to stare out of the wheelhouse windows. 'We're forty-eight miles north of North Cape,' Hooky said. 'They'll have written us off by now; they're obviously making sure that poor old *Shower* is on her way back to UK.'

In the silence, Hooky could hear the morse bleeping from the radio office. Then Sinclair turned to face his skipper. 'Reckon it's worth having a go, Skip,' he said. 'But *I* wouldn't have the guts.'

Hooky nodded and took a long pull at his cigar. 'Tell Sparks to make the switches on the main receiver, please.'

Hooky watched the mate disappearing into the office. Sinclair was all right and would make a skipper one day. Hooky spun the course control of the autopilot; the ship began to swing, heeled, then settled to her new course: 205 degrees. 'If anyone asks,' he said, 'I'm altering to the southward for a good departure. Who the hell wants to be right up here, anyway? We're almost in the pack ice.'

He began whistling to himself, as happy as a schoolboy truant.

'We'll be down there after sunset,' he called to Peter, who was still leaning against the door of the radio office. 'Couldn't be better: so long as the fog holds, we'll really get in amongst 'em this time.' He moved to the pitch control. 'I'm going full ahead, Pete,' he said, grinning mischievously. 'Here we go...'

19: COME INTO MY PARLOUR

'*Hekla*, this is Iceland Coastguard.'

Hekla's captain was standing close to the loudspeaker; the atmospherics were bad today.

'Coastguard, this is *Hekla*. I hear you strength two. Pass your message.'

Sven Karlsen turned quickly to the radar operator now crouched over the visor of the PPI. 'Bearing and distance?' he demanded.

'O-four-five, sir. Fifteen miles.'

Karlsen nodded and picked up the microphone: 'Coastguard, this is *Hekla*. Suspicious echo closing at thirteen knots, bearing O-four-five, distance fifteen miles,' he reported. 'I shall remain on station, close to our ships and inside the twelve-mile limit. Request instructions.'

'*Hekla*, this is Coastguard… Wait.'

The air went dead, only the crackling of the atmospherics disturbing the peace on the bridge. The gunboat captain strode to the for'd edge of the wheelhouse and peered at his men cleaning the 57-mm. The sun was obscured by the fog and by its strange light, droplets of condensed water glinted like diamonds where they had re-frozen along the grease on the long barrel of the Swedish gun. He watched as Seaman Jax fondled one of the new HE shells, fused to explode at the merest suspicion of contact: the fuse was so sensitive that even a cloud could detonate it, the gunnery school had said.

Karlsen knew exactly what would be going on ashore. Coastguard would now be obtaining clearance with headquarters. It was probable that the Minister himself would come on the line — the conversation was 100 per cent secure. Sven Karlsen felt keyed up this morning: he'd been seen off yesterday by that cunning devil in *English Campion*, but the Englishmen had been too clever, doubling back. *Laki* was on her way round, south about; and he, Karslen, in his superb gunboat, was fully prepared to receive this British madman.

'*Hekla*, this is coastguard.'

Karlsen picked up the H/F microphone: 'Coastguard, this is *Hekla*. Pass your message,' he replied, wishing they would get on with it.

'Minister here, Karlsen. Give me all the facts, please … over.'

'Good afternoon, Minister. This is Karlsen. May I have precise instructions, please, after you have heard my report…? Over.'

'Yes. Go ahead… Over.'

'The Britisher is the stern trawler, *English Campion* — the one who interfered yesterday with the arrest. She is, I am almost certain, doubling back to North Cape, where many of our own boats are fishing. I am stopped and I am an hour's steaming from them, so I can stand by for any developments. I want to know whether to arrest *English Campion*… Over.'

'Minister speaking… On what charge, Captain?'

'Interfering with the course of justice when I was attempting to arrest the trawler *Shower*. I am sure she was just inside the twelve-mile limit… Over.'

'So, was she definitely inside our fifty limit…? Over.'

'Of course, sir. That was the reason, on your instructions, that I attempted to bring her into Reykjarfjord… Over.'

'What are you asking, Karlsen…? Over.'

'Do you wish me to use force to arrest *English Campion*, sir? And am I to sink this Englishman should he resist arrest…? Over.'

The ether crackled during the long silence that ensued. Sven Karlsen enjoyed putting politicians over barrels — he liked them to know what the sensation felt like... The ether snicked again.

'Your incident of yesterday is now worldwide news, Karlsen. We've made the most of it and so have our Russian friends.' The unctuous voice was chuckling. 'The Americans have even put their nuclear forces on the first stage of alert. If the Englishman is fool enough to return, then we've got the whole thing tied up, haven't we, Karlsen...? Over.' The politician was evasive, trying to pass the buck as usual.

'Yes, sir — but it would be even better if we could catch him poaching inside the twelve-mile limit. All our boats are well inside and fishing like mad. If I know *Campion*, she'll try to lose herself amongst 'em in the dark... Over.'

'Let her hang herself. Present her with every opportunity to poach. Then grab her red-handed... Over.'

'Do I use force, sir...? Over.'

'Certainly: use whatever force you consider necessary, Captain, and bring her into harbour... Over.'

'And if she resists, sir...? Over.'

'Sink her, Skipstjóri ... sink her.' There was a short pause. 'Good-day, Skipstjóri... Out.'

Karlsen stood motionless, R/T microphone hanging from his hand. It was so easy for them; but, for him, it was within his own will whether to become the catalyst in the terrible escalation towards a world conflagration. He replaced the mic. He turned slowly towards the radar and peered into the screen: the echo was still there, bright now and moving towards the centre of the glowing PPI.

'First Lieutenant,' he commanded, without removing his face from the visor. 'Go to action stations.'

20: THE GREAT DIVIDE

The mate of *English Campion* stood in the starboard for'd corner of the wheelhouse. In this position, he could be alone with his thoughts. With one elbow locked against the back of the door, and legs splayed, he could balance without too much effort against the crazy motion of the ship surging down the following seas as she ran towards the North Cape of Iceland.

Peter Sinclair surreptitiously regarded the skipper who was slumped in his bridge chair, his heavy shoulders squared back against the back-rest. The strong face was deep in thought, his thick lips working rhythmically as he chewed on the new false teeth which he so detested but which he always suffered for protocol purposes during daylight hours. Those piercing eyes were as steady as a rock when they regarded a man. How could anyone, Pete thought, be fool enough to try and deceive such a straightforward appraisal?

The large head seemed particularly leonine today: a straggly mane sweeping untidily about his face, and five days' growth reaching from the shadowy chin to his sideburns. Not an Adonis for the mass media, but a leader for those content to entrust their lives to such a giant of a man. Yet he had his Achilles' heel, as everyone did, Peter thought... Hooky's obsession was to reach the top; he suffered an insatiable urge to fill the ship with fish — and during the next few hours this weakness could be their undoing, not only for all on board this vessel, but for countless millions, once the chain reaction of power politics was set in train.

Why did Walker have this blind spot? And why did he refuse to maintain communications with the outside world now?

Hooky had refused to call up the owners, even after hearing the BBC announcement of yesterday's fracas. Should he, Peter Sinclair, second-in-command of this ship, disclose his anxiety to his skipper? He turned away, his eyes drawn to the angry sunset: kissed by the last rays of the sinking sun, the layers of slab-like cirrus were streaked red, like blood smeared across a rumpled sheet. He trusted Skipper Walker and he, Sinclair, wouldn't compound a difficult decision by making it more difficult: he'd do his utmost to support Hooky. If there was any adverse comment 'tween decks, he'd squash it. There was a job to do; in two hours, they'd be shooting the trawl off North Cape, so he'd better check the net.

The radio operator had been curbing his impatience for over twenty-four hours. He'd listened in to the events of the world outside and had refrained from worrying the skipper over much with news of the deteriorating situation … but now, with the news that the Soviet fleet was reinforcing its squadrons in Icelandic waters, surely the time had come for him, Ewan Massey, to register his protest?

It was now seven-thirty; though at tea Ewan had been alone with the skipper in the officers' mess while they fed, he had failed to screw up sufficient courage to express his fears. Now he was convinced … but to collect his thoughts before blurting out his misgivings, he'd have one more look at the radar and the echo-sounders. They were entering shallower water now, judging by the appearance of the churned-up seas and the savage motion. He stooped to peer once again into the radar screen.

There were the blips of the Icelandic trawlers — big ones, small ones, all fishing with a frenzy characteristic of having found the cod. These echoes married with the string of lights dancing across the western horizon, visible for only short snatches between the fog banks. The PPI was a rash of echoes, all bunched ahead of *Campion*'s line of advance. No problem of collision here, but they were all inside the race and therefore inside the twelve-mile limit. There was only one echo clear of the melee and that was to the westward — another independent cuss of an Icelandic skipper, probably. Ewan smiled to himself; every nation had one!

Campion was bucking about now, but she must be inside the race or she would surely have been on her beam ends? By radar, North Cape was eight miles off. He raised his head and felt his heart quickening with excitement: the steady rhythm of the engine, the slapping of the seas, the silence on the bridge; the normality of routine accentuated this tense moment of decision.

As *Campion* nudged her way into the circle of plunging lights from the Icelandic trawlers, Ewan's eyes riveted on the trace of the echo sounder: wide, definite marks — no doubt at all.

'Skip,' he called. 'Look at these marks…'

Hooky stirred from his chair. 'Good God,' he cried. 'We're amongst the cod. I'll stop and have a "do".'

Ewan saw him swing round towards the watch-keeper. 'Knocker,' he ordered, 'call the watch and shoot the trawl. Look slippy.'

Ewan stood rooted by the bridge console. He could feel the fear mounting inside himself and, for better or ill, he knew that now they were committed.

Hooky realized that the next few hours would be some of the most momentous of his life. He'd gambled for high stakes, as he liked to do. He would stay on the bridge, fish two hauls then, as yesterday, get the hell out of it before daylight.

Whoosh! Away went the trawl... Sinclair had wasted no time. The hours dragged by; a magnificent haul at 0100 — a bulging bellyful of shining cod. He confessed to himself alone that the sight evoked in him an ecstatic sense of pleasure — what a harvest of the oceans!

Campion shot again, this time on the edge of the constricting fleet. Hooky wanted to be on the perimeter of the twelve-mile limit by daylight, so that nothing could be proved against him: he'd be crucified if they caught him here. The hours sped by, his skill perpetually put to the test by having to avoid the Icelanders. Shortly after 0300, a Teutonic voice bellowed at him as the two trawlers crossed slowly on parallel courses. He shouted back, 'Rhubarb, rhubarb...' and the Icelander seemed satisfied. They waved as they slid by each other, to disappear into the night. Now he was hauling again, the last before dawn. It was 0530 and he felt the weariness seeping over him: his eyelids ached from the superhuman effort he was making to remain awake.

'Last fifty, Skip!'

Mitch's corncrake cry was like music. Hooky moved to the pitch control and reduced speed; he needed enough only for steerage way.

'Short mark!'

The last twenty-five fathoms — thank God. The gamble had come off — if only this too could be a good haul... Then he saw it, a hillock of bulging fish, where the cod-end surged back and forth in the wake. The oilskinned deckies were staggering about like marionettes on the working deck — another five minutes, and he'd clear out of it... He scrambled back to the bridge console as the R/T began to crackle. The voice and the accent were recognizable...

'Hey — you bastard,' an Australian voice drawled angrily. 'Sheer off or I'll ram you.' So *Noontide* was close, amongst this lot. Digger Greaves, the Australian skipper who had returned last year from down-under, was a kindred spirit who'd chanced his arm. When he'd broken off yesterday from *Shower*, he'd been steering for Greenland. He must have been as evil as Hooky, but he was now in trouble — and then, with a jolt, Skipper Walker remembered his own son. Hell's teeth, Mark was amongst it too. Hooky picked up the mic just as the gunboat came on the air.

'You are fishing illegally,' an Icelandic voice shouted angrily, a voice that the skipper of *English Campion* would recognize anywhere. 'I am cutting your gear.'

An unintelligible oath rent the air, followed by a loud Australian twang. 'Hard a-starboard! You bastard,' Digger was bellowing. 'You Icelandic bastard — what d'you mean by chopping me?'

Hooky chipped in, before the gunboat could reply. 'Hi, Digger,' he called. 'Hooky Walker here, Digger. D'you need any help?'

There was a roar of triumph through the speaker. 'You're here, Hooky? Good on yer, mate — come and give these bastards a dose of salts. I'm just inside the edge of the race, north-west of North Cape.'

Hooky's mind raced. He didn't want to be involved, with all this fish on board and being already in a compromising position, but... 'Okay, Digger,' he called. 'I'm coming up to join you — half an hour, mebbe.' He set the pitch to full ahead and felt her racing forward to maximum power. 'On my way…' he yelled. The R/T clicked, went dead, then clicked again.

'Hey, Hooky,' Digger yelled. 'I'm going to fix these bastards — how can I cut one of their trawls?'

Peter Sinclair was pointing across the port bow. 'Aircraft, Skip,' he was shouting. 'Coming straight towards.'

Microphone in hand, Hooky waited for the roar of the plane's engines to subside. The two-engined jet swooped overhead, wave-clipping and barely clearing *Campion*'s forestay. The aircraft swooped upwards, banked and flew off to the southward towards the land.

'We seem to be expected, Digger,' Hooky spoke into the mic. 'He'll be reporting us, anyhow.'

'So what?' Digger replied. 'How can I fix 'em, Hooky, you pom?' He was excited and, from his past knowledge of the Australian, Hooky quailed for the ships within reach of *Noontide*.

'Lower your anchor a couple of shackles,' Hooky growled. 'Tow it across one of their trawls.' He regretted his advice as soon as he'd broadcast it — it was only given in fun. No sane man would try the manoeuvre when surrounded by the enemy.

''Kay, Hooky — boy!' he yelled. 'Watch out, you bloody Icelanders…' A few seconds later, the clanking of cable running through a hawse-pipe was audible over the air…

'Good God,' Hooky gasped. He glanced across at the mate. 'The idiot has taken me at my word, Peter.'

He peered around the horizon to collect his bearings… Up ahead he could see the cross-trees of pitching ships and, occasionally, a black hull. Slightly to starboard, there was the unmistakable silhouette of a gunboat — no doubt at all: there was only one *Hekla*.

The gunboat was still steaming slowly, just to seaward of *Noontide*. *She hasn't seen us yet — and what can she do about us?* Hooky was thinking, assessing the alternatives. *I'm only steaming and I'm outside the twelve-mile limit,* he mused; *international law permits me to steam through international waters — to hell with bloody* Hekla. *I'm going to stand by* Noontide. He tried to thrust behind him the image of his son: his strained, sensitive face; he was probably working somewhere on deck, feeding the needles ... but the boy's laughing eyes intruded on his imagination. Such a short while ago it seemed, since Molly had smiled softly up at her husband when she drew back the shawl to display their first-born son...

Hell, what was *Hekla* up to now? She was swinging to starboard and steering towards, on an interception course with *Campion*. The gunboat could not now be steaming at less than twenty-five knots, from the seas that she was taking over her.

'Hey, Hooky,' yelled Digger. 'Watch out — the axeman cometh.'

'Better rouse the lads, Peter,' Hooky drawled. 'Tell 'em to stay aft, will you, please?'

The mate, grim-faced, bustled down the ladder. There was little to do now because they had seen it all before. Axes, hammers, spanners, knives... They knew how to repel boarders if they had to. He peered through his binoculars at the gunboat — she was thrashing along, on an opposite course.

Hell — what's up now? Hooky wondered. *There's not much I can do, except to close* Noontide. She was only a couple of miles off now, with a hive of Icelandic trawlers around her. Hooky was enjoying himself — he'd take *Campion* in amongst 'em, slap, bang through the middle to *Noontide* — and he realized then that he'd never make it in time. *Hekla* was barely a mile off.

She was turning slowly to come up alongside on the port quarter, and to leeward. Hooky watched the seas streaming from her foredeck — saw her ease down while her captain strutted out to the wheelhouse deck.

Hooky recognized him then, the adversary he'd met before and had been fighting for so long in his mind, in his fantasies, and subconsciously through every working minute. That tall, lean streak, peering at *Campion* through his glasses, was the evil that Hooky had been warring against for too long in his life. He flung open the door and shook his fist at the arrogant captain, so sure of himself in his warship, his gun uncovered and manned by his brave sailors.

The R/T extension lead snaked across the wheelhouse deck to where Hooky stood by the doorway.

'Iceland coastguard … this is British trawler, *English Campion*,' he called. 'What are your intentions?'

The two ships were now dipping along at thirteen knots, the gunboat less than two cables off. The gunboat captain lifted his right arm to speak into his R/T. Hooky could see him turning his head to judge the manoeuvring distance.

'You will soon find out,' came the guttural reply.

Hooky's thoughts raced. What was the bastard up to? But all the time that Hooky could distract him meant the gain of precious seconds as he raced towards *Noontide*. Another few minutes and *Campion* would be between them both, so long as those Icelandic trawlers poked off…

'Don't interfere with me,' Hooky called, standing in the port doorway, left hand in his trouser pocket. 'If you do, I shall call on the Royal Navy.'

The Icelander's laughter began to stir the hate in Hooky's soul — but the bastard was at it again…

'And if you *don't* stop, you English bastard, I'll call on the Russian navy. Please yourself. You've been fishing inside the limits and I have orders to arrest you.'

Hooky thought fast. 'Your twelve-mile limit?' he shouted, hurt by the outrageous suggestion. 'I've never fished inside your twelve-mile limit in my life.'

Hekla was nearer now and almost abeam. He could see the helmsman at the wheel and the gunlayer and trainer at their sights.

'No,' the gunboat captain shouted. His face was working, and he was clearly excited. 'No, not the twelve-mile limit. You've been fishing inside the fifty-mile limit many times.'

'Yes, you bet I have.' Hooky was now enraged. 'I've been fishing inside the fifty-miles dozens of times,' he shouted. 'My Government doesn't recognize your fifty-mile limit.'

Hooky was watching him carefully — there was no immediate reply. He could not therefore know that *Campion* had been fishing inside the twelve-mile limit... Thank God for that. If the Icelander had known, he would never let go... Hooky had been damned stupid, but his luck was still holding — so far...

The gunboat was still steaming parallel, laying off at a cable and a half. Her Captain had nipped back into his wheelhouse — probably contacting Reykjavik. Hooky walked slowly back to the centre of the wheelhouse. He'd kept his head and stalled long enough to reach *Noontide*: he was on her port quarter now — between her and the gunboat. The Icelandic trawlers on the port bow had sheered off when they saw the gunboat creaming up their kilts. He could see Digger Greaves jumping up and down as he cheered from his deckhouse. The R/T mic was in his hand and he was blazing with rage.

'I got one bastard's gear. I'm going to sink that flamer,' he cried, insane with rage. 'Keep out of my way, Hooky. I'm turning to starboard.'

'You're not going to ram one, Digger?' Hooky shouted. 'The gunboat will blow you out of the water. For God's sake, stop!'

Noontide was already swinging to starboard. He could see the crazed Australian right ahead of him.

Then, to port, Hooky sensed *Hekla* hissing up alongside — her gun's crew was closed up and she was scything past, her captain in the wings and yelling through his loud-hailer: 'Clear your decks, trawler *Noontide*. I shall fire live ammunition.'

The Icelander meant what he said, Skipper Walker realized. The loading number was ramming a shell into the breach of that 57 mm. *Campion* was in the middle, like lucky Alphonse… Hooky picked up his mic, blind hate overpowering him, but Digger Greaves was in a frenzy too. He was gripping the bridge rail with one hand, shaking his fist, and was purple in the face.

'Yes, you bastard, that's all you can do…' He had gone berserk. 'Fire at us, you bastard. We're unarmed — go on, *fire…*'

There was a *whoomph!* a *bang!* and behind Hooky, a shock of air blasting against *Campion*'s windows. *Hekla* had opened fire with live ammunition. Hooky propelled himself towards the bridge door and tugged it open. Before he could protest, Digger was screaming with rage; his clenched fist shaking at the suave captain standing in the wings of the gunboat.

'Go on… Fire another, bastard… Go on…'

Skipper Walker watched the shells exploding on the defenceless trawler: four shots, deliberately aimed at *Noontide*, all for'd of the bridge and into the hull below the rail. He saw the orange flash, where the shell exploded; sniffed the sour smell of cordite. Brown fumes swirled outwards and choked him as he rushed outside on to his verandah. Shocked, Hooky stared across at the grinning gunboat captain.

'You're firing across me and I have done no harm,' he yelled. 'I am reporting you to my Government.'

The Icelander shouted unintelligibly, but while Hooky watched the long barrel was swinging round to aim directly at his own bridge. He knew fear then — he'd seen what those shells could do.

'Yes, yes,' the *Hekla* captain yelled. 'You report me to your Government. Do just that. I hope I sink you, you English bastard.' He turned to the officer standing by the gun. Hooky held his breath as the barrel swung back across him again. Five pairs of eyes squinted towards him and he could see the layer itching to squeeze his trigger. Never before had Hooky felt naked fear ... and in those seconds, he prayed to his God.

The slim barrel hung for a moment, then slowly traversed his bridge until it was clear of *Campion* and trained again on *Noontide*. Hooky never knew what happened next — afterwards, they said it was an accident.

'Fire!'

Hooky heard the guttural command. He glimpsed the flash, watched the gun recoil. The shell struck aft, in the break of the poop where a cluster of *Noontide*'s men were gathered. A red stain on the paintwork, a sudden cry and a young man's scream.

He saw the rush of men; heard the panic of their cries. A deckie leaped down from the poop deck to crouch over the prostrate body ... and he knew then, before Skipper Greaves had yelled across, who had been blown to bits.

'It's your boy,' Digger screamed. 'Hooky, it's Mark, your lad…'

Hooky felt no pain — the speed of events had shocked him into savage, animal reaction. He moved swiftly back to his wheelhouse, clicked over the rudder control from 'auto' to 'hand'.

'Full ahead,' he commanded. As he felt the spokes of the wheel firmly in his hands, he glimpsed the pitch control lever being slammed forward by the mate.

'Clear the upper deck,' he rapped. 'Everybody to the other side… Mister Mate, clear the wheelhouse and shelter behind the bridge.' He was angered to see the shocked reaction of his men — the amazed disbelief on all their stupid faces. 'For Christ's sake — *move*…' he screamed at them as he spun the wheel hard over to port.

He had never known before the exultation of being in action and under fire … and now, as he took his ship into battle, he knew that he was doing what he had been destined to do since the day he'd been borne to the sea. He saw the blue-grey bows of the gunboat; watched her side lining up squarely against his flared prow. *Hekla*'s gun was swinging towards him, pointing directly down *Campion*'s fore-and-aft line. Twenty yards to go — *Campion* would slice the gunboat open; pierce straight through her, abreast the bridge.

As he braced himself, he saw the flash — there was a roaring about him and a smell of burning flesh. Dimly he was aware, as he slid to the deck, of the warm blood pouring down his belly and into his slippers. He was dying, he knew… *Jesus, into Thy hands*… He felt the shock of collision, was aware of the screech of mangling steel; he heard the cries from the gunboat; saw her prow rearing skywards. There was a blurred image before his eyes; yes, it was the mate. *Take the ship, Peter — take my beloved ship...*

'*Abandon ship —*'

He heard the mate calling, felt the rush of icy water. There was the waving of a hand; a mewing of the sea birds and the lapping of the salt, salt sea...

EPILOGUE

The skyline stood up sharply, icy, steely grey on this December morning. The skipper of the British trawler, *Noontide*, stood motionless by his bridge rail; he was staring towards the east, unbelieving, still numb from the shock of the *Campion* tragedy. Leaping up from below the horizon was a line of grey cruisers, their flared bows mounting high in the seas as they raced westwards towards the island. From their single mastheads streamed their ensigns, large, flapping rectangles of blood-red.

To the southward of them and still hull-down, the skipper sighted the white cross-trees of the British frigates; their battle ensigns were streaming too, in the wind: blood-red crosses on a white ground, they were.

Overhead, high in the ice-blue sky, were the crescent shapes of escorting aircraft. Their wing surfaces glinted in the winter sun, as the planes wheeled and turned silently, their herring-bone trails streaming far behind them…

A NOTE TO THE READER

Dear Reader,
If you have enjoyed the novel enough to leave a review on **Amazon** and **Goodreads**, then we would be truly grateful.

Sapere Books is an exciting new publisher of brilliant fiction and popular history.

To find out more about our latest releases and our monthly bargain books visit our website: **saperebooks.com**